GOOD GUY

A ROOKIE REBELS NOVEL

KATE MEADER

Copyright © 2019 by Kate Meader

Cover by Michele Catalano Creative

ISBN: 978-0-9985178-2-7

1

LEVI HUNT HAD SURVIVED Special Forces training, which made SEALs' Hell Week look like a tweens' summer camp. He'd lived through multiple tours of Afghanistan when it seemed that everyone and his aunt was trying to kill him in wildly inventive ways. Last night, he'd choked down goalie Erik Jorgenson's surprise mac and cheese welcome meal—the surprise was pickled herring—and had not spent the rest of the evening hurling chunks for his country. But he had serious doubts he was going to get through a whole season of Theo Kershaw talking about the thickness of his own ass.

Except for a not-placed-well-enough towel in one hand, Chicago Rebels defenseman Kershaw stood naked before a full-length mirror in the practice facility's locker room gazing at his ass's reflection.

"I can't believe I'm the only one with this problem. Hey, Burnett, you feelin' me on this?"

"Unsubscribe," groaned Cade Burnett, another D-man, as he pulled on sweatpants. "Already told you I've got eyes for one ass only and that's my guy's."

Kershaw's eyebrows dipped in a V. "Not looking for your admiration, Alamo. I'm just trying to get a consensus on how big a problem this is in the NHL." He turned to Levi. "Navy, what are your measurements?"

"Navy?"

"Yeah, because of your time with the Navy SEALs. Trying it out to see if it fits."

"First, I was in Special Forces, aka the Green Berets. Second, you want to know how wide my ass is?"

"I have major problems finding pants that fit. I've got these gorgeous, trim hips and perfect waist, but the glutes ..." He slapped his right buttock, leaving a red mark and the rest of the team cracking up. "It's so hard to get pants to go up and over these bad boys."

Pretty funny what guys felt comfortable with in a locker room. Levi'd had this in-your-face camaraderie in college and in the service, but he'd expected pro hockey would be a bit more adult.

Apparently he was wrong.

His head was still spinning at the speed of his career trajectory. Four months ago, he'd received his discharge papers from Special Forces, acquired an agent, and put himself on the market. Ten weeks ago, he'd signed on for a fall start with the Chicago Rebels AHL affiliate, the Rockford Royals. Spending a year or two in the feeder league to get game-tough seemed as good a plan as any. He'd spent nine years off competitive ice after all.

But then disaster struck—for someone else. Garrick Jones, one of the Rebels' centers fractured his arm during a preseason game six days ago. The next morning, Levi was on the practice rink in Riverbrook, home base of the Rebels. Just like that.

"Get your pants made custom," Rebels captain Vadim

Petrov said to Kershaw as he walked out of the shower in a cloud of steam. The guy made millions in modeling endorsements so this entrance was definitely on brand. "Then your beautiful, thick ass will be covered."

Theo pointed at Vadim. "We're not all Russian billionaires. I'm doing okay, but I'd rather not slap down a few thousand buckaroos every time I need a suit. Not when the pants end up splitting because my glutes are so damn powerful."

The entire locker room lost it.

"You've got super glutes, Kershaw," Levi said. "Hey, that has a nice ring to it."

"Don't even think of it, New Guy. I already have a nickname."

Facing an ass-free mirror, Cade scrubbed a clump of gel through his hair. "You mean Lightning? Which you invented yourself."

Surely not. "You self-assigned your nickname?"

"And it's starting to catch on! Like Lightning."

Vadim curled his lips in aristocratic disgust. "In your wet dreams, Theo. You cannot come up with your own nickname. That is the rule."

Jorgenson walked out of the showers, munching on a power bar. Apparently the Swede brought food with him everywhere he went because who'd want to risk going hungry for ten long minutes while soaping up your balls?

"Rule for what?"

"Kershaw coming up with his own nickname," Cade said. "But the new guy thought of a better one. Superglutes."

Erik took a long, hard look at Theo's ass. "I can see that."

"He's got super glutes, super glutes, he's super glute-y!" Right-winger Ford Callaghan sang it to the tune of *Super Freak*.

Soon the whole team was singing the new version while Theo did something mildly threatening and downright unmentionable with his dick.

"Gentlemen," a soft voice cut in. "Okay if I enter?" Levi recognized the voice as belonging to team owner Harper Chase.

Huh. Were locker-room visits from the female ownership a common occurrence?

Theo covered up his super ass. "Yeah, we're decent, Ms. Chase."

In walked Harper, along with the Rebels general manager, Dante Moretti. To say that the leadership of the team was unusual would be like saying Theo Kershaw did not have an ass-splitting-pants problem that he insisted on yammering on about incessantly. Owned jointly by the three Chase sisters and managed by Moretti, the only openly gay chief executive in pro sports, the Rebels had spent the last four years smashing glass ceilings and busting every stereotype imaginable about how a team should be run. Along the way, they'd made enemies but had also found soulmates.

If you believed in that kind of thing.

Petite, blonde, high-heeled, and steely-eyed, Harper was de facto CEO and hands on, a trait Levi had admired during a hi-how-are-ya meeting a couple of days ago. He'd also been impressed by her hockey knowledge, business savvy, and faith in him. Having spent his prime athlete years in the military, he'd missed out on what should have been the most lucrative period of his hockey career. Going straight from NCAA to the army was not a typical path, and while it made for good PR copy, donning camo fatigues and dodging bullets in inhospitable climes generally didn't scream 'committed' to your chosen sport.

But the Rebels wanted him—and he planned to do them proud.

The management chit-chatted with a few of the players before Harper zeroed in on him. "Levi, if you have a moment, could you join us in Coach Calhoun's office?"

"Yes, ma'am."

They left, but not before Dante sent a significant glance toward his partner, Cade Burnett, and got a burner of a look in return. It was clear that the Rebels management didn't much care for appearances. Harper was shacked up with Cajun hockey legend, Remy DuPre, now retired and playing house husband with their three kids. Another sister, Olympic medalist Isobel Chase, was married to Rebels captain, Petrov, but she still hung around doing skating consultancy. Not to be left out, the final sister, Violet, had tied the knot with Bren St. James, former captain, also retired. It was the kind of thing that filled *Page Six*, as if the women-in-charge thing wasn't enough to keep those gossip hounds and haters hungry.

Acquiring a former Green Beret to make his NHL debut at the positively ancient age of thirty was likely just another day in the front office for the Rebels.

AFTER ENDURING some ribbing for calling the team owner "ma'am"—*sigh*—Levi entered Coach Calhoun's office two rights and a left from the locker room and found Harper seated behind the desk. Decked out in a bespoke suit complete with pocket watch, Dante stood near the window checking his phone.

"Have a seat, Levi," Harper said.

He sat, turning the chair slightly so he had both Dante

and Harper in his sightline. Old habits. Always know the location of the people and the exits.

"Good work out there, Hunt," Dante said. "Looks like you've hardly missed a step since college."

"Thanks. I'm feeling fit and ready."

Harper smiled. "Normally we'd just let PR handle this but we figure it might be better to speak to you directly. We've heard you're resistant to interviews."

And not one, but two of the senior management had descended from the ivory tower to tell him this? "Only the ones that want to talk about my time in Special Forces and what kind of work I did. I've no problem talking hockey but it seems my backstory invites a lot of nosey questions." He'd have to accept this newfound spotlight eventually, but the more he could keep undercover the better—and not just the military secrets.

Dante eyed him. "People are curious about you and they're going to be skeptical of a guy who's starting his NHL career so late. It's one thing to ease in at the AHL level. Up here, there are different expectations, and one of them is to do your part to make the team look good."

"I'm hoping my play will eventually speak for itself and I can avoid the inquisition." The first game of the season was the day after tomorrow. As the FNG—or Fucking New Guy —he was unlikely to get ice time, yet he planned to be out there cheering for his boys.

"We understand your hesitancy, Levi, and of course, we can't make you talk about your journey," Harper said in a tone that said she'd do whatever the hell she wanted. "But what if we handle it right? Give people a chance to see the hard-working professional."

"While showcasing the team's red, white, and blue

patriot cred?" Levi shot back, yielding a smirk from Harper. This woman was no dummy.

"Why not? It's a win-win. People get to know you and the team gets some good press. I imagine we'd want to play our part and ensure you're on the ice getting all the chances you can to prove we made the right decision in calling you up."

If he played their PR game, he might get a guaranteed start in the early season games? His heart thumped at the notion. It was an attractive offer. But there was one thing he knew for sure: the Rebels' bench wasn't as deep as it would like when it came to centermen. DuPre and St. James had anchored the team before their retirements and the team was having trouble filling their big skates. Losing Jones was a significant blow, which gave Levi unexpected leverage.

Leverage he wasn't quite ready to use. "I just want to be treated like anyone else. You called me up because you think I have something to offer. I want to earn that faith."

"Very noble, Hunt," Dante said, somewhat impatiently. "But you're a unique property from a public relations point of view and it would be foolish of us not to capitalize on that. We have requests for in-depth profiles of you from a number of outlets, both local and national."

Levi repressed a shudder at the mention of "in-depth." He'd rather sever his left testicle. "I play puck with your PR game and you put a word in Coach's ear about getting me ice time sooner than later?"

"We like to leave it to Coach to make game decisions," Harper said, flicking a glance at Dante, "but we do have some influence around here."

Yeah, he bet. No one would be ignoring "suggestions" from these two, but that's not how he wanted to earn his spot in primetime. Playing for the Rebels might be a dream come true, but even dreams needed hard graft behind them.

From Kirkuk to Kabul, Levi had broken bread with warlords, tribal chieftains, and strongmen, and had learned to quickly discern the true power players in a room. Dante might be GM, but Harper was queen.

He met the woman's stern gaze. "Think I'd rather have Coach make the final call. No disrespect intended, ma'am."

"None taken, Levi." Was that a flash of admiration in those sea-green eyes? "Of course, you'll be expected to chat innocuously with reporters post-game—"

"Assuming you're even dressed for a game," Dante cut in, clearly annoyed at Levi's stubbornness. Pissing off your superiors was probably not the best way to ingratiate yourself, but Levi enjoyed a perverse pleasure in going against the grain even when it amounted to self-sabotage. Patience was embedded in his DNA. Given their personnel woes, the Rebels would have no choice but to eventually give him ice time.

Still, it never hurt to be gracious. "Post-game chats with the press are fine as long as it's clear I can't divulge details about my military service."

"Of course." Harper stood, those heels giving her hardly any height, yet Levi suspected that no one would want to get on the wrong side of this woman. He'd flexed his muscles and scored a point today. The next engagement would be mighty interesting.

"I expect you're good under pressure, Levi. Looking forward to seeing what you bring."

Join the club, Ms. Chase.

2

"IT's kind of hairier than I expected."

Jordan Cooke extracted the phone from her friend's crone-like grip and took another look at the photo that had slithered into her Twitter DMs this morning. "That's all you've got? The manscaping isn't up to snuff?"

Laughing, Kinsey made another swipe for the phone. "Let me see it again. For research." She shook her head, analyzing the dick pic with the morbid curiosity of women everywhere who wonder: *why, men, why?* "So this happens to you all the time? And you just ... ignore it?"

"What am I supposed to do? Reply back with a thumbs-up? Good for you, penis-owner, you are dick and balls above the rest of your cocky cohorts?"

Kinsey raised an eyebrow. They'd met three years ago at a Women in Media event, hit it off, and tried to get together for coffee or cocktails and a good old gab every couple of months when Jordan trudged to Chicago from the sticks of Rockford. She considered Kinsey both a mentor and a friend.

"Heads up, Jordan, but this is the twenty-first century,

post-TimesUp and MeToo. And it's from a co-worker. You need to report it."

"If it were someone I actually worked with in the press, I'd make a fuss. But we're talking multi-million-dollar, hockey-playing penis here. If I complained about a player sexting, I'd quickly find myself covering pee wee games and college wankfests."

Jordan had heard the stories from her sisterhood on the sports reporter beats. The East Coast field analyst who was reassigned after calling out an NFL player with a habit of "accidentally" dropping a towel whenever she walked into the locker room. The female reporter vilified when an MLB player told everyone she'd slept with half the team and would do anything for a story. And it didn't stop with the talent. An unseemly percentage of agents, management, and owners treated women reporters as their personal playthings.

"Being in PR," Kinsey said, referring to her gig as a partner in M Squared, one of the premier public relations firms in the city, "I could make quite the meal out of this if you were willing to spin it."

Jordan took back her phone and turned it facedown on the bar at the Starbucks. Outside the window, the Windy City's denizens rushed by on their morning commutes. Having lived in Rockford for the last few years, she'd forgotten how busy the streets here were. She longed to be one of those places-to-be big-city dwellers—and soon she might get her chance.

"Right now, it's just an occupational hazard. The last thing I want is to stir the pot when I'm up for a chance at this job."

One of the most coveted beats in sports, a hockey reporting gig was currently open at Chicago SportsNet. The local network controlled the TV broadcast concession for the Rebels games and offered a multi-pronged approach to sports coverage: online articles that were less about reporting games and more about venting the collective ire of Chicago's various rabid fandoms; provocative on-air interviews to mine for sound bites; and deeper profiles to lend the network gravitas. While journalism might claim objectivity as its almighty pillar, sports journalism preferred its practitioners came loaded with deep-seated knowledge, strong opinions, and a willingness to prod a subject into revelation.

Jordan had all this in spades.

CSN's usual hockey guy, Jack Gillam, was taking time off after collapsing in the press box. That his heart attack had happened during a Rebels preseason game where the defense had looked incredibly shaky—four goals allowed in one particularly excruciating seven minute stretch—prompted the sports media to label goalie Erik Jorgenson the Almost Widow Maker. Gillam would be back in action in three months, but in the meantime, this could be Jordan's big break. For the last four years, she'd paid her dues covering the AHL in the regional Midwest and fronting a weekly, well-received podcast, Hockey Grrl (two Rs, no vowels, all sass). This was next-level for her and she was not throwing away her shot.

"What time's your interview?"

"An hour."

Kinsey squeezed her hand. "How are you feeling?"

"Like a squadron of carnivorous butterflies are gnawing away at my insides."

"You've got this. And once you have the job, we can work on getting you a date with a hot firefighter."

This again? The woman was relentless. "Aren't your

brothers-in-law spoken for?" Kinsey had married into a Chicago firefighting family, all of them very built, very fine, and very much hitched.

"Oh, plenty more where they came from. Chicago's firehouses are brimming with talent."

A hunky firefighter sounded like fun, but she couldn't imagine their schedules would ever mesh, which was fine because right now, her career was where she wanted to focus all her efforts. "The job, Kinsey. That's the prime directive."

"You're a shoo-in. If anything, just think of the receipts you're piling up in your telephone machine. Have you considered blackmail?" Half-winking, Kinsey touched a finger to Jordan's overturned phone.

"Uh, no." More than qualified for this gig, Jordan certainly didn't need to extort anyone into employing her. She still believed in what you know versus who (or whose genitals) you know when it came to landing her dream job. Eventually she wanted to work for a premier national broadcaster like ESPN, but in the meantime, perching a few rungs up the ladder at CSN would look great on her resume. "Why would I need blackmail when I have the credentials, the experience, and the—"

"Cojones?"

"And mine don't even need to be manscaped."

Kinsey laughed. "Knock 'em dead, Cooke."

"Hɪ!" Jordan smiled big at the woman on reception duty as she exited the elevator leading to the Chicago SportsNet offices. "I'm here to see Mr. MacLoughlin."

Dragging herself away from an Instagram feed, the

college-age receptionist with intern written all over her, greeted Jordan with a sullen stare. "Your name?"

"Oh, right, you'd need that. Jordan Cooke."

"Have a seat. I'll let him know you're here." Still nada in the smile department. What a wonderful face for the organization.

Jordan sat in a lobby armchair and listed off her credentials in her head even though it was all laid out in her resume. It had taken her five years to get here. Four, really, because that first year had been a wash, written off as she grieved Josh. Losing her husband at twenty-three had forced her to focus on what was important, the career she'd put aside to be a young wife, the person she needed to become in the wake of the human rubble of death and loss. She'd paid her dues in the trenches and now she was ready to seize her destiny.

Go, Jordan!

She giggled at her inner cheerleader—they went *way* back—which earned her a glower from Bored Intern. Oh, well. It would take more than that to bank Jordan's fire.

Above her, a TV mounted to the wall was tuned to ESPN's SportsFocus with host Coby "Big Dog" Dawson breaking down the NHL teams for the start of the season. A little unusual as the network rarely covered hockey since dumping their league contract years ago. It took a couple of minutes for him to get around to the Chicago Rebels.

"Man, this team is in big trouble. We have Jones out of the mix, Petrov's knee held together with duct tape, and the defense with more holes than a salt shaker. And now they're calling in the cavalry. Literally. Tweet your thoughts to @BigDogDawson and get in on the conversation."

"You can go in now," Bored Intern called out. "Through the door and down to the end."

Stepping into the open plan setup of the CSN office, Jordan inhaled the competing scents of pastrami, testosterone, and deadline despair. Strange how every newsroom, even sports beat newsrooms, looked like the typing pool in *Working Girl*. Unfortunately there was no hot, shirtless Harrison Ford in her future.

Ignored by the all-male staff on her journey through the cubicle maze, she arrived at the editor-in-chief's office and applied a firm, I-mean-business knock. At the gruff "come in," she popped her head around the door. "Hi, I'm Jordan Cooke."

Jerry "Mac" MacLoughlin waved her to the nearest chair opposite his paper-strewn desk. "Coffee?"

"Already caffeinated to the max, thanks." She took a seat and smoothed her skirt, then instantly regretted it because it drew attention to her thighs. Not that they were bad-looking thighs, but she didn't want to make them the focus of her interview. Sporty-casual was usually her look, and most of the guys she'd passed in the outer office were decked out in jeans and tees, but an interview called for a suit and heels.

Stop overanalyzing. Take yoga-quality breaths, even though you don't do yoga because you've never gotten further than the juice bar at the gym. In, out. Innnnn, ouuuuut.

Feeling calmer, she redirected her attention to the man behind the desk. On anyone else a walrus mustache might look old-school. On Jerry MacLoughlin, it looked ... really old-school, and was currently a nesting ground for pink sprinkles.

"Donut?" He raised a half-consumed pastry, mother ship for the sprinkles, which sent a haze of additional candy particles raining down over assorted paperwork.

"No, thanks, I'm driving."

He squinted at her. Too soon for jokes, apparently.

"A lot of people want this job, Jordan. Why should I give it to you?"

Despite the crusty approach, she appreciated him getting straight to the point.

"I have four years reporting on the minor leagues, Chicago experience and connections, and a proven track record of establishing relationships with players, front office, and industry colleagues." Sure, wasn't her camera roll of dick pics as good as a reference list?

Probably shouldn't mention that.

Continuing to elaborate on her opening points, she was leading into her podcast when he cut her off.

"What do you know about Levi Hunt?"

She blinked, surprised at the sharp turn of the conversation. "Thirty years old, native of Hoboken, New Jersey. NCAA All-Star. Was about to make his AHL debut after spending the last nine years serving his country in Special Forces. Called up last-minute to fill out the Rebels roster. Tons of expectation, a metric shit ton of warm fuzzies. The biggest story in hockey right now."

Aaaaand she'd just sworn in her interview.

Mac either didn't notice or didn't care. "Biggest story in *sports*, Jordan. And you know him."

"I've met him once or twice." A chill crept across her skin, gooseflesh prickling with the realization of what this was truly about. So much for hard work and the meritocracy. "Is this why I got the interview?"

"Like I said, a lot of people want this job. Hell, I could give it to anyone out there in the pen." He jerked a hand toward the glass window that overlooked the open-plan office. "But you have an in with Hunt."

"I wouldn't call it an in."

He raised a bushy eyebrow, one of a matching set that

accessorized perfectly with that 'stache. "I've listened to your pod-thing and read your copy. You're personable, knowledgeable, and clearly good at what you do. But I have a million tapes and think pieces from two-bit regional reporters ready to stab anyone and everyone in the backs to get this gig. However, you've got a couple of things in your favor."

She would normally have liked the sound of that, but now, not so much.

"You're a woman and you know Hunt."

"What's me being a woman got to do with anything?" This might be the first time her ovaries had not screwed her over.

"Did you notice the staff on your way in here? A bunch of dicks, and I mean that in every way you can take it. We've been told we need to hire more women into reporter positions." From his tone, whoever had instituted this directive would not earn a spot on Mac's Christmas card list this year. "Between you and me, I have my doubts about whether women should be spending time in male locker rooms at all. Wouldn't want my daughter in there."

"Luckily, I don't faint at the sight of dicks, and I mean that in every way you can take it."

Mac barked a laugh and refocused his attention on her, as if she'd finally said something worthy of it. "So, you can hang tough with the boys. I won't have to worry you'll take a joke the wrong way or sue me for creating a hostile work environment?"

The words hung, half-question, half-threat. This is what she'd meant about rocking the boat. She'd never get her foot in the door if every guy she worked with was too wary of being himself. In other words, your basic asshole.

"I just want to be treated like any of my co-workers." Tone and response neutral. *Check.*

"Good. Now Hunt won't grant any interviews, says he wants to focus on his game"—Mac inserted an eye roll here —"but I've talked to Harper Chase over at the Rebels. She said they might be willing to convince him if the story was framed right. And what could be better framing than a probing profile on the Navy SEAL—"

"Green Beret."

"What?"

"He was in the Green Berets, not the Navy SEALs. Big difference."

For a moment she worried that contradicting him was a bad move, but his curt nod signaled appreciation of her willingness to speak up. "A Green Beret veteran who survived a shit show in Afghanistan and is now *finally* making his debut at the highest level? This could get attention from national networks."

That chill warmed at the mention of national exposure. But, Levi Hunt? She knew she'd have to run into him at one point or another, that memories would resurface and possibly overwhelm, but she never expected her past would become so integral to her future.

"I get that this might be tough for you, Jordan," Mac said with a gravelly-sounding compassion that must have killed him to show.

"It was five years ago. An age, really."

Mac nodded, giving her a moment to dwell—and dwell she did.

On the fact that Levi Hunt was her husband's best man at their wedding.

On the fact that he had been with Josh when he died on a desert road in Afghanistan.

But mostly, she dwelled on the fact that the man didn't like her one bit. She couldn't pinpoint exactly the nature of his problem with her but she knew this much: her particular brand of cheer pissed him off royally.

Working with him on an interview? No way would he go for that. Neither was she sure that *she* should go for that.

"The last time I saw Levi Hunt was at my husband's funeral five years ago." She fought the flush of her skin and the memory of that last encounter. "We haven't kept in touch, so for me to be assigned to this interview might look like I'm trying to cash in on a very tenuous connection."

"Did you or did you not tell me that you're good at cultivating relationships? Your tenuous connection to Hunt, a veteran who served in the same unit as your husband, is the best chance we have of beating ESPN or Fox Sports to the punch. I just know those bastards will be sniffing around. Should I call Harper now and tell her we're putting you on the story?"

"Assuming he wants to talk to me."

"That's your job, Jordan. Get him to talk to you."

The drama of his lean toward her was diminished ever-so-slightly by the escape of several sprinkles from his mustache. But with his next words, he managed to recapture the moment's significance.

"Do you want to be covering piss ants in Rockford for the rest of your career, Jordan, or are you ready to make a move?"

3

@ChiRebels hoping for a strong start tonight. Can their young legs beat the @NewOrleansCajuns, NHL's current powerhouse? #ChicagoSportsNet #OpeningGame

NOTHING EXCITED Jordan more than the opening game of the season. The atmosphere in the Rebels Center in River-brook, about 30 miles north of Chicago's downtown, was electric as she exited the elevator leading to the executive and press boxes.

Was it her imagination, or did the air smell sweeter up here? The moneyed scent of success, perhaps. Or maybe it was the hint of pheromones left behind by Rebels GM, Dante Moretti, spotted heading into the home team box a few doors down.

You've made it, girl.

Okay, she had one heeled foot in the door, and she was still feeling a bit queasy about how she'd managed it: a classic case of who-you-know and not the result of her years reporting on this game she loved. Not only was she a token female hire but she was here because she had a connection that could be exploited.

Her dead husband.

Kinsey had congratulated her by ripping her woe-is-me-I-might-have-the-job-because-boobs mantra to shreds: *Who cares how you got here? You know you deserved it, and that's all that matters.*

But she could be out on her ass at any second. For now, Jordan was Jack Gillam's replacement in the press box, but staying there was dependent on convincing Levi she was the perfect person to tell his story.

She tried channeling Kinsey's no-fucks-given attitude. No one else could do this profile justice because no one else was Jordan Cooke. *Booyah!*

Giddiness restored, she flashed her press pass at the security guard and added unnecessarily, "I'm with Chicago SportsNet." Wow, that sounded awesome.

"Go right on in, Ms." Neither his blasé tone nor his unsubtle once-over could knock her off Cloud 9.

As the job didn't require on-camera work, she'd normally stick to jeans and cute tops, but tonight she planned to visit the locker room after the game, which meant her navy pinstripe interview suit and four-inch heels were pulling double duty. She stepped into the press box. A long table with chairs faced a window overlooking the ice and awaited the most grizzled, cynical curmudgeons in the business. Seeming to sense that an interloper was in their midst, the three guys present turned in unison.

"Hey, guys! I'm Jord—"

"Yeah, we know who you are, Cooke," Curtis Deacon of the *Chicago Sun-Times* barked. "What's the latest on Gillam?"

"Doing okay. I talked to his wife, Betty, today and she said he's whining about the hospital food."

"Sounds like him. Ungrateful bastard." A particularly hoary specimen—Jim Krugman, string for the *Trib*—who looked like the Ghost of Sports Reporters Past jerked a thumb at the seat next to him. "This is Gillam's usual spot."

More press straggled in, taking what were likely their regular spaces. Reporters were notoriously superstitious. No one here would be switching up seats.

She sat where she was told—and boy was she conscious that her time here was temporary—and pulled her laptop from her backpack. The press boxes for the AHL teams weren't quite so exalted, more like spare seats behind the sin bin. To be honest, she wouldn't mind being down there in the center of the action in jeans and hoodie, sans toe-pinching heels, but such was the way of the ascendancy.

Like all noble families, hockey press royalty was made up of miscreants, oddballs, and know-it-alls. Press box type number one was the veteran, of which Krugman was a prime example. Once there might have been a tweed jacket (with elbow patches) hanging on the back of his chair. These days, a tie rarely made an appearance and the shirt could do with a pressing. Veterans usually hauled around laptops that weighed more than Jordan, could expound with frightening authority on the quality of Chex Mix in each box, and wouldn't dream of starting a fresh pot of coffee—that's what newbies were for.

Which brought her to press box type number two: the new kid on the block. And *this* new girl needed to ingratiate herself—hence the presentation of gifts.

"Who likes donuts?" Jordan asked with a smile that would usually melt the iciest of hearts. From her backpack, she extracted a box of sugary, fatty, carbolicious cheer.

"Donuts?" Krugman's sneer was withering. He gestured dismissively over his shoulder. "Any idea where you are, girlie?"

On the table lay a spread that wouldn't look out of place at a Michelin-starred restaurant: cute-as-a-button pastries, baby tiramisus, and—Mary Mother of Jesus—mini-macarons. She loved mini-macarons and their alpha brothers, regular-sized macarons. No wonder the arena security had laughed at her. Her donuts were positively low-rent by comparison.

About to introduce the donuts to the trash can, she stopped when Arnie Raulson, the play-by-play guy on a visit from the broadcast booth to load up on beers, grabbed a cruller from her box. *Thanks, Arnie!* "You want to see how the game's really covered, Jordan? Stop by the booth."

"Sure will!" At least, someone was happy to see her.

The Ice Girls were doing their thing while the strobe lights and pulsing bass turned the arena into Ibiza. Determined to avail of the perks before the players skated on for warm-up, Jordan checked out the beer fridge. It was stocked with plenty of craft beers she'd never heard of, like Angry Shrub and Hops' Redemption.

A waft of very pleasant aftershave tickled her nose.

"Any Fat Tire in there?" a smooth voice asked. Looking up, she met the hazel-eyed gaze of—*no way!*—Coby Dawson.

"No Fat Tire, but there is something called The Nun's Dilemma. An IPA."

"Sounds good. Hi, I'm Coby," he said, offering his hand. "You look like you're new on this beat."

"Oh, hi, there! I'm Jordan. Jordan Cooke." Standing, she shook his hand—or she would have if she didn't try to use a beer bottle to make friends. She placed the bottle on top of the fridge and tried again. Warm, firm grip. Friendly smile. "Years in the trenches, first time in the nosebleeds. Filling in for Jack Gillam at Chicago SportsNet."

"I heard. How is he?" All concern, he cocked his head, topped with black, wavy, gel-stiff hair, like Ross's from *Friends*.

"Getting the care he needs."

"Good, good."

"So, what are you doing here?" Presumptuous, perhaps, but Jordan was currently in the presence of press box type number three: the big shot. Given their colorful off-ice antics that filled the gossip pages, the Rebels were a top draw, but Coby Dawson was far too huge a deal to be hanging with the local newsies at an opening season game. Plus ESPN and hockey weren't exactly best buds.

"The Rebels have an interesting crew this year. Could do big things."

"They did big things three seasons ago when they went all the way after the Chase sisters took over." They'd had a couple of good seasons since but nowhere near the heights they'd scaled that first go out with Harper and her sisters at the helm.

Then it hit her like a puck to the temple. "You're here for Hunt."

"He's a good story."

He was. More important, he was *her* story. She should have called Levi before the game to lock it down.

Hey, Levi, you were in my dead husband's unit and stood up with him when he married, and even though you have an active dislike of me, you were there for me when he died and that makes us sort of besties. Also there was that time we almost—okay, let's not talk about that. Want to give me an interview?

So Mac claimed Harper would prefer to keep the story

local, but what if Dawson made a better case? Hell, if Jordan was in Harper Chase's very high heels, she'd be shopping that profile to a national network, like ESP-fucking-N.

"Dressed list is up," Krugman said.

With a self-assured smile, Coby walked to the viewing bench, took a seat to the left of Jordan/Jack's spot, and set up his laptop, a brand new Macbook Pro.

The players swarmed onto the ice, starting with Erik Jorgenson, the Rebels' goalie. Then Vadim Petrov, the left-winger and captain, arrived in a dramatic flourish, followed by right-winger Ford Callaghan, and D-men Cade Burnett and Theo Kershaw. Finally—and no doubt deliberately—in skated the man himself, Levi Hunt. That he was even on the twenty-player dressed list was a surprise and demonstrated either supreme confidence or utter desperation on the part of the home team.

The photo on the jumbotron showed an unsmiling Levi, not a trace of softness in his granite features. Short, military-style dark brown hair teased hints of red; crystalline blue eyes saw everything and revealed nothing; that square jaw wouldn't look out of place in a Superman comic. Jordan had already studied his profile on the Rebels' website—added only yesterday—and knew his specs inside out. Nothing compared to seeing him projected on that screen or watching as the man put blade to ice and made his debut.

Her heart flipped in her chest, not at the sight of all two hundred pounds and six feet three inches of Hunt, but at his jersey number: 51. It had to be a homage to his unit, 5th Special Forces, 1st Special Forces Regiment.

Josh's unit.

"Putting him on the second line," Dawson murmured. "Interesting."

Agreed. Like most of the NHL press, she'd assumed that

he'd be relegated to the third, if any line at all, to give him a chance to get his bearings. That was a lot of pressure to put on a rookie, but then the Rebels never did anything by halves.

~

THE LIGHTS WERE SO FUCKING bright.

Levi had attended professional hockey games and he'd skated this rink during a preseason warm-up. He just hadn't expected the arena to be so in-your-face. Lights, noise, the contorted faces behind the plexi, who looked like they were preemptively pissed instead of fans thrilled to be here cheering on their team. Good thing he didn't suffer from PTSD because a professional hockey game would be trigger-central.

The Rebels had their work cut out for them: the New Orleans Cajuns were current holders of the Cup, and had looked hot and hungry for more glory in the preseason match-ups. When Coach told him earlier that he was dressing for tonight's game, Levi had almost blurted out "are you sure?" True, he'd felt good in practice, but playing in the opening season game was bananas. He'd made it clear to Dante and Harper that his PR cooperation couldn't be bought, so he had high hopes that Coach was making this call without interference. No one skates on NHL ice if he doesn't deserve to be there, right?

So he was thrilled. And he was fucking terrified.

"Hunt, you're in!" Coach Calhoun yelled.

Petrov came off and patted Levi's arm clumsily with his gloved hand. "Good luck, New Guy."

Thanks for the reminder, Cap. Levi skated on, surprised his legs didn't wobble, but then he was known for having ice water in his veins. He'd stared down terrorists, defused bombs, woken to the barrel of a revolver against his temple more than once. Nothing bothered him except ... *shit*. His stomach lurched, and Levi wondered for the briefest moment if Jorgenson's welcome meal was back for revenge.

The center's role in the game is to cover more ice than anyone. Good centers act as traffic control, can turn offense into defense at the drop of a puck, and make opportunities for the wingers to score. Great centers manage the game on the ice. With Ford Callaghan on his right and Travis Perez on his left, Levi was part of a line that should be rock-solid.

Slashing his stick against the opposing center's, he won his first face-off and whipped it right to Callaghan. No time to celebrate his first completed pass because it was back to center, left, center, left, dump in the blue zone.

Fast, so fucking fast.

Checked against the plexi by Hansen, the Cajuns' humungous D-man, Levi took a second to catch his breath, and that was all the time New Orleans needed. The buzzer sounded, the lights flashed like police sirens, and the crowd expelled a collective groan.

Score one for the visitors.

Fuck.

LEVI INHALED A BREATH, then another. The oxygen likely sensed the stink of failure and made no effort to enter his lungs.

He'd played like shit. No wonder Coach had pulled him after that first clusterfuck of a play, acting like he'd never skated in his life. He yanked his sweatpants on, then a long-sleeved T.

"Hey, calm down, Hunt. You wanna rip those nice clothes?"

Levi frowned at Kershaw who was grinning like they hadn't just played the worst opening season game in five years. *They didn't, Hunt. You did.*

"Just want to get out of here."

"Look, nobody played well out there. This isn't on you. Sometimes first games are like that. Everyone's rusty."

Theo was about the only one who'd had a semi-decent game. That last goal had slipped by Burnett but Kershaw had been solid during every shift he was on. Only when he wasn't on the ice, the Rebels defense was Swiss cheese, hence the 4-1 loss.

"Coach shouldn't have put me on so soon. I'm not ready."

"That's the spirit, Wee-wee."

"Wee-wee?"

"Yeah, like 'yes' in French."

Levi shook his head, hoping that would activate a Kershaw translator in his tired-ass brain. "Come again?"

"Yes in French, as in the French who wear berets, as in the Green Berets." He held his palms up. "Don't worry, we'll work on it."

What Levi really needed to do was head to the practice facility to work on his game. He'd pull all-nighters the entire season if he had to because that bumbling excuse for a performance was not going to cut it.

"Here come the vultures," Petrov muttered. He walked over to Levi, with a slight limp because his knee was acting up. If Levi didn't know better, he'd think that Vadim was shielding him from the new arrivals—the media. "Just answer their questions without being too down on yourself, Hunt. They will get bored and move on."

"Sure, Cap."

Any hope that the press might be uninterested was dashed to the tape-strewn floor when they made an immediate beeline for Levi.

"Hey, Levi, tough game out there," someone called out.

Keep your cool. They're just doing their job. Plate up the usual bromides about early days and getting my ice legs under me and ... fuck.

Jordan Cooke.

Jordan Cooke was here. In the Rebels locker room.

He blinked.

Still here.

She looked good. Damned good. Fair and freckled, with the red hair of her Irish ancestors to match. A heart-shaped face, a storybook character's peacock blue eyes, that slightly crooked, smart-tart mouth ... she hadn't aged a day in five years. Her suit was the typical uniform of the women reporters, professional but also body-hugging. If he were to trail his eyes down, he'd no doubt find shapely legs tapering to hot-as-hell heels.

What was she doing here?

Dumb question. She was obviously reporting on the game but he had no idea she'd moved up in the world. He'd followed her career and knew she was a regional beat reporter for the Midwest feeder teams. Was she based in Chicago now or maybe New Orleans, here for the Cajuns' opener?

His head, where common sense usually reigned, hoped it was NOLA. As for the rest of him ...

Someone shoved a mic under his chin, but the question came from Jordan. "Probably not how you wanted your first game to go, Levi. How are you feeling?"

The first words she spoke to him in years and she was

dragging him? *Deep breath. It's her job to ask the tough questions.* His gaze dipped to her press pass on a lanyard around her neck: Chicago SportsNet. Impressive.

"Well, I'm still getting my ice legs, finding my way. It's—"

"Early days?" She hoisted an eyebrow of *bullshit*.

Play the game, Ms. Sunshine. I give you the well-worn platitudes and you extract what you need to make your game report.

Someone else jumped in with a question about how his training here compared to the SEALs.

"Green Berets," Levi said at the same time as Jordan. Their shared look felt a little too intimate. And then the imagined intimacy magnified by a hundred when she winked one bright blue eye at him, like it was a grand joke and they'd laugh about it later over tequila.

After a few more excruciating minutes, the media moved on to interview Kershaw and his super ass. Jordan stayed behind, one hand on her hip.

"Well, hello there, Sergeant Hunt." She gave a perfect salute filled with just the right amount of sauce.

If anything, she should be furious with him for what he'd done when they'd last met, but it seemed Jordan Cooke didn't hold a grudge. Instead, she was smiling at him, just like the days of old. Back then, it was done to needle him. Every tool in her arsenal of pert and pep was sharpened to earn a reaction.

Come on, Mount Grump, show us a smile.

"You're the last person I expected to see," he said, feeling her out.

"I meant to call first, give you a heads up, but I didn't want to mess with your preparation."

Interesting that she assumed she'd get in his head. More interesting that she was probably right.

"Looks like you've moved up the media food chain. Congratulations."

"Just standing in for Jack Gillam up in the press box while he's on medical leave, but yeah, kind of my big break." Anyone else would be keeping such a telling conclusion close to their chest. Hell, Levi had kept his contract with the Rockford Royals—and the sheer pleasure of being back in the pro-hockey mix—to himself long past the need to for fear he'd jinx it. Jordan had always been a different animal, fine with wearing her heart on her sleeve.

Which was why he knew exactly what she thought of him.

"So, I—"

"Could we—"

She smiled. He did not. Why was this so hard again?

Maybe because the last time he'd seen her, he'd just shoved his tongue down her throat about six hours after she'd buried her husband, his closest friend.

So, yeah.

"I wondered if we could talk," she said. "Catch up properly."

His pulse picked up the pace. No other woman made him so itchy and hot.

When he didn't respond, she stepped in close, her floral and feminine scent curling inside his chest. "Chicago Sports-sNet wants to do a profile on you."

"They do?"

"That's why I'm here."

Of course. There was no good reason for that pinch behind his breastbone, a feeling he recognized as disappointment, as familiar to him as the terrain of scars on his body. After their last encounter, Jordan would need a damn good reason to want to spend time with him. Not because she wanted to trip down memory lane but because it meant something to her career.

Good. It put him in his place and the two of them on a professional footing.

"I'm not doing interviews beyond the post-game stuff."

Her lips scrunched up, making her look younger than her twenty-eight years. Last they'd met she was a young widow of twenty-three, mired in the tar of grief, desperate for answers and comfort. And he'd offered it. First in the form of reminiscences about Josh, better known to his Special Forces team as Cookie, the usual stuff about what a prankster he was, an all-around great guy. But as the night had worn on and his unit-mates had left, the tequila had slipped down easier and he'd started listening to this woman. How much she missed her husband. How she wished their last conversation hadn't been so normal. Banal. That was her biggest regret—that nothing special had singled out their final interaction. She could barely remember what they'd talked about.

And then the bar was closing and he was offering to drop her off at her parents' house in Georgetown, just a ten-minute walk away. On the street, she'd said something about staying in touch and he'd agreed, though really he had no intention of doing so. Knew it would be impossible because a line had been crossed, oh, *fucking years before*, and he needed to stay far away. Any promise would be all wrong.

But not as wrong as what came next ...

"I'll be honest, Levi," Jordan said, yanking him back to the present. "I got this gig because of my connection to you. Because of Josh."

Levi swallowed at the mention of his friend. Annoyance rose up, chased with guilt. Did she really think trotting out his name was going to make Levi fall to his knees and agree to being prodded and probed? Fuck, even if he wanted to do this interview, Jordan would be the last person he'd let in.

He was tired, annoyed with his performance on the ice, and just a touch pissed that she'd try to play him with their so-called connection. "So what did you have in mind, Ms. Sunshine?"

She looked surprised to be put on the spot, but more likely at his nickname for her. It had always emerged from his mouth with just a hint of sarcasm.

"Come on, Jordan. You must have some idea. An interview on your podcast perhaps?"

Her eyes flashed at his irritability. Good, let her know how this would go down. But of course, in his zeal to piss her off, he'd revealed that he knew of her podcast. May as well have admitted he stalked her every move on the web.

"That and more. My boss's idea is to shadow you for the first month of the season, then sit down and interview you at the end of each week. Find out what it's like for the newest/oldest rookie in the NHL. It would be respectful. Anything you reveal about your military service would be up to you."

"That's behind me. I'm here to play hockey. Hell, I don't even get why there's so much media interest."

"Then you're the only one, Levi." She moved closer, bringing with her sunshine and memories that fairly gutted him. "Listen, I know I'm the last person you probably want to work with—"

"Why'd you say that?"

Asking her to explain was a dick move. He knew why she said it but he wanted her to remember it just like he did.

Her cheeks reddened, and on anyone with her coloring it would be unsightly. Garish, even. But on her, it merely heightened her beauty and made her look young, unsure. She said simply, "It was a strange time."

Guilt at pushing her panged in his chest. *Grade A assholery right there, Hunt.*

"Thing is," she went on, "I'd rather not use how we know each other to get ahead in my career, but I've been given a chance. A chance to make my mark." Excitement rung through her voice, and hell, he felt every form of conflict known to man. "If we do this, the connection will be part of the story."

"Which is what your boss is probably hoping."

"But we can control it. *We* can decide how the narrative is framed." She gestured between them, inviting him into her confidence, this secret bubble of two. "I also think that Harper might appreciate a woman's perspective."

"Don't assume that," a sultry voice offered. Despite those heels, the boss had a stealthy step. Harper offered her hand. "Ms. Cooke, I presume."

Jordan shook it. "It's Jordan, Ms. Chase."

Harper studied her. "Mac called about you, said you might be the right person for the job. However, I'm not in the habit of handing out plum interviews with my prime rookie to a reporter purely because she's a woman."

"I'm not looking for special treatment but I think I can offer a dimension to this that you won't find with any other reporter."

"I have to admit your past connection with Levi definitely gives me something to think about." She didn't even look at Levi when she said this. He'd been reduced to a commodity worth bartering over.

Welcome to the NHL.

The women sized each other up, leaving Levi feeling like a gazelle about to be torn apart by two terrifying lionesses.

Likely his opinion would have no bearing on what happened here. Decisions made above his paygrade.

He could still say no, but after tonight's performance, his leverage wasn't quite so strong. He'd need more practice to get another shot, which meant buying time before they cannoned him back to the AHL—or dropped his slow-playing ass altogether.

Did he want to work with Jordan on an interview? Be forced to spend time with her, to make small talk about Josh, to endure her pity because Levi had never bought in to her happy-sappy cheer like everyone else? Perhaps he could convince Harper to go with a different outlet although in truth, his sanity demanded that this interview should happen when Satan donned skates for his morning commute across the frozen tundra of hell.

"Come to my office tomorrow, Jordan," Harper finally said. "Eleven a.m."

Well, damn.

4

JORDAN SMILED at Harper's assistant for maybe the fifth time.

The woman with big eighties hair and friendly hazel eyes, smiled back. Now, that's how you front an organization.

"I'm sure she won't be long now. Someone showed up unannounced." She added an eyebrow raise to signal that this was generally unacceptable behavior in the world of CEO appointment scheduling.

"No worries!" Jordan went back to wringing her hands, though she had no good reason to be nervous. Harper was a fellow ovary-possessor, a woman in a man's business. They had plenty in common, but she was also kind of scary.

"I'm a big fan of your podcast," the assistant said. "Never miss an episode."

"Oh, thanks so much. Always great to hear from people who actually listen." She leaned forward conspiratorially. "So is there anything you'd like to hear more of on the show? I'm sorry, I don't know your name."

"Casey. Casey Higgins. PA to the superstar CEO of the Rebels." She did a jazz hands move, then seemed to think

better of it and put her palms down with a shake of
her head.

Jordan laughed. "Nice."

"Sorry, sometimes I can't believe I work for this organization. It's really cool, especially when you love the sport."
She looked at Harper's door. "It might be nice to do a feature
on female fans. On your podcast."

"That's a good idea." Jordan wasn't saying it to be
convivial, either. Female spectator numbers were growing
and had plenty of room left to run. "I—"

The door to Harper's office opened and out walked the
woman herself shaking the hand of ... *whiskey tango foxtrot!*
Coby Dawson from ESPN.

"Harper, thanks so much for making time for me before
I catch my flight back east."

Back east. Who said that? Big shot losers like Coby
Dawson, that's who.

"I always have time for you, Coby," Harper said, loading
on the saccharine. Her gaze flicked to Jordan for a nanosec-
ond, then back to Coby. "Have a safe trip."

"Will do." Coby caught Jordan's eye, surprise pleating his
brow. "Hello. It's Jordan, isn't it? Fancy seeing you here."

Yeah, fancy that. For once in her life, Jordan found herself
with nothing to say. Dawson was stepping on her turf, trying
to finagle his way into her story, and she was feeling less
than charmed.

She stood to let everyone know that she was here to be
counted. Unfortunately, her heel chose that moment to
wobble, but she managed to right herself and caught Harper's assistant, Casey, eyeing her with interest.

"You didn't mention your connection to Hunt last night,
Jordan," Coby said.

"Can't give away all my secrets."

The man's smirk made her blood boil, and an awkward moment passed before he broke the silence. "Well, I should be going. Ladies." With cocky swagger, he walked off down the corridor toward the exit.

"Come in, Jordan," Harper said, appearing amused in the way of a Roman emperor viewing gladiators in the Coliseum.

A subtle nod from Casey gave Jordan a much-needed boost as she followed the Rebels' owner into her office. Instead of the leather, mahogany, and hints of cigar she expected, the room was bright and airy, with French décor influences such as grosgrain ribbon wallpaper and ornate mirrors.

"Wow, this is gorgeous!"

"Thanks. My mother-in-law's doing, Cajun-French-New Orleans inspired. I find it's best to let her do her thing."

Harper gestured toward a pale blue velvet-tufted sofa where a coffee service had been set out. No sign of a used cup for Dawson, so Jordan comforted herself with the notion he might not have been offered.

However, she had to know. "What did Dawson want?"

"What men like that always want: for things to be handed to them on a platter." Harper cocked her head. "Let's talk about the Hunt profile. Tell me what you had in mind."

All business, then. "Levi is obviously a very hot story. He checks a lot of boxes. War hero. Second act. Self-sacrifice for the common good, given that he put a potentially lucrative hockey career on hold to serve his country. Of course, the worry is that his time away from the game has left him a step behind. Can a thirty-year-old newbie compete with the college grads? If he doesn't play much—and worse, doesn't perform—then that dims the story's impact."

"The ideal, for both of us, is that with care and feeding

we have a war hero-turned-goal-scoring phenom on our hands. Coffee?"

"Please."

Harper poured from a tall porcelain pot with blue flowers on it while Jordan made her case.

"Mac would like me to do a weekly check-in and post to the CSN website, kind of a 'Diary of a Rookie' deal."

"Where you write the diary," Harper said.

"Right, but I think I'd prefer to do something long-form, resulting in a final in-depth profile. It would give me more time to develop a relationship with my subject. I'd schedule sit-downs with Levi and pump him for information about his background, how he found hockey, why Special Forces, hopes and dreams, that kind of thing. I would still do my regular gig of game reports." Something stopped her from telling Harper her sob story: that the entire job was dependent on getting the profile. She was still determined to snag this scoop on her own merits.

"Okay, that could work." Harper waited a beat. "I want to hear more about you. How long have you been reporting on hockey?"

Stirring a spoonful of sugar into her coffee, Jordan gave her hockey journo origin story. "I was playing and reporting as soon as I could skate. While my brothers were on the ice I was giving the commentary. Wrote for my school newspaper, then majored in journalism at Syracuse."

"But you didn't start immediately. You got married and put aside your goals for a while."

So Harper had done her research. "My husband was based out of Fort Campbell in Kentucky. Establishing myself in journalism, especially sports journalism which requires more mobility, wasn't foremost on my mind. I wanted to make my marriage work and that was the way to do it. When he died, I thought long and hard about where I should take my life next."

Throwing herself into her career had filled a void and helped heal the ache of Josh's death. So many people had implied that her marriage was so young, such a whirlwind, and in the words of her mother, "mercifully short." Mom had intended her words to soothe, and true, with his deployments, they'd only spent a total of seven months together over two years. But she and Josh had something special, and the brevity of their marriage didn't make it any less real.

"I'm sorry about what happened to him," Harper said. "It must have been a terrible time for you."

"It was, but I have a good support network. After a few false starts, I moved to Rockford to cover the Midwest regional hockey beat and now I'm working for Chicago SportsNet, though just a temp gig at the moment. This is where I'm meant to be." Her last statement emerged from her throat—and heart—with a vehemence than surprised even herself.

"I didn't mean to imply your marriage wasn't the right move." Harper looked uncomfortable for the first time since Jordan had met her. "A little projecting on my part, perhaps. I thought any man I was with wouldn't be able to compete with my empire-building ambitions or would want me to be less *me*, I suppose. And of all the men to catch my eye ..."

"The veteran center you brought on to save the team shouldn't have been it."

Harper shook her head, possibly in amazement at how it had all turned out. She'd inherited the team jointly with her sisters after the passing of their father—legendary player, coach, and owner, Clifford Chase. Immediately the knives came out, everyone ready to slash through her dreams. Engaging in a taboo affair with Remy DuPre, one of her players, had opened Harper and the organization to ridicule. Making the playoffs lowered the volume of the chatter.

Winning the Cup shut them right up.

Harper went on. "What I'm saying is that love can make us do crazy things. As long as you feel that you're still you, then any decision you make in support of that love is valid." She took a cleansing breath, evidently setting that part of the sermon aside. "I've read your work and listened to your podcasts. You have a good take on our sport but better than that, you know Levi already."

Those last few words might have sounded casual to any other ear, but not to Jordan's. Kinsey's voice echoed in her brain: *Who cares how you got the job? Just take it, then prove it belonged to you all along.*

"He and my husband were both Sergeant Engineers in the Green Berets. I met him a couple of times when the team was stateside but we're not friendly."

Harper eyed her over the lip of her coffee cup. "That's a curious way to put it. You could've said 'we hardly know each other' or something like that. 'Not friendly' is more of a ... statement."

Jordan fought the heat flushing her skin. "There's nothing there."

Harper raised an eyebrow. "I thought I picked up on some tension between you two last night."

"He's always given me the impression that he's not my biggest fan. I used to tease him because he was grumpy and moody, kind of robotic, always shooting daggers every time I opened my mouth. He obviously thought I wasn't right for Josh and anytime we met, his disapproval was like another person in the room."

And then there was the night of Josh's funeral when I kissed him like I needed oxygen and he was the only dispenser in a ten-mile radius. Where exactly was she going with this again?

"And now I've revealed that Levi and I have a history that might not be conducive to digging deep for a profile, I guess that changes things."

Harper shook her head, her eyes bright with excitement. "Are you kidding? If you're already annoying him for whatever reason, I would think that's exactly what you want."

"It is?" That kiss had certainly annoyed him. For the briefest moment, he'd not been a robot. He'd been a warm, giving, sexy man with excellent kissing skills.

And he'd hated her for taking him there.

Possibly still did. Last night, he'd not been happy to see her. That had bothered her, but only because she was human and wanted to be liked. No other reason.

"Any man can play the stoic card if he doesn't have skin in the game. Indifference is a killer to intimacy," Harper said. "A little friction is the best way to pull out a few secrets and open up those channels of communication. With Hunt, it's not just about performance on the ice but getting to the heart of why he's a good fit for this team. I don't know if it's a Jersey boy thing but he seems a little ... closed off. Not that any of these guys are paragons of communication." She grinned. "But with a couple of recent retirements, it's important that Levi becomes part of a cohesive unit sooner than later. We agreed to the profile because it's good PR. But it would be wonderful if it had the additional benefit of opening Hunt up and getting him better acclimated to his new role as a Rebel."

Harper wasn't telling the whole story, but Jordan didn't push for now.

"You mentioned this long-form piece idea," Harper went

on. "To truly make that work, I'd like you to embed with the team, travel with us, get to know us."

Travel with them? Oh, Levi would hate that, but Mac would love it, and right now he was the only man she had to please.

"That sounds fantastic."

Harper pressed her lips in a tight line. "The lawyers said I should make you sign a non-disclosure agreement, but I think that defeats the purpose of this. Instead, I need a guarantee from you."

Jordan wasn't in the habit of making promises to the subjects of her stories or their bosses, no matter how powerful they were. She remained silent, waiting for Harper's request.

"You'll be traveling with the team, getting up close and personal, likely hearing risqué comments and inappropriate jokes."

"I have tough skin."

"I don't doubt you do. But if you come across anything that could hurt Levi, another player, or the reputation of the team, I ask that you share it with me first."

Curious. "I can't promise I won't publish or report on anything that the public wants to read."

"I'm not asking that. I just want a chance to assess and come up with a plan that minimizes any potential damage. Mostly, I don't want to see any of my boys hurt."

There was no missing the steel in Harper's tone. This woman ran a successful professional hockey franchise while raising three kids under the age of four. Of course she had Remy at home clocking the house husband hours, but still.

Harper Chase was a badass in this season's Prada shoes.

"I think I can agree to those terms. And can we agree

that I'm the only reporter on this story? In other words, Dawson is out."

Harper smiled, clearly appreciative of a fellow cut-throat. "You'll have exclusive access. Do we have a deal?" She thrust out her hand.

"Deal."

Jordan took it and shook, thinking on what Harper had said about hurting Levi. True, she would be coaxing words from him he'd likely never spoken to anyone else. That was her job. But the idea that Jordan had the capacity to hurt Levi was ridiculous.

The man was a robot. One with deliciously kissable lips, but a robot all the same.

"Looks like your friend's back for more of those gourmet *huevos rancheros*."

Levi rolled his eyes at Lucy, who thought she was *so* funny, and got a laugh in return. "They weren't that bad, were they?"

Her smile popped bright against her brown skin. "I'm not kidding. Joe and a couple of other guys have been in here asking for those eggs every day for the last week. You're putting the rest of us to shame, Levi."

Last week he'd cooked up his best egg recipe at the Uptown Mission, a homeless shelter on the north side of Chicago where he volunteered once a week, usually for the breakfast shift. As soon as he'd moved to Chicago a month ago, he'd signed on for kitchen duty. Cutting a check—which he did anonymously, anyway, because he now had more money than he knew what to do with—wasn't quite enough. He was used to getting his hands dirty.

This morning, he'd arrived at six and worked with the crew to prepare breakfast for one hundred and twenty guests, seventy-five percent of whom lived on the streets. The rest were in temporary housing here at the Mission, part of a holistic program to get them clean, fed, employed, and reintegrated.

Joe—Levi's new buddy—approached with a tray, over-long hair in his eyes and his head dipped, but clearly seeking out Levi. Last week, Joe had shared with Levi some details of his army service about three years prior. They'd bonded over it. Well, bonded was a stretch. They'd acknowl-edged their common frame of reference and didn't think the other person was an asshole.

"Hey, there," Levi said.

Joe offered a shy grin. "Got any of those eggs?"

"It's French toast and bacon today, I'm afraid. I had to let someone else pick the menu"—disapproving cluck from Lucy—"and even though it can't beat my eggs, it's not bad."

"Bacon's good, I s'pose. French toast, too. You got syrup?"

"Sure do. Over on that counter." Levi loaded a few slices of the thick, egg-battered toast on his plate and extra strips of bacon. "Come back for seconds if you're still hungry."

Nice going, idiot. Hollow bellies were these guys' normal.

A brief nod was Levi's reward. Ten minutes later, the entire line had been served, and the dining hall was abuzz with the sound of cutlery scraping against plates and the low murmur of conversation.

"I have to change my day next week," Levi said to Lucy, who was the shelter's director and handled the scheduling. "I'll be out of town."

"Somewhere nice?"

"Philly. Business." It was the first away game of the season against the Liberty, one of the Rebels' age-old foes.

No one here had figured out who Levi was and he was hoping to keep it that way for a while longer.

Because as soon as people figured it out—and by people, he meant intrepid cub reporter, Ms. Sunshine herself—there would be the inevitable questions. *Why this? Why here? Why now?* Which would lead to puzzle pieces being moved around and slotted together into whatever mosaic suited her damn profile. Moretti had informed him yesterday that Jordan would be "embedded" with the team for the next month, whatever the fuck that meant, and Levi should cooperate with her "to the best of his ability." No doubt she'd be shining a light into the dark crevices of Levi's life, looking for creepy crawlies to give her story background color.

"Can you do Monday?" Lucy asked.

"Shouldn't be a problem." He thumbed over his shoulder toward the seating. "Mind if I join Joe?"

"As long as you're back in ten for dishwashing duty."

"Yes, boss." Levi grabbed a cup of mud-awful coffee—better come up with a plan for donating a decent stash of beans—and headed over to one of the tables with a few strips of bacon on a small plate.

"Hey, need more?"

"Won't say no." Joe wrapped the offering in a napkin and put it in his pocket.

Levi took a sip of his coffee and settled into a comfortable silence. From what he'd gleaned, Joe had left the army on a Big Chicken Dinner—better known as a Bad Conduct Discharge—after going AWOL during a visit stateside. Clearly suffering from some form of untreated PTSD, he'd been offered one of the beds upstairs, but preferred the streets. Levi wondered why. He could get away with that in October but the cold descended on Chicago pretty quickly.

"You sleep under the viaduct on Wilson last night?"

Joe nodded. "Rumor has it they're gonna clean it up. Move people on."

"Got somewhere else?"

"A few places. Viaduct's better, though. Good cover."

Levi wished he could do more to help, but throwing his weight around was probably not the ideal move despite the special connection he felt with a man who had served his country and now lived under a train bridge. Too many veterans got left behind in this, the supposedly best country on God's green earth.

"Lucy said there might be a bed here, if you're interested."

Joe raised his gaze, which was usually averted, and Levi saw the directness that must have served him well during his time in the military.

"Not really a mixer."

Levi laughed because damn if that wasn't himself to a T. "You're looking at the guy who'd rather poke a fork in his eyeballs than play nice with other people. But sometimes you gotta join the team to get to the next stage, y'know."

"Rah-rah, school spirit."

"Something like that."

Joe smiled, then his mouth straightened into a grim line as he looked around the cafeteria. "In these places, some-one's always trying to steal your stuff."

Usually a fear of assault or having valuables stolen topped the list of reasons to stay out there.

"Figured I'd mention it in case you changed your mind." Levi stood to let the man finish his breakfast in peace.

"What you been doing since your discharge?"

"This and that. Keeping busy."

"Be careful you don't think about it too much."

Levi sat again. "Think about what?"

"It." He shrugged, then wrapped his hands around the mug of coffee like he was trying to draw the warmth into his bones or transfer bad mojo to the porcelain. "You think about it too much and then next thing you know ..." He flashed his hands, mimicking an explosion. *Boom.*

Every guy Levi had met in the service had memories they'd rather bury, images they'd prefer surgically removed from their brain. What shit had Joe seen and had it led him to where he was right now? Linking the two seemed like a job for Captain Obvious except there were a million decisions and branches in between those bookended events.

"You think about it too much?" Levi asked, testing the temperature of the conversation.

Joe tapped the side of his head, but didn't speak.

"Levi," he heard Lucy call out behind him. "These dishes aren't gonna wash themselves."

"Guess I've been told," Levi said which yielded a chuckle from his new friend. "You take care, buddy." *And think about that bed.*

Joe smiled secretively and headed off to get a refill of coffee.

Levi checked his phone, which had buzzed earlier, and lo and behold, if it wasn't Susie Sunshine with a message just for him.

"Hi, Levi! Jordan here. Well, you know that! So, I called yesterday but maybe you didn't get that message? We're a go on the profile and I'd love to sit down and discuss the parameters, the scope, and what I have in mind. And of course, hear your thoughts on the direction of the piece. Oh, I've got a joke for you. How did the skeleton get to the hockey game? Driving a Zamboni! Get it? Ah, good one, Jordan. Okay, call me, bye."

Levi stared at the phone, then hovered a finger over the

delete option. How the hell was he supposed to get through this?

Be careful you don't think about it too much, Joe had said. Good advice for a multitude of situations.

Pocketing his phone, he headed to the kitchen to lose himself in the thought-suppressing power of dish duty.

5

*Got questions for Levi Hunt? @HockeyGrrl is in the house! DM
me and help me do my job ;)
#ChicagoRebels #OldestRookie #ChicagoSportsNet*

CLIFFORD CHASE, the late owner of the Rebels, once famously commented that hockey was not exactly civilized given that it involved thousands of pounds of brute force distilled to superhuman physiques. Throw in knives on feet, clubs in hands, and a no-holds barred, full-contact environment, and you had society-sanctioned war with water breaks.

God, it was exciting, though.

Sitting rink-side during a Rebels practice session, Jordan was in awe of the effort levels going into drills. Pity her subject didn't seem as in awe of *her* effort levels to schedule a sit-down interview.

Three calls ignored in two days. More than ignored, she suspected, because she had taken to imagining he wore a sneer when he listened to her cheerful voice mails. Maybe he played her messages on speaker for his new teammates while shaking his head, scratching his balls, and ... spitting. Yeah, she could see that.

Today, the man was doing an excellent job of continuing their non-relationship. He had to have seen her, especially as Theo Kershaw had gone out of his way to skate over and say hi. She knew Theo from his early days on the feeder team in Rockford. He'd spent close to two years out of hockey after a brain aneurysm ruptured one night during a game. Open and easy with the press about it, Theo was the perfect subject with an outgoing personality to match.

Speaking of personality, or lack thereof ...

She waved at Levi, hoping to throw him off his mental stride without having him trip on the ice. Like the pro he was, he continued to ignore her.

Time to bring in the big guns.

She shot off a text message to Tommy Gordon, Levi's agent, who she knew because he also represented Theo Kershaw.

Her phone rang immediately. "Tommy Boy!"

"Welcome to the big leagues, Jordan. I assume you're calling about Hunt. Heard you were on the story."

"He's not playing nice, Tommy. Can't you impress upon him how good this will be for his career? Or more important, *my* career? At minimum give me some nugget I can use as leverage."

Tommy chuckled. "Sell my player down the river? Jordan, honey, this game is about trust."

She managed not to scoff. Just. "The Rebels brass is on board and I'm on site, but your player is avoiding my calls to set up a sit-down. A word in his ear from my favorite agent might grease the skate. Besides, you owe me for that juicy nugget I slipped you about Nate Barker." She'd overheard that Nate, a goalie with Nashville, was unhappy with his representation and passed it on. Tommy had been *very* pleased at the chance to swoop in before anyone else.

He growled. "Let me see what I can do."

A shiver ghosted through her, maybe a premonition because a text message popped up from ... ugh, the Dick Bandit returns. No pics this time, thank the gods.

Hey Red, been thinking of U.

Good Lord, didn't he know that people no longer needed to abbreviate because of autocorrect? It took more effort to capitalize that damn U! And as for whether he'd been thinking of her, she'd prefer he not think of her at all.

Billy Stroger, or Dick Bandit, was a player on the New York Spartans who had started following her on Twitter four months ago. A notorious troublemaker and total goon on the ice, he'd offered to guest on her podcast at a time when she was anxious to build her audience and a name for herself. While she had no problem chatting with players— encouraged it, frankly, to start building those relationships she'd bragged to Mac about—an indecently swelling percentage assumed it gave them license to spill their most intimate thoughts and anatomy pics.

Stroger was one of them.

"Thanks for helping out, Tommy. Maybe I'll see you at a game one night." She signed off and refocused on the messages coming in from DB.

Heard U got a promotion. Maybe I'll see U when Ur in town for the Rebels away game in NYC.

In three weeks. And not if she could help it.

Kinsey was right. She really should report it, but her position was precarious. Having promised Mac she could hang tough with the boys, she'd get short shrift if she made a fuss. He'd say she was too thin-skinned (read: lady-skinned) to be doing this kind of job. And who else would care? Stroger's bosses in New York? Like anyone would go to bat for the temp at the local network.

Better to use a tried-and-tested female strategy: kill it with politeness, bury it with lies.

Probably not. My boyfriend might not approve.

Should she add a smiley face? She hovered over the emojis and after a few seconds of internal struggle, decided to go for it.

That damn smiley face felt like a sellout, but better that than risking the wrath of the species all women knew well: Butt-Hurt-By-Rejection Male.

Another text came in, this one accompanied by a pic. Abs—nice abs, to be sure—with a trail of hair crowning his ... *really*?

The text said: *U sure about that?*

"Hey, Jordan, want to come to lunch with us?"

Guiltily, she looked up into the pretty face of Theo Kershaw. His green eyes flicked through the Plexi to her phone, lingered, then returned to meet her gaze.

She turned the phone over in her lap, mentally cursing that Stroger's penis was so close to her non-consenting lady bits. "Us?"

"Yeah, I heard you have to get close to Envy for some exposé you're doing. Swapping stories over massive amounts of carbs is probably a good way to do it."

"I wouldn't call it an exposé, more like a profile. And why Envy?"

"That's the nickname we're trying out for Hunt because of his time in the service. Green Berets, green with envy, get it?" He grimaced. "Sorry, that's probably insensitive. I get accused of that a lot. No filter."

She smiled her instant forgiveness. "It's fine. Mentions of the armed services roll right off my back."

The rest of the team were heading to the locker room, so Jordan stood and walked along the row to the exit while Theo trailed her on the ice.

"Levi's not too excited about the prospect of me hanging out here, I gather."

Theo chuckled. "He's got that military, just-the-facts-ma'am thing going on, so he probably hates talking about shit." At the entrance to the tunnel, he leaned in and not even the smell of sweaty guy could diminish his shine. "I've a better idea. You know your recording device just wants to listen to me talk about my favorite subject."

"As in you?"

"Totally! Interview me for your podcast, Hockey Grrl." He rolled the Rs dramatically.

Jordan laughed, trying to sound assured. Was he flirting with her because he'd seen that graphic photo and thought she'd be receptive? The last thing she needed was to give anyone ideas. Since Dick Bandit had led the charge into her Twitter DMs, every interaction with a player was tainted with suspicion as to motives.

Another glance at Theo confirmed that he was just a happy puppy, excited at the chance to get air time and spread the Word according to Kershaw. He'd make a great guest, but it was almost more fun to pod-block him.

A shadow fell, obstructing the light shining off Theo. Mount Grump, himself, because he was tall and craggy and cranky. This was a much better name than Envy and she'd be happy to license it to Theo.

"Off to the showers, Kershaw," Levi grunted with a glare at his teammate.

Oblivious, Theo winked at her. "See you for lunch, Hockey Grrl."

The sudden tension intrigued her. Maybe she could give

Levi a severe case of FOMO. "Oh, Theo, we should definitely sit down and chat about your return to the game. I think your fans would love to know more about that."

"Yeah, they would," Theo responded with another wink. It's a wonder he didn't pull an eye muscle.

When he was out of earshot, Levi turned to her. "Lunch?"

"Why, I'd love to!"

Levi growled. "I mean, why is Kershaw saying he'll see you for lunch?"

"Because I was invited. No better way to get a feel for the team dynamic than by eating with the crew. I'll also be traveling to Philly with you guys on Thursday."

He looked pained, which strangely, was sort of hot. Stupidly hot. That made no sense whatsoever.

Thrown by that conclusion, she collected her wits. "You haven't returned my calls."

"I don't really have time—"

"To do what your bosses want? Have you already forgotten how to follow orders?"

That one earned her a grunt. Ah, the sweet sound of progress.

Perhaps they needed to clear the thick-enough-to-smother air. "Or is it just that you can't stand that fate has thrown us together after all these years and you have to spend time with your sworn enemy?"

His mouth twitched. "Fate? Sworn enemy? When did this happen?"

"You're obviously still holding a grudge about what happened back in the day."

"You think I have a problem with *this* because I kissed you?"

Oh. *Ohhh.*

"Pretty sure I was the aggressor."

He narrowed his gaze. "You? Jesus, Jordan, is that what you think?"

"Why else would you be so mad at me?"

"I'm not mad at you." He scrubbed a hand through his dark hair, like he was mad at something. Maybe his hair?

No. It was him. He was mad at himself. Still, after all these years.

In that moment, something unfurled inside her. A twist in her stomach that had her reassessing the man before her. Levi Hunt was six feet three of Special Forces badassery, his body a honed weapon, his gaze sharp enough to fell the enemy or a weak-willed woman at fifty paces. Objectively, she'd recognized this when she first met him. He had a gruff, dangerous quality that would appeal to many.

She had never considered herself one of them.

Yes, there was The Kiss from Yore. But it had come at a strange time and existed outside the rules of regular attraction. Sad times sometimes led to sexy times.

But she was no longer sad. She was on a mission, and the last thing she needed was present-day sparks with the subject of a story.

Why, Lord? Why must you torment me like this?

"You seem mad? Just a smidge?" She rubbed her finger and thumb together.

"I just don't like being the center of attention," Levi said. "I've lived my life under the radar. In my previous job, shining a light gets you killed, so getting chatty and opening a vein isn't my favorite thing."

Her heart checked for him. That night after Josh's funeral, he'd been the consummate listener. Just watching, taking her cues, waiting for her to open up about her pain, and not indulging in what must have been his own.

Then she took advantage by eating his face off.

Subtlety wasn't her go-to, but she might have to change it up here. "Okay. How about you just pretend I'm not around for the first couple of weeks? I'll be part of the furniture, a warm body on a plane, just another mouth stuffing my face with——what's for lunch?"

"It's usually pasta primavera on Mondays. There's an Italian place that delivers Moretti-approved meals."

Right, the Rebels GM was well-known for his cooking skills and heavy hand in the Rebels' menus. Now she knew who to blame for those mini-macarons in the press box.

"I love pasta primavera! I'll blend in, get a feel for the team energy, and then when you've settled and scored a few goals, I'll pounce with all my pesky questions."

"You'll pounce? Probably not the best threat to make to a former Green Beret."

Acknowledging what sounded like an attempt at humor, she smiled at him.

Zip. Zilch. Zero. *Game life lost, back to square one.*

"You'll be aware whenever a conversation is on the record and I promise I won't try to pull a fast one. I'm just looking for a shot here, to find a good angle on this profile."

"There are no good angles." Pronouncement made, he skated back to the center of the rink and started shooting drills with pucks even though practice was long over.

Well, Grumpster, I call liar. From the back portrayed a perfectly pleasant angle because Levi Hunt had an excellent ass.

While he was being an impossible one.

~

"Dad?"

Her father peered from the iPad screen, set up on Jordan's kitchen counter. Owllike behind his glasses, he blinked as if he'd just woken up and was surprised that somehow he'd managed to press answer on the FaceTime call.

"Jordan? Is everything okay?"

"Of course it is. I usually call at this time, remember? A move to Chicago isn't going to change my weekly check-in with the parental units."

"Oh, right. Of course." He lowered his bifocals and eyed her over the rims. From a swivel chair he usually had too much fun with, he leaned in closer. "How's it going, Jo-Jo?"

"Settling in. Is Mom there?"

"She's at the conference in Copenhagen."

"Forgot about that." Her mom, better known as Dr. Tamara Wilson, world-renowned expert on human rights abuses and the law, was giving the keynote at the World Child Rights conference. Just another day. "Have you eaten?"

"Not yet. There's no food in the house." Her father was the epitome of the absentminded professor, especially when her mom wasn't around to remind him to eat.

"Can you take a break?"

"I'm at a good point to stop. And I've got something to show you." He moved out of frame and rummaged about. When he returned, he was holding up a hardcover book titled *The Rise of the Sharing Economy*.

"Oh, you got your copies!" Somehow her father was making bank on long-ass treatises about Airbnb and micro-lending. A three-time *New York Times* bestseller, he also had a named professorship at Georgetown in DC. The man made economics sexy.

If she ever told him that, he'd die.

He placed the book down, pride on his face that he didn't bother to hide. "Don't you have a match to watch?"

"Game, Dad. They're called games and tonight they're not playing. I'm heading to Philly to see the first away game of the season in a couple of days."

"How's your new place shaping up?"

"Stuff's still in boxes for the most part. I'm going one room at a time, so I'm at the living room."

"With the kitchen last?"

She laughed. "You know it." Her parents were big fans of eating out and ordering in as they were far too busy being intellectually productive to cook. Along with her parents' neuroses, she'd inherited the can't-boil-water gene.

"Tell me more about this new job, sweetheart. Sounds like a step up from reporting on the matches." He shook his head in apology. "I mean, games."

She smiled, grateful to him for trying. Passing for a mere mortal in a family of intellectual giants was mentally exhausting, probably because her brain was too small to begin with.

"I have a chance to do a profile on one of the players. A lot of people want it, but I'm getting behind-the-scenes access." She took a sip from the half-drunk wine glass on her kitchen counter. "It's Levi Hunt."

Her father squinted. "That name's familiar, and not because I follow the sports pages."

"He was one of Josh's teammates in the Berets. Best man at our wedding and he came to the funeral."

"Ah, yes. Serious, stone-faced, not much to say." Yep, got it in three. "He plays professional hockey?"

"That's the story—this guy who gave up a guaranteed pro career to enlist in the army. To be honest, he's kind of a dick."

Her dad grimaced at her word choice, which proved her expensive education was largely wasted. "To you or to everyone?"

"To everyone but particularly to me. He's a complete robot, not into sharing. I just don't know how to reach him."

"You thought because he was Josh's friend that it would make it easier?"

"Smoother, I suppose? And my boss is expecting something in-depth. Something that hasn't been seen before. But I hate the idea of poking him about his service or his past. It's all sort of—"

"Seedy?"

She barely managed the shrug she felt the situation needed. Her father's opinion on how she was wasting her talents was well-known. Her oldest brother, Jeremy, was a civil rights lawyer in DC. Her other brother, Will (aka St. Will), ran a nature reserve for endangered birds in California. *I mean, come the hell on.* She was well aware that covering men bashing a rubber disk around an ice rink was not really what her family had in mind for her.

The screen beeped and another smiling face appeared.

"Hi, Mom!"

Her mother waved, which she seemed to think was the best way to get attention on a family conference call. "Hi, darling! It's one in the morning here, but I remembered that you'd be calling about now. Hope I haven't missed anything good."

"Just filling Dad in on my latest assignment."

"It's the statue from Josh's funeral, Tam," her dad said. "The one you said looked like a millennial Zeus. Moody—"

"But beautiful and fierce," her mom picked up. "Logan something."

"It's Levi, Mom. Levi Hunt. He's a pro hockey player now and a big story."

Her mother smiled. "I'm sure he is."

Jordan bit back her exasperation. *They love you. They just don't get sports.* "I'm hoping to make parallels between Levi's work ethic in the military and in the NHL. Try to get to the heart of why someone would make the choices he did."

Her father cleared his throat. "Well, you know how I feel about our country's military-industrial complex, the glamorization of war, and state-sanctioned murder—"

Jordan mimicked falling asleep, and her father smiled.

"Okay, no more lectures from the professor. But surely this Hunt character's choice to serve his country shouldn't be so strange. He saw something greater in service than he could obtain with a ball."

"Puck."

"Language, young lady."

She laughed. As much as she wished her dad better appreciated what she did, she did enjoy listening to how his brain ticked over.

Her mom cut in. "Sounds like Levi Hunt is more interesting than the usual players you work with, darling. At least he chose to do something of benefit to the human race."

"I know this doesn't seem important, Mom, but sports drives a lot of people. It's like a religion to the fans, as organized and untouchable as a faith, and these players are their gods."

"The new opium of the masses," her dad said.

Here we go. When her dad started paraphrasing Karl Marx, she knew they'd veered off track and into one of his favorite subjects: the dumbing down of American culture.

Though her mom would claim it wasn't all that smart to start with.

"Speaking of faith, darling," her mother said, "I'm starting to lose mine. Are you getting any action, dating-wise? Because one of my former students just moved to Chicago. I gave him a reference and he is very smart, very handsome, and *very, very* single."

"Did you put that in the reference? Because very-very-single sounds like a commitment-phobe and basically unemployable." Jordan knew the conversation was winding down as soon as her love life made an ignominious entrance. "I really don't have time to date anyway, not with the game schedule and all the travel."

"Well, I'll send him your number and you could get coffee. Everyone has time for coffee."

"Mom—"

"I have to go, darling. Early flight. Tootles!" She shut down the connection before Jordan could make her case for not having her number be disseminated to Very-Very-Single and whoever else her mother deemed fit for her.

"Dad, I'm not interested in dating."

"Why do you think that is, Jo-Jo? It's been a long time since Josh."

In his voice, she heard his love and concern, so she gave the question the consideration it deserved. "I put my career on hold when I was with Josh. That's not to say I regret it. I don't, but now it's *my* time. It's been easier to box that part of me away and focus on working toward having a fulfilling career. Once I'm established, I can worry about my personal life. And I know the job's not what you or Mom had in mind for me, but this is what I want. And wanting it means giving it my all and not being distracted."

Her father smiled. "We just want you to be happy, sweetheart. A job you love, and maybe when you're ready, a man who loves you almost as much as I do."

Aw, her heart melted. "Thanks, Dad. I better go. Before she does any real damage, I need to write a stern text to my matchmaking mother."

6

"So you'd let your mom find you a date but you won't let me?"

Jordan grinned at Kinsey, seated next to her at the bar in Dempsey's, a firefighter-owned, and as of this moment, wonderfully occupied bar in Wicker Park. Quite a few specimens of the hot 'n' hunky variety were rubbing shoulders with each other and Jordan was basking in the pheromones.

"I am *not* letting her find me a date. I've been screening my calls all day because my mother said Very-Very-Single doesn't like to text."

"Weirdo."

"Right? This guy apparently is a debate champion, won all the mock trials in law school, blah, blah. Dude thinks he can ethos-logos-pathos me into a date."

"You've got to answer your phone first."

"Which won't be happening." Jordan clinked her wine glass against Kinsey's. "Sucker."

"Another round, ladies?" The spectacularly built bartender with shocking blue eyes leaned over and dropped a panty-melting grin.

Kinsey leaned right back. "Only if you want to get me sloppy drunk and take advantage of me, handsome."

"You're giving my clientele the wrong idea, lady."

"Which clientele?" Kinsey looked around dramatically. "Who do I need to take down to keep you all to myself?"

Jordan chuckled at their cute dynamic. Kinsey had certainly lucked out with Luke Almeida: firefighter, bar owner, husband, and per his wife, amazing dad. Clichéd as it sounded, all the good ones were taken.

Or gone.

Seeing a couple as in sync as Kinsey and Luke sparked envy and more than a hint of sadness for what Jordan had lost. Maybe her parents were right. Maybe she should be dipping her toes in the dating pool.

Luke poured another glass of tolerable Pinot for them both. As awesome as Dempsey's man candy options were, the wine selections were only so-so.

He turned to Jordan. "How's Hunt shaping up in practice?"

"Pretty good, actually. I'm thinking that maybe he got nervous on that first outing."

"He'll need to get up to speed soon. Everyone enjoys a feel-good story but if he can't back it up, he'll lose fans real quick."

"Which means you need to strike while the iron is hot," Kinsey said. "In a few weeks, Levi Hunt might be yesterday's news."

Didn't she know it.

"Oh!" Kinsey waved her hands. "I almost forgot. I have a gift for you! Luke, babe, I stashed it behind the bar over there."

Luke retrieved a shopping bag, placed it on the bar away

from the full glasses, then stepped away to help real customers.

Jordan couldn't stop smiling. "You got something for me?"

"Yep! Open it. Open it now."

She pulled out the box and blinked at the label: Kate Spade. Her mouth made an O, because even though she wasn't a fashionista she knew this was a top-quality purse. She also knew it wasn't cheap.

"Kinsey, you shouldn't have."

"I should. You can't travel on chartered jets, scarf down mini-macarons, and hang with Harper Fucking Chase sporting a backpack. You're in the big leagues now."

Boasting soft pebbled black leather with a pink-striped lining, the handbag had room enough for a pony or a laptop. Actually, only a laptop. "It's gorgeous. But it must have cost a fortune."

"Outlet bargain. I *never* pay full price for anything."

"I will get you tickets for a game or access to the press box. Anything." She hugged Kinsey, so grateful to have this woman in her life. Friends were hard to come by when you moved around a lot, mentors even harder. In Kinsey, she'd found both.

Kinsey smiled, obviously pleased with her gift's impact. "So, Hunt. He's not coming around?"

"Not in the slightest."

"When you knew him before, he wasn't all that friendly?"

Jordan bit her lip. "Uh, the guy hated me. Thought I was too perky or happy or sunny. If I showed enthusiasm for anything, he'd give me the stink eye, like I'd offended him and his ancestors. He was so different from Josh that I wondered how they were even friends."

"Work friends, especially in the kind of work they were doing, is a different kettle of fish. Outside of that, they probably wouldn't have even registered as likely buddies, but when you go through things together—missions or whatever they did—that creates a bond."

"I suppose."

Kinsey put down her glass and tilted her head. "You're blushing."

"What? No, it's just toasty in here. Sexy firefighters, y'know?" She gestured to a Thor-lookalike at the other end of the bar. "How many hot brothers-in-law do you have again?"

"Five, each more delicious than the last. What happened?"

"When?"

"When? With you and the Marine."

Damn her choice of interrogative. She should have said "what."

"Green Beret. And it was nothing."

Kinsey steeled her gaze.

Jordan caved. "A little too much tequila." Her shoulders sunk lower, her eyes narrowed further. "On the night of Josh's funeral."

"You mean you and Levi Hunt ...?" Kinsey did a twirling gesture with her finger.

"God, no! It was just a kiss, I barely remember it." *Liar, liar.* "I made a dang fool of myself climbing him like a tree and he set me back down on the earth where I belonged."

"So what's the big deal?"

"I think you're overlooking the part where I'd just buried my husband." She covered her face with her hands, the memory of how she'd embarrassed herself as fresh as a sliced-open wound.

Kinsey squeezed her arm. "Do not beat yourself up. You were going through the most heart-wrecking period of your life and he was someone who empathized because he was hurting, too. No judgment."

No problem because she had judged herself plenty enough that she didn't need Kinsey to play pinch hitter.

After a pause to allow Jordan to gather herself, Kinsey said, "Maybe he feels as embarrassed about it as you do. Give it time, but not too much time."

Indeed. Time was a luxury she didn't have. She had to turn in the copy in less than four weeks. Mac was worried about being scooped, though from what she could tell no one else would get the level of access she had.

For now, she'd skate around the edges and figure out a way to crack the code of Levi.

LEVI RACED from end to end, pivoted, and raced back again. Two lengths, three, four. Only when he'd done it five more times did he attempt a shot between the pipes.

Wide open. Score!

Not a sound, only his heavy breathing and the thump of his heart. For the last three mornings, he'd arrived at 5:30 to practice alone. He needed it. Keeping up with players half his age was work. Sure that was an exaggeration, but the effect was the same. He felt old.

He'd kept fit in Special Forces, but the schedule for an NHL player was more demanding than anything in the military. Most days started at 9 a.m. with treatment and muscle taping, followed by a ninety-minute morning skate with puck drills, 2 on 1's, 3 on 2's, PP and PK practice, and shootouts. After a short break to wind down and eat with the team, most of the guys spent time on the bike or tread-mill, in the weight room, or power-napping. And that was on a home game day.

Levi's fitness would never be in question, but his reflexes and stick skills had fallen below par. It was a wonder the Rebels had even bothered with him at all, but then they weren't known for their clear decision-making. Making a splash—that was their MO. So here he was taking advan-tage of their need to bring on a novelty act, the league's oldest rookie, someone the press wanted to write all about.

Well, he'd ride that train all the way to another ... goal.

"Yes!"

The pleasure of which was kind of ruined by the sound of a slow clap.

Levi spun around and almost tripped over his skates. *The* Remy DuPre was gliding toward him, dressed for prac-tice, stick in hand. Levi had never understood the word "twinkling" as it applied to eyes, but he did now. The man was a legend, largely responsible with Bren St. James and the Chase sisters for turning the Rebels' fortunes around when he was traded under duress from Boston a few years back.

"Up kind of early, Hunt," DuPre said with his distinctive New Orleans drawl. He shoved a gloveless hand in Levi's direction.

Levi took off his glove and clasped the offered hand. "Thought I had the place to myself."

"I try to get out here a couple of mornings a week before my girls wake up because once they do, there's no peace."

Sounded like "no peace" was an enjoyable problem to have. "Heard you liked being a stay at home dad."

"While *ma femme* brings home the bacon? Yeah, *c'est bon,*

mon ami." He drew on the glove he'd stashed in the waist-band of his shorts. "What you working on?"

"You saw the game. What do you think?"

"The speed will come, but I'm guessing you could improve your hand-eye coordination."

"I was a bomb disposal expert, so I assumed I had that. But this is a different level."

"Okay, that's just a tiny bit impressive. You play video games?"

Levi shook his head.

"You should."

"Cheatin' on me, brother?"

Levi looked over Remy's shoulder to the source of the voice, tinged with a Scots burr. Bren St. James, Highlander himself, skated toward them, coming to a halt in a spray of ice shavings.

Remy smiled. "Couldn't sleep?"

"Aye, Violet was snorin'. Figured I'd get in a few laps." He raised an eyebrow at Levi. "He told you to play video games yet?"

"He might've mentioned it."

Bren's glance at his brother-in-law was affectionately amused. "He's one of the players featured in the Hockey All Stars video game and always looking to boost his income streams. But he's not wrong about it being good for your hand-eye. Hit up Burnett—that kid kills on the console. Kershaw's good, too."

Levi filed it away.

"How about a little two on one?" Bren cut in between Levi and Remy, whipping a stray puck with his stick as he went. "And I think you know who the one is, Hunt."

No preamble, few niceties. Levi had never met either of

these men before, but he already felt like a member of an exclusive club.

Remy put on his second glove. "Let's see what you got, soldier."

7

Can the @ChiRebels catch a break against the @PhillyLiberty?
Check out the @HockeyGrrl podcast to get the inside track.
#ChicagoRebels #PhillySteakExtraCheese

"Read 'em and weep, gentlemen."

Kershaw lay a flush down on the table in the mini-lounge on the Rebels' chartered plane to Philly, which had the obviously desired effect: everyone threw in their hands and groaned, except for Erik who threw his cards at Theo's head.

"Hey, watch it, Fish!" Theo picked up the cards. "This beautiful face could do without the paper cut threat, you know."

"That's the third hand you've won. You're the luckiest son of a bitch who ever played cards."

"Yeah, Lucky's my middle name." He shuffled the deck. "Maybe we should ask your shadow to join us, Hunt."

Over Theo's shoulder, there was no missing that crown of red hair topping the seat in the third row.

Jordan.

She'd kept her word. For the last week, she'd attended practices, games, locker-room interviews, and team lunches. Every time he turned, she was talking to someone on the staff, the fitness coaches, even the guy who drove the Zamboni. The only person she hadn't talked to was him.

Which he shouldn't be mad about. Not that he was mad, exactly, but he was something. Irked about covered it. Was she talking to other people about him? What was she asking? What were they saying?

He was starting to sound like a middle-schooler.

"No wonder she doesn't want to talk to you if all you're gonna do is scowl at her," Theo said.

"She said she was going to hang back a bit, get a feel for the team dynamics."

"No better way than to join us for a game." He whipped out his phone and shot off a text.

"You have her number?" Levi had it, all the better to ignore her calls. He didn't realize Theo did, too.

"She gave it to everyone."

"In case we think of anything interesting." Erik picked up his hand. "About you."

"She's been asking questions about me?"

"Of course I have."

Something floral filled his nostrils. He looked up and there she was—a copper-haired vision in a blue top with a sheen to it, dark-rinse skinny jeans, and boots that made her look ten times taller. When he'd kissed her all those years ago, she wasn't so polished. But then how polished is a woman on the day she buries her husband?

He mentally squirmed, uncomfortable once more at the memory of that night. But it wasn't so much his inappropriate behavior. It was because he'd enjoyed it and a part of him wanted to enjoy it again. Cup her jaw, curl a hand around her nape, and touch his demanding lips to her soft, giving ones.

She'd moaned. He remembered that, along with the clutch of her hands to his shoulders, digging in. Claiming.

"Levi?"

He blinked to find Jordan and the entire team looking at him.

Say something. "You get your story yet?"

She smiled, a secretive curve to her lips he wanted to— nope. Nothing. He wanted nothing.

"You're hard to get a bead on."

"Me? I'm an open book."

Everyone at the table apparently thought that was hilarious. Jordan waved a hand of "see."

His agent had called a few days ago and told him to make an effort—though he didn't phrase it so nicely. (*Asshole* and its many variants might have been used liberally.) Wanting to demonstrate that he wasn't nearly as difficult as she painted him, he asked, "What have you discovered so far?"

"Let me see. Theo says you like"—she consulted her phone—"hot sauce on your fries, which I *guess* is sort of revealing?"

"I like it spicy. What's wrong with that?"

Kershaw made a noise of discontent. "It's all we've got! What music do you listen to? Are you a T or A man? Who's your favorite player in the NHL besides me?"

"That's what people want to know?" Levi couldn't believe this was what passed for "in-depth" these days. He raised his gaze to Jordan, who looked amused and perky and pretty and ... *stop right there.*

"It adds color to the newsprint," she said with a shrug.

He didn't buy it. No one really cared about that shit, and

if they did, then civilization had probably come to an end. He'd made it back to the States in one piece, a thousand times luckier than all the guys who would never come home. Here he was, living a dream he barely deserved and people wanted to read about his music preferences? He hadn't even made it more than a few minutes on the ice! Profile someone important, for Christ's sake.

It also chapped his dick that Kershaw would use such disrespectful language around a lady. *T or A man? Really?*

"Ms. Cooke, I'm probably the dullest guy in the NHL. I eat the same food every day. I work out at the same time. I get antsy if I don't pull down eight hours sleep."

Jordan leaned in, bringing more of her perfume. His body pleasantly tensed. "Favorite color?"

"Don't have one."

"Everyone has one."

He shook his head. "I'm not a preschooler, so no."

"Best James Bond?"

"Lazenby."

"The one who got married. Interesting. Is our Mr. Hunt actually a romantic?" He had no chance to comment because she was on a roll. "Favorite Beatle?"

"George."

"The quiet one?"

"Underrated talent overshadowed by superstars who eventually comes into his own. A late bloomer."

That made her smile, and he wanted to think it was different than the standard ones she dropped on the rest of them. He wanted to think it so much that he had to mentally slap himself upside the head and put her straight.

"Not exactly deep stuff now, is it?" That he sounded like a dick made something in his chest lurch.

"Got you talking, didn't I?" Another grin to let him know

she'd won a battle in a war he hadn't realized they were fighting.

Erik held up the deck of cards. "Jordan, you in?"

She shook her head. "I've got some notes to write up. Talk to you boys later." She walked away, with everyone watching the sway of her hips. Everyone but Levi, who didn't enjoy the power she held over him.

"Fine woman, that," Erik murmured.

Levi rolled his shoulders because it was either that or shove Erik hard through the plane's little window. The guy had made a perfectly legitimate comment about Jordan's fineness, yet Levi felt that unconscionable violence would be a proportionate response.

"Heard you knew her husband back in the service."

Levi looked up at Theo, who'd made that observation. "Yep. Good guy."

"So you already know Jordan?"

His neck felt prickly and hot. "Met her a couple of times. Don't know her well."

Theo held his gaze for a beat, came to some conclusion in his head, and dropped this gem: "She's dating someone."

Erik sighed. "The good ones always are."

Levi couldn't help but bristle before spitting a question at Kershaw. "You and she besties now?"

Theo looked at his cards, then up at Levi. "Just information I have. Must be pretty serious because they're sharing X-rated pics. Saw her phone screen."

Bristling would no longer cut it. "Kershaw. A word. In private."

Theo blanched, peering up at Levi who had unfolded to his full six-three and squared his shoulders, waiting not-so-patiently for his teammate to stand. "Now?"

"Now." Levi headed back to the galley, his fists clenched,

his body so tense it would repel bullets if necessary. He debated folding his arms before Kershaw moved into position but figured that might delay any much-deserved beat down that needed to happen.

Theo appeared, half-smiling, clearly nervous. "What's up?"

"I need you to understand something about how you'll be acting around Ms. Cooke from here on out. You will not be commenting on T or A in her presence. Neither will you be discussing private messages or images you happened to see on her phone."

"Hey, it wasn't *her* naked!" He flapped a hand toward the main cabin. "It was some guy's dick—"

Levi held up his hand. "Don't need to know and neither does anyone else. That's Ms. Cooke's business and you need to remember that she's a guest of the organization, and as such, will not be the subject of locker-room talk or gossip. Got it?"

The man looked suitably ashamed. "Yeah, I got it. I didn't mean to offend her. Or you. She's a fun gal to be around and she's never implied that what we say is a problem."

Well, she wouldn't, would she? As a female reporter surrounded by penises, she had to walk a fine line. Play it cool enough to take an inappropriate joke or risk being viewed as a bad sport.

"It's okay," Levi said, feeling a touch sorry for the guy. He was young and clueless. "Just watch what you say around her and about her."

"Sure, man. We good?" He held out his hand in a fist bump.

Levi gave it back. "Yeah, we're good. Just make sure to apologize to Jordan when you get a chance."

"Will do."

Left alone, Levi leaned against the galley counter, breathing hard, willing his body to return to a state of calm. Except he wasn't likely to get there, knowing Jordan was at risk of disrespect and worse every time she tried to do her job. His body hadn't experienced a calm moment since she'd strolled back into his life.

What did this guy she was seeing think? He was sending dick pics, so he probably had no problem with any of it. Modern dating was an enigma to Levi.

Would Josh have approved of Jordan's job? Hard to say. The guy was a total goof, not a cynical bone in his body, who saw the good in everyone. But surely he'd be concerned about his woman waist-deep in this testosterone-soaked culture, forced to play along with every dumb brah joke and leer.

"Okay there, Levi?" Harper appeared from the opposite side of the galley and opened a small fridge. She took out a soda and snapped the tab.

"Fine, ma'am."

"That ma'am business? Have to say I enjoy that."

"Sorry. Just slipped out."

"Oh, never stop." She cast a glance toward the cabin where Theo had returned. "How are things with our reporter guest?"

He folded his arms, realized that looked defensive, and unfolded them. A subtle uptick at the corner of Harper's mouth was his reward. These perpetually amused women would be the death of him.

"Not sure what you're expecting. All this profile stuff seems kind of ... surface level."

She considered that. "Our fans love to hear about the day-to-day, and if a couple of interesting tidbits emerge out of your chats with Jordan, that's just icing. Also, I had no idea you had such good defensive skills in your repertoire."

"Excuse me?"

She finger-waved toward the main cabin. "Your chivalry does you proud, but ..."

"But?"

"Jordan can probably handle herself. If it bothered her, I imagine she'd say something."

Perhaps, but it would be better if Jordan wasn't in this position in the first place. Not that he'd deny her an opportunity to report on the games, but this "embedded with the team" aspect exposed her to all sorts of threats.

And exposed Levi in ways he didn't want to examine.

JORDAN ROLLED her suitcase into her hotel room and flopped backward onto the bed. Then she stood immediately because she'd heard horror stories about the cleanliness of bedspreads. Germ-ridden, semen-soaked horror stories.

This one was soft, fluffy, and doing a fine impression of harmless.

Kind of like Levi Hunt. But she knew better. There was nothing soft, fluffy, or harmless about the man.

Annoyingly, after a week embedded with the team, she knew hardly a thing about him. His family. His friends. The inner workings of his stubborn mind.

What she did know wasn't really suitable for publication and could barely fill a double-spaced page in Word:

1. He'd been a good friend to her husband
2. He was a great listener

3. His lips knew just the perfect amount of pressure
for a kiss

Not exactly riveting stuff for CSN readers. And to be
honest, she'd rather block out her knowledge of point
number three.

Her phone rang with a call from ... *shit*, Mac. She considered ignoring it but decided she was a grown-up. Most of
the time.

"Mac! Just landed in Philly. How are you?"

"Where are we on Hunt?"

I'm fabulous, thanks for asking. "Oh, great! It's mostly background right now which is really helping me set the scene."
He doesn't have a favorite color. Isn't that so revealing? Subject
change needed, stat! "The game reports and opinion
columns seem to be getting good responses." Hers had more
comments than any of Jack Gillam's columns, she was happy
to say. And yes, she'd counted.

"It's good work, Jordan, even if we have to moderate
more than usual because some readers can't handle a
woman reporting. This embedding opportunity is better
than I expected, though. With you deep in the belly of the
beast, keep your ear to the ground. Players screwing up,
trade rumors, gossip—I want to hear it."

She supposed reporting was a form of espionage, but
she had enough trouble getting Levi to open up to her.
Expecting more scoops was the kind of pressure she could
do without.

Still, all stakeholders must be kept happy. "I'm on
the case!"

He hung up without saying goodbye. Charming.

She had an hour before the team dinner, where she was
determined to sit beside Levi, probe better than a Roswell

alien, and failing a good result from that, see if his carb-inhaling technique could give her any clues. First, a shower to slough off the grime of travel.

Ten minutes later, she was towel-drying her hair when a rap sounded at the door. She checked the peep hole and barely withheld her gasp.

"Levi," she said as she opened the door. Her story stood before her in his game day duds, looking rumpled, annoyed, and like he was ready to tear his jacket off and do violence to it. What was it about beefy guys in suits that got a woman's pulse racing?

His gaze skimmed her Juicy sweat bottoms and George-town tee. "Could I have a word?"

"Sure, come on in."

He moved past her, taking up considerable space in the entryway despite her placing her back against the wall. She led him to the cozy love seat near the window because sitting on the bed was just ... strange.

Also sperm-cooties.

"What's on your mind?"

"You."

She opened her mouth and gaped for a few embar-rassing seconds before finally managing a witty "Me?"

"I feel like we're playing a game here," he said. "Like we're both waiting for some inflection point that will kick start the real interview."

"I've been trying to respect your wishes not to get up in your face. And in the meantime, it's been interesting watching your interactions with the team and hearing what people say about you."

"According to you, people say nothing because I'm a cipher."

"You're not as forthcoming as some of the other players, but I've talked to you before. I know you have things to say."

His brow crimped, making him look like a confused Easter Island statue. Her stomach wriggled not unpleasantly.

"I think that's part of what's making this weird," he finally said. "We *have* talked before. And—"

"We more than talked."

His jaw tightened at her interruption. "And now you're here, using that connection between us to get the inside track."

She suspected he'd wanted to describe it differently. Yet she understood exactly what he was implying with the word "used."

"You're right." At the widening of his eyes, she continued. "Without our previous connection I wouldn't have even got my foot in the door because there are plenty of other reporters willing to chase down this story. I'd like to say I have what it takes to stand apart but it's a dog-eat-dog world in sports media. My employer saw an opportunity. As did I."

The silence in the wake of her speech seeped into her bones. Working in this business, she was used to dealing with men unable to adequately express themselves. Josh hadn't been like that, though. Her husband had been open and guileless, with no artifice to him. Levi was like a hunk of rough-hewn marble that needed constant chiseling to reveal its glories.

There was also the kiss-sized elephant in the room, and it was likely blocking the free flow of information.

"Maybe we need to lay our cards on the table," she said.

"I would have screwed you that night."

His words impacted like a blow, deliberately inflicted to shock her. Into giving up?

Or giving in?

There was a power game at work here. She needed to meet him at his level.

"I would have let you."

He growled, and Lord above that did something hot and liquid to her insides. "It would have been a mistake," he grated.

"I know."

The volleys back and forth made her blood fizz like champagne. She snatched a breath to get some balance.

"I'm not a good person, Jordan, certainly not whatever you need for this profile. I wanted you that night. A wounded, vulnerable woman, the wife of my friend."

"It's not the kind of thing that would go into any profile of you."

"Maybe not. But it gives you an edge."

"And you don't like when someone has the upper hand."

"I don't like to feel at a disadvantage. In any situation."

Who did? But women—and especially women reporters —encountered it so much more often in their battles with men, their bosses, and the targets of their stories. Probing for a vulnerability was her job.

"There's more equality here than you may think. You've seen me at my lowest point. Ugly crying, half-drunk, nymphomaniac tendencies—"

His snort sounded impossibly like a laugh. "Hardly nymphomaniac."

"What else do you call a woman who scales a guy outside a bar and tries to stick her tongue down his throat?"

No response was forthcoming.

"Exactly." She smiled, trying to lighten the mood because boy did it need lightening. "So neither of us is proud of our behavior that night. But there's no reason why it should interfere with what we're trying to do here. Today."

His scowl said that it was already interfering. "The Rebels management want you to paint a picture of a war hero. Some noble guy who gave up the money for his country. That's not me."

"You saved people's lives."

"Not everyone's."

The one he didn't save sat up between them. "Are you talking about Josh?"

"Among others. I—" He inhaled a ragged breath. "It could have been any one of us. We always think we could have taken another path, turned a different corner, had that second cup of coffee. Would it have changed anything? Would he still be here, me in the ground instead?"

It was the longest speech she'd ever heard him give and was weighted with so much: regret, pain, but most of all guilt that he'd survived. No one should ever feel bad for living.

"You can't change what happened, Levi."

"No, but Josh had so much going for him. A lot of people who cared about him. Who mourn him."

Her instincts fired: human, female, and reporter.

"You think no one would mourn you, Levi?"

His face crumpled—how had she ever thought it expressionless?—and it was a moment before he spoke. "I don't have the connections that Josh did. My father's dead. My mother skipped out on us when I was a kid. No siblings. I have friends back in Jersey and in the service but I didn't build a life like Josh or have a woman worth coming back to. He was crazy about you."

Her throat tightened with unshed tears, not all for herself. "I know. We were a good fit." Josh was the life of the party, always full of cheer, so unlike Levi who was reserved and insular. Yet her husband had nothing but good things to say about this man.

This was the man she wanted to profile. These were the conversations she wanted to have.

"He thought very highly of you. You were a good friend to him."

"Until I tried to screw his wife the night he went into the ground."

She blew out a breath, her patience with it. "Is that why you're here? To tell me what an asshole you are and scare me off the story? Because I'm not buying it."

"The tactic or the asshole status?"

"Neither." She pointed at him, but because he'd leaned in at the last moment, her finger met the center of his chest. Sensual awareness of just how hard that chest was dripped through her, all the way to a hollow spot between her legs.

I would have screwed you that night.

I would have let you.

Did she mean that or was she just trying to one-up him in this game that suddenly felt far too dangerous?

He placed a hand on the finger still idling away in Levi pec territory and wrapped his big palm around it. Rough, calloused, a working man's hand.

A voice in her brain started up a chant: *Put it in your mouth. Lick it. Suck it.* She should pull away, but every muscle in her body—including her traitorous finger—had frozen.

"You're not giving up on this, are you?" His voice was a raspy murmur, so low she had to inch closer to be sure she wouldn't miss another precious word out of his mouth. Precious, because of the story, she insisted. Everything happening right now—breathing, thinking, speaking, being —felt fraught.

And exciting.

This emotion racing through her veins was the most alive she'd felt in years.

"No, I'm not giving up, Levi. We need to figure out a way to work together. What are you so scared of?"

"You think I'm scared?" His hand still covered her finger, cocooning it, warming her through. Something flickered in his eyes ... was this man really that concerned about spending time with her? Did breathing her air threaten him so much?

No, she was merely projecting her own insane concerns onto him. Frankly, she was terrified of the pull she felt toward *him*.

"I think you're scared of something."

Ignoring her response, he released her finger. "Team dinner is in thirty minutes."

He didn't ask if she'd be there, probably because he already knew the answer.

It was her job after all.

Alone again, she grabbed a mini-bar bottle of scotch, dumped it into a glass, and downed it in one desperate gulp. Her heart still beat erratically, unnerved by Levi's visit and the sensual connection they'd just shared.

Perhaps it was her imagination. Perhaps those blue eyes weren't on fire as he held her finger.

I would have screwed you that night.

What was more terrifying is that she would have let him.

8

THE DOORBELL RANG. The cluster of guests on his sofa looked at Levi, given that it was his door to answer.

"Thought everyone who said they were coming was already here."

He gave a quick eyeball interrogation of the team-mates over to play video games: Jorgenson, Kershaw, Burnett, and Remy DuPre, who might be retired but had a permanent invite to extra-curricular Rebels events. No one looked especially guilty until Levi circled back to Theo who wore the smirk of a man up to no good.

"Who'd you invite to our video game-playing, ball-scratching, man festival, Kershaw?"

Theo was all affront. "Why'd you assume I've got anything to do with this?"

"'Cause you're a troublemaker, Superglutes," Remy said, sipping his beer. "That's right, I heard your new nickname and I fucking love it."

The doorbell sounded again.

Cade put the controller down, which was about the only

way to beat him. The guy was a savant at Playstation. "I can get it, Kraken."

"Kraken?" Levi stared down Cade, then switched to a more likely suspect: Kershaw again. "Explain."

"Your name's Levi, so we have ancient sea monster Leviathan with a quick sidestep over to the Kraken."

"It's also aspirational. Release the ..." Cade waved a hand to fill in the rest. "If we scream it at you on the ice, that's your cue to go ballistic into the blue zone."

Probably no shade was intended, but it reminded Levi that he had to start improving, and fast.

He caught Remy's eye. "You had your chance to put all this behind you, yet you're here. By choice."

Remy laughed. "Have another beer, Kraken. They sound better after more beer."

"Speaking of, anyone need a brew while I'm up?"

They all affirmed that yes, indeed, they needed more sustenance of the beer variety.

Levi answered the door and found exactly who he was expecting: Jordan looking fresh-faced and perky. What he wasn't expecting was the pizza she was carrying.

Was there no peace to be had?

"I come bearing gifts." She shoved the pizza boxes— three of them—against his chest.

"Jordan!" Kershaw appeared behind Levi and elbowed him aside to collect the boxes. "You didn't have to do that."

"Okaaaayyy, except you distinctly said the price of admission was three large cheese and pepperoni."

"What, no spinach?"

Jordan caught Levi's eye with a cute-as-a-kitten curve to her lips, the both of them sharing a joke at Theo's absurdity. His heart leaped and his brain stutter-stepped, remembering how close he'd come to kissing her in that hotel

room two nights ago in Philly, on the tail end of the conversation about Josh. Keeping it classy as always.

Reel it in. There would be no joke-sharing. No intimacies.

He was annoyed that she was here. He was annoyed that
she was pretty. And he was especially annoyed that she was
so damn chummy with Kershaw.

Begrudgingly, he stood back to let her in.

"Pizza break, boys!" Theo called out. "The lady from the
press is buying."

Levi dug for his wallet and extracted three twenties. "You
shouldn't pay for these bozos. I was about to order in but
Kershaw kept saying he wasn't hungry yet." The same
Kershaw who was now stuffing his face with a giant—no,
two giant—slices.

"Keep your green, Hunt. I'll expense it."

"This interview business is supposed to be during
work hours."

"In case you've forgotten, I've yet to get a single, decent,
useable word out of you." As she slipped off a long cream-
colored parka with a fur-trimmed hood, he sneaked a better
look at her. The early November chill had given her cheeks
a rosy glow. Her freckle-splashed nose, too. A soft gray
sweater hugged her curves, figure-forming to her breasts
and hips, and when she turned to hang her coat on the hook
inside the door, his eyes couldn't help being drawn to her
ass, perfectly shaped in dark-rinse jeans.

Back to face him, she caught him ogling her.

"Take the money," he said, holding it out, which made it
sound like he was offering cash to atone for his wandering
eyes.

Waving him off, she walked past him into the kitchen, so
all he could do was follow her.

Unsurprisingly, she knew everyone, even DuPre, and no

one but Levi seemed to have a problem with an attractive woman who could talk hockey, hang with the guys, and toted pizza. Soon Remy was turning on the Cajun charm, never mind that he was happily married.

"So what's it like following Hunt around, Ms. Cooke? Kind of dull, I'd bet."

"Oh, please, it's Jordan. And yeah, he's pretty tight-lipped. I'm hoping that seeing him in his natural habitat might loosen him up."

She bit into a slice, the greasy cheese leaving a shine on her lips that he wanted to—*nothing. He wanted nothing.*

"Don't know about natural," Remy said, his gaze arcing over the living room of the two-bedroomed apartment the Rebels org had stashed Levi in. No chance of getting lonely, either. Kershaw lived across the hall and had a habit of dropping in unannounced, usually to raid Levi's fridge.

Remy continued to wax nostalgic. "I used to live here and it's just a weigh station for the newbies until they settle down into a place of their own. Got fine memories of that sofa, I have to say."

Levi shut his eyes. "DuPre, do *not* start reminiscing about sex on that sofa with my boss."

Cade chuckled. "Bren said he found condoms in the seat cushions one day."

"Stowed 'em there for convenience. Cookie jar, too." Remy tipped his beer bottle at Jordan. "Pardon the off-color talk, miss. I hope that won't find its way into your column. My wife would de-ball me with her very sharp stilettos if it did."

Jordan laughed. "Your secret's safe with me. I'm just here to soak it all in. Anything you guys say tonight is off the record."

A likely tale. Levi would be keeping his lips zipped.

As he watched Jordan's easygoing way with the guys, the memory of their first meeting rose as fresh as the pizza they were chowing down on. Seven years ago, he'd been out drinking with Josh and Kelly at a bar in Clarkesville, Kentucky, one night after returning stateside. It had been a particularly brutal op, with one of their team getting shot but expected to make a full recovery. They were there to unwind with no expectations. That is, until Jordan showed up.

Levi saw her first. Heard her, in fact.

That laugh, so husky and big, had done him in. It was the laugh of a woman who enjoyed life and looked for the good in people. Everyone around him in that bar had been talking and shooting the shit, and Levi wasn't even on this planet anymore. He was alone on another world with this woman who laughed like she meant it. She wore a dress as blue as her eyes with delicate straps; her hair fell like a waterfall of autumn leaves over her shoulders; her gilded skin glowed. Only later—on her wedding day—did he realize that she had a parade of freckles on her arms and upper chest, like twinkling stars.

His heart thumped rabbit kicks in his chest, then and now. He wanted to shut down, to not relive the night that had ended so differently for them both. But his mind raced, the images coming hard and fast, triggered by hearing her big, boisterous laugh and seeing her in her element in his kitchen.

That night in Kentucky, she'd turned their way and looked—right through Levi. He saw it, that moment when she and Cookie clashed gazes for the first time, like something out of West Side Fucking Story. Tony and Maria alone, the room fell away.

Only they weren't completely alone. Levi was still in the

room, existing on the fuzzy edges, watching his best friend fall in love with the woman Levi wanted. Watching the dream of her slip right through his fingers.

"Quicksand."

"That was your childhood fear?" Levi sized up Kershaw, who had just uttered that gem. "You grew up in Michigan."

"Every movie and TV show I watched had someone getting sucked to their death in sand. Way less of a problem in adult life than I was led to believe. That and killer bees."

Somehow they'd landed on the topic of irrational childhood fears. Remy had been terrified of some weird Cajun boogeyman under his bed, who snacked on crackers and paté, mind you. Cade was convinced his next-door-neighbor in San Antonio was a child catcher like that creepy dude in *Chitty Chitty Bang Bang*. Poor Erik lived in fear that a snake would come up through the toilet and bite his balls. In Sweden.

Every man in the room filed that away for a check later of their respective bathrooms.

Jordan had chuckled at everything the boys vomited out, leaning in to her one-of-the-guys bit. He shouldn't be so suspicious—she'd always been so sweet after all—but there was something different about her these days. A glow in her eyes, a set to her jaw, a determination to be counted.

Jordan had always been the most beautiful woman in the room, and she still was, not that she had any competition in *this* room. But now, with her hair pulled high in a fiery pony-tail, her cheeks blush-pink with the heat, she simply slayed him.

"What about you, Jordan?" Theo asked. "What were you scared of?"

"Okay, don't laugh now." She sent a mischievous look around the crew. "I was pretty sure that everyone was a robot and we were living in the equivalent of the movie *Westworld* but without the murderous cowboys."

"Yul Brynner," Remy muttered. "Classic."

"Yep. I'd look into the eyes of everyone I met trying to determine if they were mechanical."

"That's pretty specific," Cade said. "When'd you grow out of that?"

She stood and leaned across the sofa, staring right into his eyes. "Oh ... ages ago."

"Does not compute," Cade said in a robotic voice. "Reporter is onto us."

Jordan laughed again, and it didn't sound fake. But then she'd always been like that: chockfull of cheer, completely authentic. When she was his friend's woman, it was easier to dismiss her influence on him. That was the code. But now, being around her was hell. An exquisitely beautiful hell.

"And you, Levi?" Jordan asked, her lips in a suggestive curve. "What frightened you?"

"No irrational fears. Just rational ones."

She waited, staring hard enough to pierce his armor. What would she say if he told her the truth? How he'd been afraid of the dark and the damp, of having no food or shelter. How his bogeymen were real and they weren't munching on crackers, either.

Spending time with Jordan on this interview wouldn't just be annoying—it would ruin him. One look like that from this woman and he would tell her *everything*.

The moment of silence held taut between them, broken only by his doorbell.

"It's like Grand Central around here." But really, this was good because he'd gotten a little lost in the glory of Jordan's blue eyes. He headed to the door, shaking his noggin and trying to scatter thoughts of this woman to the four corners of his apartment.

This time, the person at the door was definitely not expected. Eloise Butler stood before him, an off-kilter grin cracking her face.

"Elle!"

"Hey, Hunt, up for a visit?"

His gaze moved from the wobbly smile to the duffle bag at her feet. He'd worked with Elle at Fort Campbell where she was in Special Forces support. She'd left the service a few months ago and the invitation to visit was always open, but usually people called first.

He grabbed her bag and gestured for her to come in. "What's up?"

"Not much." She stopped, her ear attuned to the noise from the other room. "You've got company?"

"Just a few of the guys from the Rebels."

"Oh, yeah. The hockey thing."

He snorted. No one did a better job of keeping a man grounded. "Uh huh. The hockey thing."

"So that's going good?"

"Rocky start but getting better." With more ice time in Philly, he'd managed an assist and helped the team to its second win of the season. Not exactly lighting the NHL on fire, though. Yet.

"Nice, nice." She sounded distracted. "So, this is kind of awkward but I need a place to stay. Just for a couple of days. I promise I'll put bread and milk in your fridge."

"Not a problem."

"Hey, Hunt, you never said you were inviting your girl."

Theo had appeared to check on the new visitor because with Kershaw around, no man's—or woman's—business was their own.

Levi knew Elle pretty well, and when someone put her back up, she could get as snooty as all get out. Ignoring Theo, she turned back to Levi. "Listen, I'll stay out of your hair while you hang with your buddies."

Something was definitely up with her. The edginess, the small talk, the urgent need for shelter.

"Come into the kitchen with me. I need to get beers."

She followed him and took a seat at the island.

Theo trailed them and bless the child, he tried again. "I'm Theo, one of Levi's teammates."

Elle merely nodded at him, a curt dismissal.

If he must. "Theo, this is Elle Butler. She and I worked together at Fort Campbell for a couple of years and she's here for a visit. Elle, meet Theo Kershaw, D-man on the Chicago Rebels."

"D-man? What the hell is that?"

"Stands for defense," Theo said. "And other things." He added a big grin that usually had the ladies melting.

Elle raised both eyebrows, clearly not in a melting mood. "Way to sell it, Dick-Man."

Levi passed off a couple of beers to Theo with an expression that was half-apology for his friend and half-fuck off because it was none of his business. "Go ahead and play without me."

"Sure." He passed a bottle to Elle. "Welcome to Chicago."

She blinked, evidently surprised by Theo's gesture. "Uh, thanks."

Kershaw grabbed a couple more beers from the fridge and headed out.

"Are all the players as pretty as that one?"

"Christ, don't tell him that. We'll never hear the end of it." Not that it was news. The tabloids made a meal out of Kershaw's good looks—the blue-black hair, green eyes, and jaw that could cut a hole in the ice were a winning combo, apparently. "Want to fill me in on what happened? Or why you landed on my doorstep without warning? Or why you need a place to stay all of a sudden?"

She pursed her lips and ran a hand through her dark, wavy hair, which was longer than he remembered. "Told you I'd eventually be moving out this way."

"Yeah, but—"

"Oh, sorry, didn't realize you had company." Jordan placed a couple of empty beer bottles on the counter. "Recycle?"

"Under the counter." He made the introductions, keeping it to jobs only because theirs was a purely professional relationship, right?

"You're a reporter?" Elle asked Jordan.

"Yeah, I'm here to do one of those all-access deals on the marvelous Mr. Hunt."

"What's so interesting about this guy?" Now Elle was baffled, which made him want to give her a bear hug. *Exactly.* He was not worthy of this attention.

"You'd be surprised. People love this junk." Jordan rubbed her hands together. "Just need to check the medicine cabinet, grope around in the underwear drawer, and study the laptop browser history to see what we're truly dealing with."

"You'll be sorely disappointed," Levi muttered, though the words *grope* and *underwear* certainly gave him ideas.

Jordan smiled at Elle, in that friendly way she had that put people at ease. "Hanging with the boys gives me good background information, a feel for the team and Levi's place on it."

"I can probably help you there," Elle said, animated for the first time since she'd shown up. "Hunt's strategy for cheering up the boys on his Special Forces team was Disney ice cream cakes."

Jordan's eyes shone in pure amazement—and complete calculation. "I can't imagine it for a second. Disney?"

"Oh, yeah. He remembered everyone's birthday, was always buying a Princess-themed cake for his guys." Elle pulled out her phone. "Pretty sure I've got some video here."

"No one will be sharing video, especially about events that did not happen." He glared at Elle, retracting the imaginary hug he'd given her. Where was the code?

"Right, sir. Nothing happened, sir." Elle didn't even try to hide her wink at Jordan, who winked right back. *Aw, hell.* The last thing he needed was for these two to buddy up.

"You probably should be heading out," he said to Jordan, his inner grouch grumbling.

"Yeah, I have to drive back to the city. Thanks for *not* inviting me, Levi. See you at the game tomorrow." Still with the shade but he could tell it wasn't sharply intended. She left the kitchen, her pony tail bobbing because the perk was never-ending.

Elle shot him a dark look. "Shouldn't you walk her out?"

"She knows where the door is. She used it to come in uninvited." But he wondered where she'd parked and if it was well-lit and ...

Jesus wept.

He found her at the door, putting on her coat. "Jordan."

She looked up, eyes bright like nothing, not even the surliest vet-turned-hockey rookie, could throw her off her stride. What would it take?

Annoyed with this entire situation, he grabbed his jacket. "I'll walk you to your car."

"No need for that."

Disregarding her protest, he plucked his keys from the hallway table. "After you."

9

OUT IN THE HALLWAY, they headed toward the elevator, the air as thick as the cheese on those pizzas. He'd have been fine with silence, but that wasn't Jordan's style.

"Elle seems nice. You two good friends?"

"Good enough for her to feel okay showing up out of the blue without calling ahead." He stabbed at the down button for the elevator.

"Like us, then?" she said with not quite so much pertness in her voice.

Finally, he was getting to her, which was better than her getting to him.

"Was this night worth your time? Don't you have a boyfriend who'd like to see you once in a while? Or a life that doesn't revolve around work?" They stepped into the elevator and he slapped at the lobby level button. *Stab. Slap.* He was angry and he didn't know why. He hated not knowing something.

"This *is* my life, Hunt." She giggled, the sound going straight to his dick where it proceeded to tease, caress, and kiss the traitor wide awake. "God, playing video games with you guys is gold. And then when your pal showed up proving you're not such a cold-hearted, friendless Terminator type after all and that you might have a personality underneath that hard-ass demeanor? Icing on the cupcake."

He opened the door to his building, ushered her out, and tried not to enjoy her bobbing pony-tail.

"So is it true?" she threw out over her shoulder.

"Is what true?"

"The Disney ice cream cake thing?"

"Where are you parked?"

"Around the corner. You don't have to—"

But he was already eating the ground with every stride like it had offended his honor.

"Levi, what is your problem?"

"Nothing. Just making sure you get in your car and leave." He was pissed and horny and only now realizing that he had no idea what Jordan's car looked like.

"Here I am." She stood by a Honda Civic, two cars back.

Retracing his steps, he tried to get his emotions under control which should not have been a problem. Emotion-wrangling was his bag. Controlling the narrative was his forte. At least, he'd thought so until he met Jordan again.

"I don't have a boyfriend." She pushed her key into the lock.

"Say again?"

"You seem to be under the impression that I had someone I could be spending time with tonight instead of enjoying Erik's weird winking and odes to herring, or Theo's conspiracy theories as to why Chicagoland has so many mattress stores, or your curmudgeonly ways with hints of Tin Man." She hummed *If I only Had a Heart* from The Wizard of Oz.

He passed over the Tin Man reference, probably

because he was inexplicably relieved at the implication of her other statement. "Don't have an opinion on your dating practices. Just something Kershaw mentioned."

"And you believed him?"

"I didn't *not* believe him. Strange thing to make up." Especially with the graphic detail of naked photos. If she wasn't seeing someone, then what was all that about?

She opened the door a couple of inches but still stood there. Pertly perking. "You know, the sooner you cooperate the sooner I'll be out of your hair."

"I'm doing everything management has ordered."

"Under sufferance."

"What you see is all you're getting." He was done here. Done with her teasing scent and dick-springing laugh. Done with trying to negotiate a truce between his hands and his cock. Just. Done. "Safe home now." He turned to walk back, but didn't get far.

"Coward."

He pivoted. "What?"

"You've never liked me for some stupid, God-knows-what reason and now you can't be man enough to sit still for a few questions."

He ignored the last part which was half—okay, *all*—true, and focused on the first part. "I've liked you fine."

She took a step toward him, then another until she was right in his space. She looked up at him, her expression filled with fury and spirit. Typical, maddening, heart-stoppingly gorgeous Jordan. "Admit it. You can't stand me. When I kissed you five years ago—"

"We're not talking about that."

"*When I kissed you five years ago*," she insisted, her voice rising with each word, "it was as if I ripped out a piece of your mind! You didn't like me. You certainly didn't think I was right for Josh and then when we had that moment, when we were at our lowest, we were drawn to each other. You hate that of all people, it was me who made you go to this fragile, needful place. It happened and you need to get over it so we can do this interview and you never have to see me again!"

Hell and damn, she was so right and so very, very wrong. Of course he liked her—that was the fucking problem. It had always been the problem. He'd been holding on to this guilt he'd felt for betraying Josh, not just the night of the funeral, but all the nights before. Lust in his heart, someone had once termed it. Making a move on his friend's woman had been the logical culmination of the envy Levi had bottled up, and he was letting it color all his decisions in the now.

She'd worked hard to get where she was and so had he. They could do this interview. They could salvage something from this messy, unexpected intersection of their lives, and move the fuck on.

Clean, simple, done.

Which is why he probably shouldn't have placed one hand on her hip, pulled her close, and stamped his lips on hers.

❧

LEVI HUNT WAS KISSING HER.

This man she didn't like all that much and who definitely didn't like her was kissing her.

The subject of her story was ... okay, *we know, we know,* her brain chimed in.

Kissing. Her.

Maybe he was doing it to prove a point. *See how much I*

don't like you? These lips are filled with so much dislike it's practically dripping off them.

But there was proving a point and there was kissing so deep and wet and oh-my-God sexy that Jordan was fairly sure she and her chatty brain knew the difference. There might be dislike but there was plenty of lust, too.

He tasted of beer and need, and the way he felt ... so hard and good and groan-worthy. It had been too long. The last man she'd kissed was ... *no, no, no.*

This one.

She pulled back, more shocked at that factoid than the act itself. Since Josh's death, she had gone out on a few anemic dates, more to please her parents or friends who thought she "needed to get back out there." Inevitably date chatter would stray into widow territory and she hated it: hated talking about him. Hated how her dates would offer pity first, then quickly transition to viewing her as a sure thing. The woman whose grief could so easily be replaced by mind-blowing orgasms.

She hadn't needed it. She was getting her kicks in her budding career. Subsuming those desires was necessary while she carved her path to sports reporter glory. But now ...

Tonight, she'd pushed Levi hard, intending to make him mad and force a misstep. Only now she wasn't so sure of her rationale: to reap a benefit for the story or for her sorely neglected love life?

Levi was panting, his eyes dark, shining buttons under the street lamp. His hand still laid a possessive claim to her hip, which aligned her favorite parts of him with what she imagined would be his favorite parts of her.

"What was that for?" she managed to croak out.

"I don't regret that kiss." His voice sounded like he was speaking through gravel. "Five years ago. Or now."

"You don't?"

His breath sawed in and out. "I understand that you do. Of course you do. But I needed it then. So bad."

So had she. So *did* she. Here, now, while pinned between his hard body and her Honda Civic. All the guilt she should be feeling was refusing to percolate to the surface. In all honesty, she was attracted to Levi. Immensely so.

And that was a problem as big as what the Special Forces vet was packing below the belt. "We shouldn't do this ... the story."

His hand moved to cup her ass and hoisted her a few inches off the ground until she landed on the hood. "The story can wait."

Expertly, his mouth sought hers, parting her lips and introducing his tongue to the mix. *Well, how do you do?* She moaned, a heartfelt, deep, desperate sound because she'd missed this. Being wanted. Desired. Needed. Her thighs fell open, wanton, wicked limbs inviting him in, and he took her up on the offer because he was a damned fine player when he saw his chance, both on the ice and off. Strong hands shaped her ass, gripping and magnetizing her core to all that glorious hardness behind his zipper.

The kiss continued, mutating into something wilder and deeper with each luxurious sweep of his tongue. Underneath this gruff and stoic exterior lay a man of passion. She'd known this—after all, they'd kissed before. But back then, it was mixed with grief and sadness and tequila. She couldn't separate the man from the moment.

But this Levi, this person with his lips locked to hers was very much his own man and this was very much its own moment.

The sound of a car's engine forced their mouths to separate. But their other body parts remained well and truly engaged in the getting-acquainted mode. And it felt shockingly right.

The car passed, the lights illuminating Levi's chiseled jaw and what she'd always thought of as expressionless eyes. Not now. Those eyes were supernovas of emotion.

"Jordan—"

"Don't apologize, Levi. Takes two to kiss like that."

"Wasn't planning to. I was going to say you need to get your sweet ass off that car before I lose control."

Ah, okay.

He drew back, the void of his departure chilling her through. But he dragged her with him, which felt nice. Like they were going in the same direction at last.

"You've got skills in the kissing department, Levi."

"Gonna put that in the article?"

"God, no, you're under enough pressure to perform as it is."

He laughed, the first time she'd ever recalled hearing that.

"What strange sound is this?" She pushed at his chest, feeling that she had a right to while they were still in this friendly bubble that would burst the moment she slipped into her car.

"I laugh. You've just never said anything funny. Until now."

She thumped his arm lightly. "Are you kidding? I am a total cut up. Ask anyone. Jordan with the Jokes, they call me."

"They do? And who's *they*?" He looked skeptical, a reasonable reaction given that she'd just made it up, but he also looked amused. Why did she feel so giddy? Perhaps because Levi Hunt didn't seem so opposed to her existence after all, and the relief that came with that conclusion made her dizzy.

"Uh, my sports reporter colleagues, barfly acquaintances, and the nice man at the dry cleaners."

"The only audience that matters."

"Yes!" Well, look at them, bantering like pros, the ease of it both electrifying and comforting. "You probably should return to your guests."

"Kind of hoping they'll take the hint and be gone when I get back."

"Except Elle." Remembering the sudden arrival of the young—and pretty—woman shot Jordan's chest with a ridiculous bolt of jealousy. "Is she staying long?"

"For a few days. But there's nothing between us, just in case you thought that angle might work for your story."

She hid her smile. Was that his way of telling her she needn't worry on that score? Had they both declared their single status tonight for ... reasons?

Reasons be damned. Nothing more could—*would*—happen here. She had a story to write and anyway, Levi Hunt was most definitely not her type. Too broody, too bad-tempered, too uptight.

Although there was nothing uptight about that kiss or the erection that heralded good times ahead if she wasn't writing a story and this was actually a thing that could happen in the current universe.

Sheesh! Shut up, Jordan. No, you shut up ... other Jordan.

"I should go," she said, not wanting to at all. Hoping that like her, he'd prefer to hold on to what they'd found in the cold, dark night that didn't seem so lonely anymore.

She'd missed this human connection.

He stepped back to give her space to open the door. Reluctantly, she slid by him as she clambered inside.

"Want to start tomorrow?"

She blinked back at him. "What?"

"The interview, for real. After morning skate and lunch with the team, I usually come back here to take a nap."

Was he asking her to join him for a nap? She let that seep into her bones, the comfort implied in it and—oh, he was still talking.

"... back at the practice arena and find a spot to sit down and talk."

Were they going to talk about the kiss some more? Or perhaps his rush to finish the interview was so that they could do something else? Or so she could be ushered out of his life more quickly?

So many questions (yay, journalism!), yet all she could manage was a cheery "Okay, see you then!"

He closed the door before she could get another word in, not that she had anything profound to say. They had come *this* close to dry humping on the hood of her Honda and it was both weird and not weird.

She'd take that as a win.

Starting the car, she was keenly aware of him watching her as she pulled out of the space, standing soldier-tall and motionless. And she waited until he was a speck in her rearview mirror before she touched her kiss-ravaged lips.

10

Levi walked into the front office suite at Rebels HQ and looked around. He'd been here before during a meet-and-greet but they'd connected in a conference room, so he had no clue which office belonged to Harper. Jordan had texted this morning to meet him here after his post-lunch nap, so here he was ready for the vivisection.

Did he say "ready"? He meant "dreading it."

Last night, the woman had tasted so good, a million times better than he'd remembered, and he had an excellent memory. A small part of him had hoped it wouldn't live up to that previous encounter but for it to go and surpass it? Not fair in the slightest.

He wasn't fool enough to think she might like him, but she certainly liked prodding him. Her version of fun—and he was beginning to think he liked being the source of that fun. She made him smile with all the effort she put into drawing him out.

One of the doors opened and out walked Cade Burnett with a big old grin on his face. Right behind him was Dante with his hand on Cade's back. Moretti said something that made Burnett chuckle, then turn back to him, his gaze lit with that special understanding that exists between couples.

A savage kick of envy struck Levi.

His time in the military had never been conducive to relationships. Some guys made it work, like Josh, but Levi didn't have the skills to keep something so fragile alive at a distance. Small talk, texting, all the minutiae required to feed a relationship were beyond him. He needed to be close enough to touch, to taste, to take. And even then, no one had made him want to go there. Until Jordan.

"You're looking mighty pleased with yourself, Hunt."

Levi snapped to attention and found himself the subject of Cade Burnett's scrutiny. He liked Cade, or Alamo as he was nicknamed because he hailed from San Antonio. A great defenseman, he sported an easygoing attitude and had a way of cheering up the locker room after a bad game, a skill he'd been forced to call upon for these early efforts. They were 1 and 2 on the season, a pretty slow start for sure.

"Burnett." Levi nodded at Moretti who was leaning against the door frame. "I'm looking for Harper's office."

"She's at home today." Awareness dawned on Dante's face. "Ah, you're here to get grilled by the press."

"Maybe that's what he's smiling about," Cade said. "You were gone an awful long time last night while walking Ms. Cooke to her car. And you had that same self-satisfied look on your face when you returned."

Perfect. "Harper's office?" he asked, ignoring Cade's smirk.

Dante pointed. "Down that corridor, to the right. But could I have a word first?" He turned to Cade. "See you later, *polpetto*."

"Sure, *borchia*," then to Levi with a hammy wink, "Have fun, now."

Pet names. Adorable.

Annoyed that his emotions were apparently playing like a movie on his face, Levi schooled his expression while Cade walked away.

Dante still leaned against the door, waiting for Cade to leave. Once they were alone, he spoke. "I hear you're getting extra practice in, Levi."

"Just some early morning drills. I've cleared it with Coach."

"You played well in Philly. I know it's been a quick adjustment for you, and I appreciate you putting in the effort. We all do. Just be careful not to overdo it."

Levi took a deep breath. "I want to make more of an impact in the games. And I know my limits."

It was hard to tell if that was what Dante wanted to hear because all he said was, "Jordan's waiting for you."

He headed down to Harper's office, outside which a familiar, bright-eyed woman with dark, wouldn't-look-out-of-place-in-Jersey hair sat at a desk. She looked pleased to see him.

"Oh, hi, Levi! Go right in, you're expected."

"Sorry, we've met, but I don't recall your name."

She waved his apology away. "No problem. You can't be expected to remember someone like me. I'm Casey, Harper's PA."

"Good to see you again, Casey." Usually he was better with names and faces. Since leaving Special Forces, he found himself losing a step in all the things that had once made him a logistical mastermind in the field. Or maybe it was Jordan's kisses fogging his brain ...

"You know, she's just a reporter," Casey said, because apparently, he'd stopped outside the door to day-dream about kissing Jordan again.

"Actually, I know her. But you're right, I don't really enjoy this kind of thing."

Casey scrunched up her nose. "Maybe think of her naked? You know, like what you do to get over public speaking."

"Not sure that would help here."

Casey smiled. "Then, just be yourself."

That won't help either. He inhaled deep and opened the door.

Seated by a window, Jordan looked up from her laptop and flashed him a huge smile, as if she was actually pleased to see him and the last time they'd connected, they hadn't been making out like horny teenagers.

"Hey, there." Suddenly, his skin felt too fucking tight.

"Levi! Come in! Have a seat. How was practice?"

He sat on the too small velvet sofa near a window that overlooked a landscaped garden he'd never seen before. Tucking himself away in the corner, or as much as someone of his size could "tuck," he magnetized his back to the sofa and tried to track the conversation.

"Good practice?" she prompted.

"Fine. Skating drills. Trying to increase my speed which was always my weak spot." Though he'd moved on Jordan pretty fast last night.

"Mind if I record?"

"No, go ahead."

She pressed record on her phone and put it down on the coffee table, but before she could ask anything, it rang. The image on the screen looked familiar—was that Hollywood superstar Chris Evans dressed as his Avengers alter-ego?

"Oh, sorry about that." Before she declined the call, he could've sworn the screen name flashed Very, Very Single.

"You're screening calls from Captain America?"

"What? Oh, no! Well, sort of. My mother's trying to set me up with a lawyer she knows, one of her former students, and she made him sound like some all-American superhero. Believe me, if Chris Evans was really calling, this interview would be toast."

His pulse went haywire, though where to start? Was it the fact she was being set up by her mother, the fact that she was actively dating, or the fact that she'd bump him for Captain America?

Okay, Levi would probably bump him for Captain America.

"You said last night you didn't have a boyfriend, but you're dating?" Kershaw's mention of that intimate image on her phone tugged at him.

Two spots of color tagged her cheekbones. "I'm not, actually. I really don't have time, but my parents are worried I'm not opening myself up to the possibilities. Like my job's not satisfying enough."

"They must be proud of how far you've come in your career." She remained silent, so he prodded again. "Aren't they?"

"Sure they are." Her cheer didn't quite convince. "You know how family is. They don't really get what I'm doing."

Her parents were Georgetown University professors, but surely the air in DC wasn't that rarified. "Not sporty types?"

"Ah, no. They're supportive but they don't really understand my career path."

"Let me guess. They think sports are for lugheads lacking in the brain cell department?"

"Oh, they'd never be that rude. They'd just prefer I was a lawyer or an economist or running a public policy think tank that changes lives."

Jesus. "Sports changes lives. It changed mine. It changes the lives of kids everywhere."

"I know. But they were disappointed that I didn't do anything big—or bigger—after college."

"You got married. Found your soulmate. What's bigger than that?"

She peered at him. "My mother was annoyed that I became an army wife. She thought I was too young. And perhaps I *was* rebelling in some small way."

"She sounds like a peach."

She laughed. "She's great, really. She and my dad invested a lot of their time and money in me and my brothers, so I can see why they don't feel the return is so great on their youngest."

"Jordan, you're not a freaking mutual fund. You're a flesh and blood woman with ambitions and goals and desires." So that came out with more passion than he'd intended. Something about introducing the word "desires"—plural—into the mix sent a wave of desire—singular—through him.

The air thickened between them, that word floating lazily on it. He searched for the right follow-up to break the tension. "Do you like what you're doing?"

"What I'm doing?" She licked her lips, chewed on her plump lower one, a move that had his cock twitching.

"Your job. You like it?"

"I do."

"Then to hell with them. To hell with anyone who says you can't."

Why did he feel so protective over her? He had no doubt she could handle her parents or anyone who came at her. She'd been handling him since the minute they met.

Needling, taunting, provoking ...

"Guess we should get started," she said, and for the first

time he could recall, she refused to hold his gaze. "If you don't want to answer a question, just say so and we'll move on." At his nod of acknowledgment, she consulted a list. The pen in her hand shook slightly. "Tell me how you got into hockey."

Starting him off easy. "My dad was a big fan of the Devils when they were based in East Rutherford. They were just starting to come into their own after a long drought and that year they came back from a 3-1 deficit to win. That Game 5 turned it around."

"The game when Stevens hit Lindros. Ended his career."

"Guy was headed out. Had more hits and concussions than anyone in the league."

Jordan raised an eyebrow. "Not much sympathy?"

"This is a physical sport. Everyone on that ice knows what he's getting into. What did Clifford Chase say? Hockey's not for pus—well, you know."

"He wasn't known for his political correctness."

"The man was an asshole for a whole lot of reasons but he was right about that. No man or woman can play this game and not expect to come out of it unscathed."

She remained silent for a beat, then seemed to make a decision. "Does that apply to women on the sidelines—the PTs, the reporters, the locker-room cleaners? Are they fair game?"

"Fair game for what? Getting knocked about on the ice?"

Her smile was thin, fake, not Jordan-like at all. "These male-dominated environments create their own ecosystems. Bro culture where men think it's okay to drop a towel before a female reporter just to earn a reaction. Or get a little handsy with their masseuse because she's employed by the team."

This had taken a surprising left turn, one that had every

cell in his body itching to fight. "Did something happen to you, Jordan?"

Wait, had *he* happened? Was this about the move he'd put on her?

"Oh no!" She waved it away with a smile that *appeared* genuine? His instincts were completely out of whack. "But you hear stories. I was curious about your stance."

Apparently, he was being tested, and on the record, too.

"I've worked with women in the military, a male-dominated environment with its own ecosystem. Sure, there's plenty of that, where a woman is expected to take a joke or develop a thicker skin or put up with some BS about her tampons. I've witnessed it and I can guarantee you I shut it down whenever I came across it. Could I have done better? Probably. But anyone who disrespects a woman in my presence, whether she's doing her job or not, won't get a second chance to make that mistake."

"Good to hear it," she murmured. "Sorry, we got off track there. Tell me more about your love of the New Jersey Devils."

The topic she'd raised gnawed at him. Something felt off. "What kind of shit are you putting up with when you do your job, Jordan?" He'd already taken Kershaw to task about running off his mouth. Who else did he need to "talk to"?

"Nothing. As I said, everyone hears stories of athletes thinking they can do whatever they want because their million-dollar contracts act as insurance against bad behavior. I can handle any of the bullshit that comes my way."

It was the same thing Harper had already made abundantly clear: Jordan was perfectly capable of handling herself.

"I've no doubt you can. You're tougher than I remember you."

"I was a different person then. Josh and I married so young and he was big into taking care of me." She lifted a shoulder. "Well, you know what he was like. After he died, I had to figure things out. My family was there for me, but I needed to forge my own path. This business doesn't really reward tentativeness, so I'm working on being more assertive. Taking what's mine."

He'd liked the Jordan of before with her lusty laugh and cheerful personality, but this new, go-getter Jordan was something else. "Josh would be really proud of you, Jordan."

"You think so?" She blinked those big, storybook eyes at him, imploring for affirmation. "Because if he was here, I might have taken a different road."

She would have led a different life for sure if he'd lived. Kids, probably, and with Josh in the service that would have made it tough for her gain traction in her career. Something lurched in his chest at the idea of her potential being wasted.

"Maybe. But you've done amazing things under your own steam. Come a long way. As for your parents, they're probably just worried that you're pushing yourself too hard. All work and no play, etcetera."

"Yeah, they mean well. I love what I do and I'm good at it, but it's tough for relationships, dating, my sex life." She closed her eyes briefly, clearly admonishing herself. "Not that I'm trying to steer the conversation around to ..."

"Last night's hot make-out session on the hood of your Honda Civic?" He'd wondered when they'd get to it.

Her hand flew to her mouth. "Oh my God, I can't believe I"—she grabbed the phone, pressed pause, and whispered loudly—"did that!"

"You seemed to have no regrets last night." *Please don't say you do now.*

"Oh, I still don't," she said with a cheeky grin. God, her mouth. So lush, so mobile. Levi wanted to do very wicked things to that mouth. "However, I need to be professional because it wouldn't look good if I was seen kissing the man I'm supposed to be reporting on. That gets out, and it'll just make the profile sound like a puff piece."

"Instead of hard-hitting journalism about some guy's favorite color and which Pokemon he self-identifies with?"

She tilted her head, a sly smile quirking her lips. "Uh, respect the process, Levi."

"Sure. The process. Got it. No more kissing." Which took him back to last night's lip lock and how damn good it had felt. How good it would feel to do it again.

"No more kissing," she murmured, and he imagined he heard a touch of regret in there.

11

Using his army stealth skills, Levi crept from his bedroom, destination: the kitchen. He was determined not to wake Elle, who, for the last three days, was usually asleep when he left or came home. He was worried she might be depressed.

She refused to talk about why she was here, which he put down to the army culture embedded in her bones. Military guys didn't share their troubles, and Elle had always been one of the guys.

Satisfied he'd analyzed the shit out of the situation, he entered the kitchen and found Elle at his kitchen table, drinking what looked like scotch and scrolling through texts on her phone. "Hey, Hunt."

"Hey." He turned on the under-cabinet lighting and grabbed his coffee cup.

"It's oh-five-hundred," she said. "Are you seriously heading out?"

"I have an early practice." He leaned against the counter and folded his arms. "We haven't talked much since you landed here."

"Just trying to keep out of your hair. Stay under the radar."

Something about the way she phrased that sent a shiver through him. *Stay under the radar.* Like she was running from something.

"Want to tell me what's going on? Are you in some sort of trouble?"

"I'd rather not talk about it."

So there *was* something.

Before he could think of a response that wouldn't make him sound like a pushy ass, she added, "But you'll be the first person I tell when I'm ready."

He nodded, both hurt that she wouldn't share and touched that she'd made the promise. "You can stay as long as you like. Mi casa and all that."

"I appreciate it. What I really need is a job. Anything going at the hockey ... uh, place?"

"You really don't know a thing about it, do you?"

"Bunch of toothless goons chasing a piece of plastic while trying not to fall over. Sounds awesome." She chuckled at her joke. "But seriously, if you hear of anything, let me know."

"Will do."

"Maybe your lady reporter friend could help me out. At the reporting place."

Levi kept his expression blank.

"She was married to Josh Cooke, wasn't she?"

"Correct."

"Never met him, but people used to talk about him. Good guy."

"Yeah, he was."

"And now you have a thing for the widow."

He gripped the countertop so hard dust creation was imminent. "Don't have a thing."

She shrugged, went back to her phone. "She likes you. I can tell."

His heart skittered with the pleasure of that. Pathetic.

"She's just doing a job. Trying to provoke a reaction." It was working. The last time they'd spoken a few days ago, he wasn't nearly as annoyed as he could have been. He'd enjoyed her candor about her marriage and her family, coming funnily enough at the same time he started opening up to her. Possibly some psychological mirroring skills they taught her in journo school, like the interrogation techniques he learned in Special Forces training. If she was playing him, he'd go down with a smile. (On the inside. Always on the inside.)

"I'll be heading to New York this afternoon ahead of tomorrow's game. Keep the place tidy while I'm gone and no parties."

She saluted and grinned. "Yes, sir."

Control the narrative.

Levi imagined that was probably the mantra for a lot of professions: politics, journalism, public relations. But it was also what he was taught in the military. Constantly check your six. Know every exit. If a situation wasn't to your liking, make it so or get out.

Hockey was no different. Every player on the ice had a part to play in the story of the game. An in-sync line could write a chapter for how a play went or how a puck ended up between the pipes. An in-sync team could write a goddamn novel that ended with "Win."

So here Levi was in the lobby of the Marriott in midtown Manhattan waiting for a woman who'd taken up far more real estate in his brain than was good for him. Because waiting for the narrative to be crafted was the opposite of what he'd been trained to do. Nine years ago, he'd enlisted because he knew he had more to offer than a pair of strong legs and a killer instinct in the blue zone. All his life he was used to making his own decisions, calling his own shots. This was no different.

Control the narrative.

He tugged at the collar of his button-down before realizing that he wasn't wearing the suit and tie he'd walked into the hotel with. It just felt that way. Fuck, he was nervous.

Jordan made him nervous. Mostly, he had no idea how to act around her.

He'd tried the asshole approach. She'd seen right through that.

Plan B was the kiss-her-breathless strategy that had only made him hot, bothered, and blue-balled.

Now he was going for Plan C: Cool politeness. He'd "yes, ma'am" her into a coma and ensure any sparks he imagined between them were well and truly dampened.

"Kraken!"

He turned to see the boys heading his way: Petrov, Burnett, Jorgenson, and Kershaw.

"You waiting for us?" Theo looked behind them back toward the elevator, out of which Jordan was (in)conveniently stepping. Her cute, floral print dress showcased her perfect legs. She bent over, fixing her heel, and gave everyone a peek-a-boo view of the shadow between her breasts. "Or you waiting for her?"

Jordan approached, her smile luminous and catching

somewhere right in the middle of Levi's chest. "Hey, guys! Heading out to paint the town?"

Erik's gaze turned dreamy. "We're going to dinner, Jordan. You should join us."

"Wish I could, but I'm on the clock, Fish. Got to pry some words out of this guy." She thumbed in the direction of Levi.

"Sounds dull," Theo said. "Tellin' ya, Hockey Grrl, I have so much to share with your listeners. I've been doing some research on average hip-to-flank measurements for NHL players and—"

The boys groaned.

"All right, enough of this." Vadim slapped a big paw on Theo's shoulder, encouraging him forward. "Our new star has important media duties to perform. Let us leave him to it. No revealing any locker-room secrets, Hunt."

"Aye, captain." At least Petrov understood that this was just business. Dinner with the media. No big deal.

The ragtag crew headed off, but were accosted by a group of women near the revolving door. One of them screamed, "Theo!" and thrust a sharpie at him so he could sign her Rebels jersey. Big grins all around, then Theo was signing T-shirts and purses and even a forearm. Levi almost envied the ease with which the kid took it all in his stride.

"Kershaw *really* wants on your podcast," he muttered to Jordan.

"Yeah, I got that. He's such a sweetheart."

Of course she'd see him like that. The guy was a charmer through and through, and if the big-assed doofus wasn't such a ladies' man, he would probably be a good fit for Jordan.

Idle thought: Had she hooked up with the lawyer yet?

She grabbed his arm. "Oh! So I've got a good one: why do hockey players never sweat?"

He raised an eyebrow.

"They have too many fans! Get it?"

"I do. Unfortunately." *Stop being so cute.*

Two minutes later they were in the back of a slow-crawling taxi and Levi was questioning every single one of his life choices. The cab had the usual weird odor of New York transport, barely masked by a car freshener Levi thought wasn't even made anymore. But Jordan's scent still rose above it and made his balls zing.

"What's your usual routine the night before an away game?"

"Eating with the crew. Video games in Petrov's suite. He usually books a bigger place."

"Right, all those inherited rubles. So no heading out to have a little fun like the other guys?" She raised an eyebrow at the mention of the word "fun," no doubt, teasing him because he wasn't known for his outgoing manner.

"Not really my style. And tonight, I have to talk to you."

She gave a look of faux-pity. "You get a lot of offers since you got the call to the big leagues? Or even before?"

"Pro athletes aren't hard up for company. Guys at this level are in their prime and women are usually throwing themselves at them. But there's a midnight curfew that the team is serious about."

"Hmm," was all she had to say to that.

A few minutes later, he was holding the door open to a taqueria on the lower east side. He'd been coming here since he was old enough to ride the train from Hoboken into the city. A hole-in-the-wall, it was about as far from romantic as any place could be. No one could mistake this for a date, especially him.

Pretty busy, it took a few minutes for them to clear off a table in the corner. Chips and salsa were thrown down with attitude.

"You want a margarita? They're really good here."

"You having one?"

He shook his head. He never drank the night before a game.

"I'll stick with water then." When the server had left, Jordan took a good look around, which gave him a chance to watch her. She wore hardly any makeup, which highlighted the smattering of freckles across her nose and made her look young and vulnerable. "How'd you find this place?"

"My dad boxed at a gym around the corner, and I'd take the train in from Jersey to watch him."

"He passed away when you were pretty young, right?"

"Yeah, when I was fifteen. Pneumonia."

"Who'd you live with after?"

"A couple of distant relatives until I started college on my hockey scholarship. This is all common knowledge. Rebels PR probably has a one-pager on it." When she didn't look interested in that version, he went on. "My dad wasn't that good a boxer, to be honest, and he stayed in the business long past his prime. Got pounded one too many times, had constant ear infections, which lowered his immune system." He rubbed his mouth, trying to eliminate the bad taste at the memory. "He encouraged me to play hockey. Always said that's how I'd make the family proud. And when he was gone, I wondered if that was good enough. If hockey was good enough."

"If you were good enough."

Levi met her gaze head on. "When someone leaves us too soon, you start to question everything. You want to be sure that you're honoring them with how you live."

"That's a lot of pressure to put on yourself," she said quietly. "Might be enough to do what makes you happy."

Christ, how did this get so serious so fast? But that was Jordan. She made him think and say things he'd never think or say around anyone else. He cleared his throat. "Anyway, I put in my time in the service and when I was done, I figured I had this second act left in me."

"Talent doesn't fade."

"Oh, it fades. I just work my ass off to make sure I can stay with the pack. Every team turned me down but the Rebels. They seem to like going against the grain."

"Three women and an openly gay GM—yeah, that might be considered going against the grain." She dipped a chip in the house salsa. "Some people have big problems with the team management. Think it's a little unorthodox."

He let his eyes indulge for a forbidden moment while she popped the chip past her lush lips. "You trying to get me to trash the Chase sisters and Moretti on the record?"

"Just want to hear what you think."

"All I care about are results. Their first year out they won the Cup, the second year, they made the finals. Last couple of seasons weren't so great for them, but they had a few changes with St. James retiring and throwing off the dynamic. Guy was a recovering alcoholic and by all accounts, a bit of an asshole—"

"Your kind of player."

Do not smile. "But he and DuPre held the team together. New blood can take a while to start flowing to the heart and get all the limbs pumping."

"You've got to prove yourself."

"We all do, but especially me."

A little divot appeared between her brows. "Because

you're not sure you deserve your place?" She paused and added, "On the team?"

He rolled his shoulders, seeking a tension drain that refused to come. *On the team, on this earth, breathing her air ...*

"We all suffer from impostor syndrome on occasion. Well, except you. You've always seemed so sure about everything."

Her mouth twitched in surprise.

Shit, he'd made a mistake. Not the impostor syndrome comment but his remark about her. An astute observer might think he'd spent a little too much time analyzing one Jordan Cooke.

"Everyone has doubts," she said, slowly, and he could almost hear the wheels turning as she figured out how to use this new information to press home an advantage. An even more astute observer might say he'd given her the opening—on purpose. "But I've always been fairly comfortable in my own skin. Is that why you don't like me? Or at, least didn't back then?"

"You keep saying that. I'm not sure where you got that idea."

"How about the fact that every time we met back in the day, you scowled at me like I'd killed your puppy or cat or hamster or cockroach because now I'm doubting you'd have a normal pet?"

Levi wanted to laugh, such a foreign impulse. He fought it off, but there was no fighting off his next words. No wanting to.

"Jordan, I like you plenty. In fact, I think you're the sexiest, most beautiful woman I've ever met."

～

JORDAN'S MOUTH DROPPED OPEN. She'd clearly fallen through a trap door in this universe and had landed in an alternate reality. Levi Hunt had just called her beautiful and sexy.

No. The sexiest, most beautiful woman he'd ever met.

Bonus: he liked her! He'd said it out loud, before God and everything.

"But, the scowling!"

"Did you see me smiling at anyone else?"

She thought about it for a second. "Well, no. But you dealt extra servings of disgust in *my* direction."

"I can't really help that I have resting scowl face, Jordan. I'm not the most expressive guy."

With anyone else she'd buy that. Might even feel sorry for them, forced to navigate a world of happy-sappiness that went against their natural makeup. She was innately cheerful and recognized that not everyone had it in them. But she wasn't mistaken in thinking Levi had once had a particular gripe with her.

"But you were *such* a jerk."

"I'm going to be honest here." This clearly pained him greatly. "When you and Cookie married, I didn't approve."

"What? Why?" She'd suspected this but hearing it confirmed threw her.

"You were both so young. I mean, really young. Working in Special Forces is already stressful enough. Add to that, the weight of trying to make a relationship, a marriage, succeed, a lot of it long-distance, and that's hell on anyone. You seemed like a nice girl—"

She cocked her head.

He cocked his right back, which made her laugh. *What the hell.*

"Woman. But Josh was on months-long missions, doing things he couldn't share with you. He told me that it was tough on you both because you're the kind of woman who wants to talk. All the fucking time."

She smiled, accepting that as a compliment. "It makes me good at my job. I have thoughts. I ask questions. I use my words. You should try it sometime."

Briefly, he looked to the heavens, but for the first time since she'd met him, he didn't seem to take offense. Or perhaps she was learning to read him better.

"I know that Josh not being able to confide in you on everything as well as the time away on missions took its toll."

"We made it work."

"You did. What I'm trying to say is that I thought you were beautiful and funny and perfect for him. This was never a case of not liking you. If anything, I ..." He halted, grimaced.

"What?" *Don't stop now, Hunt!*

"I was jealous. Josh had found his soulmate and I would have liked to have something—someone—to fight for like that. Like you."

Jordan's heart melted at his sincerity. Josh had always looked up to Levi, who seemed older than everyone on the team. Actually, only by a few months but in spirit, he was wise beyond his years, who knew himself and his men. She wasn't mature enough to understand that at the time, and instead assumed his attitude was based on something superficial like her raucous laugh or her in-your-face personality.

She took a chance. "Were you attracted to me back then?"

"Yes."

She'd thought it would be hard to get Levi to open up. Not at all. She just had to ask the right questions.

"And now?" She held her breath.

"Did you not hear what I said about you being the most beautiful, sexiest woman I've ever met?"

He *had* said that, and she'd dismissed it as impossible. Yet Levi was honest to a fault, every word from his mouth deliberately chosen. Something was happening here, something miraculous, strange, and more than a little terrifying.

"We should get back to the interview." She flipped a page on her notebook. "I have all these questions."

He didn't respond and suddenly, she was afraid to look at him. Afraid of what she'd see in those damnably blue eyes, things she'd ignored all those years ago.

Before she could shape her next query, he said, low and husky, "I keep thinking about how you taste."

She inhaled a shuddering breath. Moving forward and ignoring that comment would be best. What was it she wanted to know? Something about the NCAA? Hockey player diets? The words blurred before her eyes as a heavy heat pumped though her veins, slow and syrupy.

"How did I taste?" *Wrong question!*

"Sweet. Hot." His inhale sounded labored. "My end."

My God. "Levi ..." She looked up, meeting his gaze at last. It was only a kiss. Why was it imbued with all this significance?

Because of Josh?

She'd felt guilty when she kissed Levi that first time, the day she buried her husband. But not now. Now she felt torn because she couldn't kiss or touch or stroke or—*stop, stop, stop*—do anything with the subject of a story. Besides, it was merely lust. She and Levi had nothing in common beyond the sports connection. They weren't compatible in any way ... except for how their mouths and bodies fit. Pure chemistry.

"Why would I taste like ... your end?"

"After that kiss, I brushed my teeth, sloshed with mouth-wash, tried to gargle you away. But it was like your scent was in my pores and on my sheets, embedded in my pillow. Woke up the next day as hard as granite."

Was it her imagination that he had leaned in? Or perhaps she'd inched toward him, drawn to his solidity and maleness and every crazy-hot word passing from his crazy-hot lips.

"That kiss, your mouth, is all I can taste," he continued. "And you here, so close, is making me hard again."

"You mean ...?" Her X-ray vision was on the fritz tonight so she couldn't see through the table. She would, however, take his word for it.

His nostrils flared and his lips parted, but no words emerged. He was waiting for something—perhaps, for her to make a move or ask a question.

Does it hurt? That was what she wanted to ask, followed by: *What can I do to help?* But she couldn't help. This was all so deliciously wrong.

"We probably should ..." She gestured at the phone to indicate that they still had an interview to complete but her fingertips brushed against his. "Sorry."

"That's okay," he said in a way that assured her it was most definitely not okay. The tension between them smothered.

"Would you rather we continued this another time?"

"Is my hard-on interfering with your ability to ask questions?"

She laughed, and—amazingly—he joined in.

"I'm sorry," he said, self-deprecating humor she hadn't heard before in his tone. "That was inappropriate of me to even bring it up." He blushed—*blushed!*—at the phrasing, which sent her into a giggle fit.

Bring it up. Oh God.

Might be best to just lean into it. "Want to *expand* on that? Your fans would love that inside angle. Have you ever had, uh, a similar problem on the ice? During practice? At a game? Let's discuss the erection-suppressing power of cups!"

"Jordan ..." he warned, but he was still laughing, his eyes crinkly at the corners, his lips curved with the joy they were sharing. Hearing him let loose like this was a revelation.

"No, seriously, Levi. This is why I got into sports journalism, to be able to ask the *hard* questions. Don't tell me you've never seen another guy's stiffie in the communal shower. Your public deserves to know."

"The answers to your questions are no, no, no, and I don't look at any of my teammates' junk if I can help it. Got enough problems having to listen to Kershaw's moaning about his thick ass and how suit pants are not built for a man of his superior glutinous proportions."

"Wow, you guys really get deep in that locker room." With a giggle-quashing inhale, she looked at her notes again, then back up with a sly glance. "Calmed down a bit?"

"They say humor can deflate the biggest problems but a beautiful woman's smile won't help in the slightest."

She had to say she was fairly pleased to hear that.

12

"To new jobs and new opportunities."

Jordan clinked the wine glass of her friend Sandra Watson, a baseball reporter living in New York. They'd graduated the same class at Syracuse and Sandy had made a name for herself as the Mets beat reporter for the *New York Post*.

"Thanks, lady. It feels pretty surreal."

"Always knew you had it in you. How are you handling the trolls?"

Jordan lifted one shoulder. "Like any job, there's always going to be some toxic elements, but I can manage."

"Because if you say you can't, you look weak. We all do."

Sandy had been doing this longer than Jordan, so she undoubtedly had terrible tales to tell. Of course, every woman had damage. Pro sports was a patriarchal system, with a deck stacked so high that not even a woman in high heels could see over it.

"Can't exactly bite the hand. But I have to say that so far all the guys I've encountered on the Rebels have been nothing but respectful." A couple of weeks ago, Theo had even apologized to her for a slightly risqué comment that had gone ten miles over her head.

"Respectful can be just as much of a problem," Sandy said.

"How so?"

Sandra took a furtive look around the hotel bar, still relatively quiet as most of the Rebels players, staff, and hangers-on were at dinner. After a sip of her fruity Cab, she tapped the table with a sharp nail. "There's this old-fashioned idea that a woman can't be one of the guys, so the men have to tone it down around her. But when your fellow journos are toning it down so much they don't invite you to the weekly poker game where the good gossip is doing the rounds, or everyone goes quiet when you enter the locker room because they'd just been giving so-and-so shit, it's just as damaging. Your presence changes the dynamic."

Jordan thought about this. "So you want them to treat you like one of the guys? Swear and ball-scratch and walk around naked in front of you?"

"I'd rather that than the sullen silences, like I've tainted the bro-vironment."

"But most female reporters I've talked to are looking for that level of respect."

"You call it respect, I call it lost opportunity."

This was an angle she hadn't considered before. How the gender dynamic changed male behaviors to the extent women were missing out on a locker-room landscape that might inform their stories.

Sandra shrugged. "But then it goes to the other end of the spectrum when you have guys thinking your presence in the locker room is you showing interest. Sure, why else would you be there but to get a sneak peek at Johnny Baseball's dick!"

"Exactly. You've found the perfect job to support your voyeuristic tendencies. Flash your press credentials and it's an all-you-can-see penis buffet!"

That sent them both into hoots of laughter.

Jordan asked, "So how often are you hit on?"

"Often. Majorly often. Even with this damn fine rock on my finger." She held up her left hand, though it was a wonder she could with the weight of it. "They don't care. One GM used to text me at every hotel to let me know he'd be happy to give me the latest scuttlebutt and to 'stop in any time' because he's a night owl. I told him my husband wouldn't like it and he said that's okay, he was married, too. Just in case I was in any way confused about what he was after. Once I said I wasn't interested, he cut me off."

"From the harassing texts?"

"From everything. No insider details about how Player X was doing after his rotator cuff injury. No gossip about who they were scouting for the next season. I was persona non grata because I wouldn't play along." She leaned in. "The trick is to keep the game going to give them hope without letting yourself be compromised."

"But you shouldn't have to keep *any* game going!"

"Oh, to still have your innocence, Jordan." She smiled wryly. "Egos needs to be stroked."

"More than egos from the sound of it. Don't you worry there's only so much you can tease before they expect you to pay up?"

"Oh, I'd never have done anything. I'm not going to sleep with anyone for a story, though if I had Levi Hunt in my sights—"

"And you weren't happily married."

She grinned. "That, too. Let's just say that the hot soldier could get it. Guy's got BDE."

"Big dick energy? Levi?"

"Hell, yeah. Confident but not cocky."

Jordan shifted in her seat, uneasy with how her body seemed to so readily agree. "He's a pain in the ass." And other things, too. Back at the restaurant, he'd called her sexy and beautiful. *My end.* And then they'd laughed like schoolgirls about his erection!

"No chemistry there, then?"

"None whatsoever," she lied, expecting the ghost of Gordie Howe, Mr. Hockey himself, to strike her down any second.

A shadow darkened her periphery. *Gordie?*

"If it isn't my two favorite reporters." Billy Stroger, defenseman for the New York Spartans loomed over them, hands in jeans pockets, a wide grin lighting up his face. Fair-haired, blue-eyed, and with all the charisma of a carved potato, he attracted a lot of attention in the form of fights on the ice and ladies off it.

Yet he still needed the extra validation of sending Jordan dick pics. Amazing.

"Oh, hi, Billy," Sandra said. "You feeling good about the game tomorrow?"

"Yup. The Rebels haven't really gotten their act together this season yet. Too many gimps and novelty acts."

Sandra shot Jordan a look of *this guy, right?* More curious was why a hometown player was hanging at the visiting team's hotel the night before a game. Rumor had it that he liked to stop in to get a head start on the gamesmanship.

Stroger zeroed in on Jordan. "We should get together later, Red. No doubt I can come up with something exclusive for you."

Given that she'd seen several pictures of his most intimate anatomy, she seriously doubted he had any more "exclusives" to offer.

"And Sandy," he went on, "I know you don't cover hockey but I'd be happy to let you join in. Sure I could handle you both." He added a lascivious wink.

Ugh.

One of his teammates called him over to the bar, and he backed up, a smug smile on his face.

When he was finally out of earshot, Sandra shuddered. "MCP, right?"

Most creepy player. "You, too?"

"It's been a while since he's sent me anything." Sandra lowered her voice. "Gets bored easily, which I assume relates to all those hits to the head."

Jordan hoped he'd get bored with her soon. She could bring out her best bitch and slap him down, but she didn't want to risk alienating a player who might spread rumors about her. It had happened to colleagues and ruined careers.

At this point she was becoming expert in walking that fine line.

Any sign of Joe today?

Afraid not.

Levi frowned at the text from Lucy. During his last shift at the shelter, Joe had been a no-show so Levi had taken to texting daily to get an update. Short of contacting the Chicago Police Department and asking them to check under the viaduct at Wilson for a homeless vet who liked coffee and bacon, Levi didn't have much leverage here. He'd seen too many former servicemen tap out once they got home for all sorts of reasons, chief among them the inability to adapt. Levi knew he was lucky—he had a skill that was marketable and paid well. But not everyone was so fortunate.

He slumped on the bed, turned on the TV, and flipped through the channels. Dumb sitcom. *Law and Order*. That idiot Coby Dawson on *SportsFocus*, trashing the Rebels. More *Law and Order*.

Antsy as hell, he wondered who was up. If he was being honest, he wanted company. Female company.

That phrase sounded old-fashioned, yet the only person who fit the bill as far as Levi was concerned was the thoroughly modern Ms. Cooke. It was okay to fantasize about her, right? To think about her perky smile and lush lips and freckles he wanted to lick and ass his hands were made for ... Yeah, it was okay, but it would get him nowhere.

The bar it was.

Stepping off the elevator, he heard her before he saw her, that big, dirty laugh that haunted his dreams. She stood in the lobby bar, surrounded by the entire Rebels defensive line and then some. Kershaw was on his feet, thrusting his arm toward her so she could test his biceps or something. Whatever he said made her laugh again, the sound now grating.

Life and soul, that was Jordan. No one could fail to be charmed by her, but he wouldn't be one of her victims. *Law and Order* was starting to look more attractive.

Funny how his feet refused to cooperate. Stuck at the bar entrance, all he could do was stare as she took a few steps back, her goal the bar. Looked like the next round was on her.

Abruptly, someone appeared beside her: Billy Stroger, a defenseman with the Spartans. Levi knew him by reputation only, namely his ability to piss off everyone on the ice, including his own teammates. He hugged Jordan, and every nerve-ending in Levi's body went haywire. Her back was to him, so he could only see Stroger's face. Pretty pleased with himself by the looks of it.

Levi's situational analysis skills clicked on just as Jordan took a step back. Subtle, but enough of a tell. She was not a fan.

He flicked a glance to the Rebels players, crowded around a table about twenty feet away, too wrapped up in their bro banter to even notice that Jordan might be in an uncomfortable position.

"Hey," Levi said, his arm touching Jordan's shoulder after he'd closed the gap in two seconds flat. "Glad I caught you."

Her eyes glinted with surprise and he liked to think, relief. "Oh, hello. Do you know Billy Stroger?"

The Spartans' defenseman assessed him with dark eyes, glazed over after a beer too many. "The army guy. Guess I'll be seeing you on the ice tomorrow."

"Guess you will." Dismissing him, Levi turned to Jordan. "You ready to leave? Figured we have some time to talk." Remembering that Jordan was sensitive about how their relationship might be perceived, he added a line for Stroger. "She's following me around for a profile."

"Right," Jordan said as several drinks appeared on the bar. "I just need to deliver these."

Levi peeled off a couple of twenties, placed them on the bar, and called over to his teammates. "Kershaw, drinks are up. Get your super ass over here." Ignoring Stroger, he cupped Jordan's elbow and headed out.

By the time they'd made it outside the bar into the hotel lobby, he was spitting Chiclets.

"You didn't have to do that," she said, stopping and facing him.

His palm still held her elbow, and he let himself luxuriate in the warmth and silkiness of her skin. "I think I did. You didn't look like you were having a good time. With Stroger, that is."

She slid out of his grip. "He's a jerk but I had it handled. Instead, you made it look like you had some kind of investment in rescuing me."

Investment? He supposed that wasn't completely inaccurate.

"I don't like to see a woman disrespected, and I could tell that something was up. I've no doubt you can extricate yourself when necessary but I'm also aware that there are times you may need to play along and act like one of the guys so you can establish trust."

Surprise lit up her eyes. "That's ... an astute observation."

"Military training, Jordan. Body language is something I'm generally fluent in." And right now, his own was speaking loudly and thundering out a biological imperative.

Protect. Take. Own.

He needed to escape before he said or did something he'd regret, but he also needed her to be safe, which meant there was only one way this could proceed.

"I just hauled you out of there under the guise of doing this interview, so we—"

"Probably should keep up the pretense?"

"Correct." He stalked toward the elevator bank, both relieved and on edge that she accompanied him.

"Were you headed to the bar to meet up with someone?"

"Just feeling restless in my room. Looking for company."

"And I ruined it by making you think you needed to play target extraction."

The elevator doors opened and when they closed again,

he was inside and sharing the sultry air with Jordan. He pressed the button for the tenth floor. "You didn't ruin it. Something else took precedence, is all."

You.

In that moment, when he saw her, all thoughts of a night of dumb jokes with his crew dispersed to the outer limits of the Tri-State area. Sure, he noticed her discomfort with Stroger but even if he hadn't, even if it had been Jordan in a room full of supermodels, there would have been no one else. Only her.

This was not controlling the narrative.

This was a fucking mess.

The elevator reached his floor and he stepped off, with her following.

Please. Fucking. No.

"Well, like I said, Levi, you didn't have to rescue me." She placed a hand on his arm and squeezed, probably intending to be friendly. Her touch flayed him. "I had it handled."

He snapped. "Did you have it handled, Jordan? Because from what I can see you're a beautiful woman forced to play nice with a bunch of jocks who probably think they have a shot with you."

Her eyes flashed. "No one *forces* me to do anything. I do this job because I love it, and yeah, the guys I cover usually enjoy a laugh and a joke. Unlike some people who'd rather scowl everyone around them into the grave. But I know where the line is and I've no problem redrawing it when necessary."

Fury shouldn't have made her more attractive. It shouldn't have given that wrinkle between her eyebrows new purpose or the lips he wanted to kiss a plumpness that made his mouth water. It shouldn't have made her chest heave with effort, which only drew his attention to their lush swell and the hint of cleavage he wanted to explore.

"I'm not saying you don't. I'm saying that guys in this environment tend to turn into entitled asses and wouldn't know a line if it was steamrolled all over their faces. I don't want you to be in any situation where you have to even think about the line. Case in point, maybe you shouldn't be fondling Kershaw's biceps!"

She did a double take. "Fondling?"

"Yes, fondling. You're a journalist. Haven't you heard of it?" *Weak, man. So weak.*

"Yeah, I've heard of it," she said, a rasp to her voice. "It's one of my favorite words, actually. Are you seriously jealous ... of Theo?"

Yes. All the yes. "Of course not. But he's a dumb kid, and I don't want him to get the wrong idea."

She was closer now, close enough to share a breath. To stumble headlong into her. To fall into madness.

"And what would be the wrong idea?"

His lungs were filled with her, her scent fueling his fall. "That you want him to touch you. To taste you. To take you."

"No," she whispered as she took another step toward him. Close enough to taste. "I don't want that. Not with Theo."

Not with ... did she mean ...? "Christ, woman, you're driving me crazy."

"Not as crazy as you're driving me." She tilted her head, met his fire head on, because this moment seemed inevitable, as fated as the night she walked into the locker room after that first game.

No, further back than that. The moment he saw her in that Kentucky bar, hesitated, and lost.

Not this time.

Following the beat of his heart, the thrumming, pulsing drive to possess, he found himself wrapped in her or maybe she found herself wrapped in him. Either way, they were melded together in the only way that mattered.

"So fucking crazy," he murmured before sending them both to hell by kissing her senseless.

13

HE'S A PLAYER.

He's a story.

He's an ethics violation waiting to happen.

Correction: Already happening.

He's ... so getting some tonight.

In Levi's words, this was "so fucking crazy," and if she gave it the thought it probably deserved, she would be slamming on the brakes. But she was tired of overthinking their chemistry. Jordan knew in her heart she could trust him to be discreet. The guy had made a living out of keeping secrets and helping people, both traits that she needed him to dial up to the max right now.

She especially needed help with removing her clothes.

But first, privacy was top of the list. One, two, five doors from the elevator and they were inside Levi's hotel room. A single table lamp cast the room in a muted glow.

Sex lighting.

On closing the door, he pinned her against it. "You sure about this, Jordan? I don't want you to feel pressured in any way."

Said while she felt the lovely pressure of his cock against her abdomen. Even with that obvious evidence of his arousal and the perfect, sensual weight of him, his words were the words of a gentleman—only not what she needed in this moment.

"I can't say for sure that I know what I'm doing. But I can guarantee that this is what I want. You're what I want."

He flipped their positions and walked her back until her legs met the bed. Then her butt. Her back. Her head.

Levi loomed over her, his eyes ablaze. "You want it slow, fast, gentle, rough? What'll make this beautiful body sing?"

"Seeing you naked would be a start." She longed to savor yet she needed him inside her now. Those competing desires would have to be dealt with.

He stood and started to unbutton his shirt. Really, she should have been working on her own clothes removal but she suspected multitasking was not her strong suit right now. This was too good to miss.

He fingers halted midway through the reveal. "Just to warn you, I have a tattoo."

Warn her? "Is it a girl's name? A big heart with Brandi inside it? No, I know. John Wayne because of The Green Berets movie." She'd seen those tattoos and they were troubling on many levels. She was also babbling because she was nervous.

Finished unbuttoning, he pulled his shirt apart to reveal the Green Beret insignia and motto: De Oppresso Liber. To free the oppressed. At its center was the inscription "51" which stood for the unit and regiment—and now his number on the ice. Along his lower torso, a couple of scars created an intriguing map, badges of honor she wanted to follow to wherever this night would lead.

She stood and splayed her hands over his chest, then she

applied a kiss to the insignia, right over his heart. It was impossible not to think of the man who connected them and she knew that's why Levi had warned her.

For a moment, she pressed her forehead to Levi's chest and said a brief prayer for Josh. Levi remained silent, letting her have this space to work through it.

When she looked up, he was watching, waiting for her to make the next move.

"Thank you," she whispered, unbearably moved by his concern.

The clouds on his face parted and the sun peeked through with the curve of his lips. He curled a hand around the nape of her neck, so strong and warm and life-affirming, then tilted her lips to his. The kiss was sure and sweet, an invitation back into the sexy moment they were sharing.

It felt so good to be here, the focus of his desire.

"Let's see what we're working with." She fumbled for his belt, unbuckling and unzipping and unpacking and ... *oh yes*. Her palm cupped the treasure she'd discovered as his moan filled the room.

"Jordan."

She pulled down his briefs and watched as he kicked off his pants and removed his shirt completely. The man was a flawlessly formed tower of muscle. Thighs she wanted to hug, abs she wanted to kiss, chest she wanted to caress, and the most interesting muscle of all. Perfectly thick and standing at attention, like a good, not-so-little soldier.

"You're ... wow."

"Nice vocabulary, Ms. Reporter."

"Would you rather I commented on your rigid manhood, your swollen tumescence, your engorged—"

"Wow it is."

Chuckling and more than surprised to be doing so in the

presence of the artist formerly known as Mount Grump, she gripped all that wow and stroked, loving how it came alive in her hands.

"Something's wrong with this picture," he murmured.

"Not from where I'm sitting." She tilted her head, taking him in *Playgirl* centerfold style. Having been out of the game for a while, she wanted to savor.

"Jordan, you're overdressed."

"Really?" She kissed the head of his cock, then swirled her lips around like a lollipop. Salty goodness triggered something in her sex-memory. It had been a long, long time.

He cupped the back of her neck and held her away from him. "Strip. Now."

"Strip me. Now."

She lay back on the bed, waiting for him to take charge. With one knee on the bed, he leaned over and placed a hand over the V of skin revealed by her silk shell. There was something wonderfully possessive about it as the heat of his palm branded her chest. Something in his eyes, too, told her that the fun and games were over.

Levi Hunt had spotted his prey.

He undressed her, never breaking eye contact, as if sheer discipline required he shouldn't look below her neck. Stripped to her bra and panties, she watched as he gently pushed her to the bed and hovered over her. His scrutiny rendered her breathless.

"Levi, you can touch me."

His mouth quirked. "Oh, I can, can I?"

"Yes. It's just ..."

"It's just what?"

He still hadn't explored beyond the necessary to remove her clothes. This was as frustrating as it sounded.

"You've barely looked at me."

His brows slammed together and a few seconds passed before he spoke. "You've got a problem with eye contact?"

"No." *Maybe.* The way Levi did it was unnerving to say the least. Such intimacy with that hot gaze, the ultimate in eye-fucks. "But you're allowed to move your eyes around the bod!"

"I am? You mean, I can look here ..." He removed a bra strap from one shoulder, his eyes scalding the same path as his finger. Then the other one, his midnight-dark gaze smoldering at the sight (a shoulder-smolder!). Finally, he unhooked her bra at the back and starting at the base of her throat, traced his index finger over her breastbone, down her cleavage until it met the apex of her bra cups, both still covering her breasts.

With a slowness that killed her he pulled the bra down to reveal her nakedness, a reverse striptease where he was the one controlling the reveal.

Predictably, her nipples went on high alert.

His gaze magnetized to her breasts and she longed for the moment thirty seconds ago when he was all about the eye contact. Not that she was embarrassed by the girls, but it had been a while, and she wasn't all that in the boobage department.

He coasted a thumb over her nipple, yielding a delicious shiver. "So pretty." His voice sounded rough and reverent, and then her voice sounded high and squeaky when he inclined his head and sucked.

"Oh!"

Strong, callused fingers plumped her sensitive flesh while he fed on her breast and scraped his teeth across the damp peak, the sensation so delicious and decadent.

"Levi," she moaned, enjoying the sound of his name on her lips. The forbidden shape of it, but more.

His hand trailed down her ribs, over her hips, to cup her butt and squeeze. He hooked a finger under the thong's band and peeled it down, not all the way, just to the tops of her thighs. That large hand curved around and covered her now-exposed mound, the palm separating her thighs except they couldn't go far as they were cuffed by her panties.

She wanted to widen her legs, open up to give him complete access, but he seemed to prefer it this way. The big palm inverted to two fingers—then three—stroking and slipping and sliding through all this wetness she'd created for him.

"You feel so silky. So soft." She heard that reverence in his tone again, an awe that made her feel beautiful. His mouth found hers while his fingers continued to drive her insane. Meanwhile on the all-important erection front, his was tip-tapping against her thigh demanding attention.

Moving her hands over his amazing muscled chest, she skipped down and gripped his cock.

"Fuck," he grunted against her lips. "Fuck fuck fuck."

"Nice vocab."

He rubbed his nose against hers and something about that intimate gesture reached a part of her she'd thought inaccessible. *No, that's not with this night is about.* It was about liberation, letting go, tapping into the needs she'd suppressed over the last few years. She shooed away the notion that this was more than lust.

"You keep doing that, Jordan, and I'll blank every word in my dumb brain."

She kept doing that. He kept doing what he did best, all while holding her captive with a Levi Hunt scorcher of a gaze. *Look away*, a small voice of protest demanded. *This is too much.*

Perhaps, but it was spectacularly sexy. In this one

amazing moment, she was the center of Levi's world, and it was truly the most wonderful place to be. How had she ever thought him cold and unfeeling?

There was nothing cold and unfeeling about the sensations streaking through her. Desire surged and ebbed, climbed and receded. He knew the right pressure, the right stroke, the right touch, and when he glanced a rough finger over her clit, she lost it right there.

"That's ... yes!"

Of course, in the midst of that lovely orgasm, she neglected her one job: make Levi feel good. But coming like that had left her weak as a kitten and frankly, not in any condition to finish what she'd started.

Bad sex partner.

He reached down to the floor and extracted a condom from his wallet.

"I want inside you. That okay?"

"You don't have to ask."

"I do."

Consent check-in for the win. "I'd love that, Levi."

"Love what?" He tore at the condom wrapper, his scorching gaze still on her.

"You."

You.

Damn if his ears hadn't done a double take at that. Of course that wasn't what she meant, but a guy could dream.

He quickly rolled on the condom over his aching cock, hoping he hadn't left it too long because there was a fair to middling chance he might embarrass himself. But the feel of her under his fingertips, all that slippery, sensual flesh as he slid through her soaking pussy was about the hottest thing he'd ever experienced. Guiding her to that orgasm was worth the wait.

But he didn't have any more wait left in him.

He drew her panties down and off, then placed both of his palms on her inner thighs. "Lemme see all that sweetness, baby."

His heart pulsed hard along with his dick as she spread wide for him. She was majestic. Pink and wet and ready—and damn, she had more freckles dotting her pale skin.

"Levi," she panted. "I need you."

Christ, his dick was gonna get so mad at him. "And I need ... a taste."

He'd waited this long—years, if he was being honest and now was probably the only time he would *ever* let his brain admit that—and he would take his sweet damn time.

He kissed her pussy first, a ghost of a touch, though really he wanted to drink long and deep. She shuddered against his lips and shifted to begging position. Oh, he'd have her begging all right.

With two hands gripping her perfect ass, he lifted her to his mouth and gave her one long, deep stroke of his tongue. So sweet and good.

Unfortunately, his dick did not agree. Balls started getting in on the action, too, demanding their turn. The ache hurt something fierce now, sending waves of pleasure/pain racing through to every nerve ending.

She yanked on his hair. "Levi."

"Kinda busy here."

"Levi. Please."

"Sounds like you and my dick are on the same page." He walked his hands up on either side of her and kissed her slow, wet, and deep. "You taste so good, I had to have some of that honey."

She gripped his sheathed cock, lining it up at her entrance. "Well, now I have to have some of this. Don't make me beg."

"You sure? Kind of like the idea."

"Levi!"

He slipped inside in one smooth thrust, watching how her face changed, needing to see the effect he had on her. Her moan was as dirty as that laugh of hers he adored, while his own groan threatened to inform the entire hotel that he was one happy hockey player. Rarely was he this loud. Expressive. Containment was key to so much of his life. Sex was something he usually maintained a rigid control over. It was necessary, a biological function to relieve pressure, but with Jordan, he wanted to let go in a way he'd never permitted for himself. With this woman there was no staying inside the lines.

He couldn't take his eyes off her. Her skin glowed with freckles across the top of her pretty tits, and before the night was through he would kiss every single one. Watching her react to his touch, his body, his invasion was the best feeling in the world. She couldn't hide her joy—it flowed off her like cartoon wavy lines. She was lusty and funny and a sensualist to her core.

Another thing that surprised him: how much he wanted to talk to her. Listen to her. Connect with her. All the fucking time, even now, when he really needed to focus on his balls not exploding.

"Feel good?"

"So, so good." She grasped his ass, giving it a chunky squeeze. "Don't be gentle."

"It's been a while for me, so I'm trying to go slow."

"It's been a while for me, too, so I need you to go hard."

Jesus, did she have any idea what she was asking? And when she said a while, did she mean ... no, not going there.

Instead he'd go deep. He gripped her ass, relishing the feel of that curve in his palm and held her in place for the next thrust. And another. Harder and deeper than he would have thought possible. Each stroke consumed them both, yielding new sounds, new depths, new meaning.

Pleasure checked him hard, the build like a jet engine taking off. Sizzling sensation rocked the base of his spine, filling his balls, thickening his cock until a single word from her—"Levi"—triggered first her release, and then his. Just hearing his name on her lips sent him into another dimension, falling, falling, fallen.

And he had serious doubts he'd be getting back up.

"I SHOULD PROBABLY ..." She thumbed toward the door. "I don't want to risk being caught here."

Barely five minutes. That's all she was putting into the post-coital segment of the evening. So this had placed her in an awkward position—okay, *he* had done that—but he'd hoped she'd at least spend the night.

He stroked her cheek, marveling that he actually had the freedom to do that and annoyed that he might not for much longer. "I'll protect you, Jordan. I'm not going to be gossiping with the boys."

"I'd deny every word."

Said with that saucy tone, yet it unsettled him. She had understandable self-preservation reasons, but it still bothered him that she wouldn't claim him if it came to that.

Seemed he'd already projected a future here and was disappointed that she'd dismissed it so readily.

"Not that I'm ashamed of you, Levi," she said in a nice stab at mind reading. "I've no regrets on a personal level but on a professional level, I have to be careful. This wouldn't look bad for you, but for me ..." She left it hanging, the words spoken with her bare back to him while she leaned over, looking for her underwear.

He dropped a kiss on her shoulder, tasting a clutch of freckles with it. "I get it, I do. Just saying I have your back. And to be honest, I think you should stay a little longer."

"Oh really?"

"It's not even midnight and that's the boys' curfew. They'll be filling the elevators and roaming the floors, so you might run into them. Better to sneak out in the early hours. I'll set an alarm for you."

She hesitated for a moment, but then he saw when she became resigned to his plan. "And how will we fill the time?"

"We'll think of something."

14

Time to step up, @ChiRebels, and show us where the money is being spent! @BigDogDawson breaks it down on @SportsFocus

ON HER WAY to the press box in the Spartans arena, Jordan's phone pinged and she slipped it out of her purse. The text was from Coby Dawson.

Want to meet for a drink after the game?

Interesting. They'd texted a couple of times after crossing paths at the Rebels' opener and the next day outside Harper's office. He'd congratulated her for getting the Hunt gig, adding a few shamrock emojis to let her know she was lucky, she supposed.

They weren't in the same league professionally, but he was clearly angling to see if she'd discovered anything of note when it came to Levi. *Great lips. Amazing body. Cock that could go all night.* Probably should keep that scoop to herself.

As for Coby Dawson, the old adage of "Keep your enemies closer" seemed applicable here. About to return his text, she was interrupted by someone calling her name. She turned to see the Rebel Queen approaching.

"Oh, hi, Harper."

"How's the profile coming along?"

"It's coming ..." *And coming.*

"Care to join us in the visitors' executive box today? Get another angle for the story?"

"I'd love to."

Once inside, she spotted Dante Moretti, several of the Rebels' front office staff, and ... surprise, surprise, Mr. Coby Dawson of ESP-fucking-N.

"Hey, Jordan. Fancy seeing you here." He smiled that superior grin she'd like to slap off his face. "Get my message?"

"I did. Thought I'd see you in the press box."

"Harper asked me in to see how the other half live." He gave a self-deprecating eye roll.

Not buying it, dude.

"You spent much time in the executive surrounds? Beats the crappy pizza in the press box."

"Not our press box," Dante said a little stiffly. "I oversee those menus myself."

And fine menus they were. "Hey, I'm a fan of your pastry choices in the Rebels press box, Dante."

His eyes lit up. "A fellow mini-macaron connoisseur?"

She nodded solemnly. "I would eat them three meals a day if society didn't frown upon it."

He laughed. "What can I get you?"

She pretended to think about it. "Got a pomegranate mojito per chance? If you don't, scotch would be lovely. Lagavulin."

Dante grinned, all Italian hotness. "Got it."

She sat, taking in the surroundings and the excellent view of the ice. Warm-up had started and her eyes were drawn to Levi in his number 51 jersey, which reminded her of his tattoo and his chest and kissing his chest and moving her greedy mouth down, down, down ... Quickly she averted her gaze when Dante handed off her drink, which she would sip slowly because loose lips sink relationships.

One night only. Neither of them had said it, but it had definitely been implied. Her efforts to slip away as soon as those orgasms had screamed their way into existence was evidence enough. And when his alarm went off at 4 a.m. this morning and he checked the hotel corridor, then kissed her slow and deep, she'd known it couldn't happen again. Sneaking around with the subject of her story, no matter how wonderful the sex was, would be career suicide.

Dante handed off her drink and Harper touched her arm. "Come sit with me over here."

Once they'd settled at a decent distance from Dawson, Jordan waited for Harper to get to the point of why she'd invited her to the box. The owner remained silent so Jordan filled the void.

"Thought I was getting exclusive access." She gave an unsubtle side-eye toward Dawson.

Harper hummed. "You are. I just like to stay in the good graces of all our media contacts."

Was this some power move to make sure she provided a PR-friendly profile of Levi and the Rebels? Jordan wouldn't put it past Harper to play both sides.

She slid a glance to Dawson who was watching her with interest. He raised his glass and turned back to the game. *Ass.*

"I've been meaning to ask," she said to Harper. "Would you and your sisters like to come on my podcast? It's called Hockey Grrl, so—" She waved a hand between them to acknowledge the obvious.

"Sounds like we're your prime demo. Let me run it by them. Isobel loves talking hockey, Violet not so much."

"If Violet doesn't want in, that's okay."

"She'll show up to anything if wine and cupcakes are involved."

A woman after her own heart. Jordan's phone pinged. Reflexively, she checked it and immediately wished she hadn't. The purple-splotched truncheon couldn't be swiped away fast enough, except trying to remove it enlarged it to proportions it likely couldn't achieve in real life.

"Well, hello!" Harper said. "Looks like you're having fun."

"Uh, no. That's not anything I've invited." This pic wasn't from Stroger, who was currently on the ice, but was courtesy of some catch called @LovePump99. Subtle. She shrugged it off, not wanting to upset her host. "Hey, it's an occupational hazard."

"That's from a player?"

"Not this one. But that happens."

Harper stood. "Let's take this outside for a second."

Okay.

Out in the hallway, Harper turned to her, her expression one of genuine concern. "When I first inherited the team with my sisters, we got a lot of blowback. Sports reporters, jock radio, superfan troll boys—you name it, everyone had an opinion. Still do. Part of it was people forwarding unsolicited photos of their junk to let me know I was playing with the big boys. I also had problems with players, both in my org and out of it." Her usually placid expression darkened. "If anyone on my team is harassing you, I need to hear about it."

"It's not someone on the Rebels."

"Someone on the Spartans, then? Billy Stroger?"

Interesting that she went there, but maybe not. Billy's reputation as a troublemaker was well known. A couple of years back, Remy DuPre was suspended after an unprovoked beat down he dealt out to none other than Billy Boy during a game. Rumors swirled that Billy had been an old boyfriend of Harper's from her pre-ownership days, but nothing was ever confirmed.

Jordan didn't quite feel the need to make trouble for anyone—yet. But the kernel of an idea was forming in her head. "No. Someone else."

"I can talk to any owner and GM on your behalf. This needs to be dealt with, Jordan."

"It's better I handle it myself. Reporting it just gets me a rep for being difficult."

Harper threw up her hand. "Be difficult."

"With all due respect, that's easy for you to say. You run an NHL franchise with a Stanley Cup under your belt. You can be as difficult as you want."

"Oh, for the day of unmonitored Tumblr porn and Violet's Dicktabase," Harper said wistfully. "We could have done a name and shame, but then she was pretty picky about what she added."

"You mean, the Dicktabase was real?"

Rumor had it that former wild child and youngest Chase sister Violet Vasquez had catalogued dick pics and gifs, which sounded like the perfect defense strategy for a stream of unsolicited junk mail.

"We had to scrub it after we won the Cup. Plus Violet's training to be an elementary teacher, God help us all." She laid a hand on Jordan's arm. "If there's anything I can do, I want to you to come to me."

Jordan smiled her gratitude. "I'll keep it in mind. Now, I think I spotted a platter of adorable mini cheese cakes in there, so I probably should get on that before Dante puts them away."

15

OMFG. Just saw Theo Kershaw at the Empty Net and he's as hot in person as he is on TV. Forget Captain America! TK's booty is #AmericasAss.

"So you're going to write this puff piece about hockey's hottest rookie while gathering evidence to prove that pro athletes are asshole sexual harassers?"

Jordan grinned at Kinsey, who had left the cozy confines of Chicago to meet her at the Empty Net bar, the regular hangout for the team when they weren't playing hockey, video games, or poker. Located on the main drag in River-brook, it was packed by 7 p.m. on a non-game night, mostly with men and women looking to score with the single players.

"You said yourself I should report it."

"To your boss. To the team owners. To the NHL and whoever else runs these things."

Jordan wagged a finger. "That's just picking away at the problem instead of rooting it out. These organizations are built on the premise that men are placed on this earth to be worshipped, that money talks, and that the word of a woman who's been harassed is worthless." Hearing the experiences of her reporter friend, Sandy, and even someone as high on the NHL food chain as Harper Chase had got her thinking.

"While I'm working on the Levi piece, I'm perfectly positioned to—"

"Play Harriet the Spy?"

"To observe the power structure and gender imbalances at play, Kinsey. Do try to keep up."

Kinsey lowered her voice. "You think the Rebels players are guilty here?"

"There've been a few off-color comments, nothing really actionable. But, I've been talking to women on the front lines, fellow reporters and the like, and I could easily use the cover of being embedded to speak with other women in this space. The physical therapists, the front office staff, the PR people. The women in these orgs are dealing with entitled, richer-than-God, think-their-shit-don't-stink jerks every day. Someone needs to tell their stories."

Kinsey looked impressed. "Go, you."

Jordan arced her gaze over the crowd. Even the player-fan interactions might contribute to a meatier exposé. Ethnographic research to make her mother proud.

Because let's face it, as much as she enjoyed talking to Levi, he was never going to give her full access to his puzzle-box brain. Now that they'd crossed the line, the story's integrity was spiraling out of control, anyway. Better to have a backup plan. There was a better story worth exploring that might get her into Mac's good books.

Three days had passed since New York. They'd traveled back on the same plane, ignoring each other like it was an Olympic sport (gold medal for him, silver for her). Sensual awareness of him kept her glued to her seat, headphones on, her gaze trained on a blurry page that refused to form into anything legible for the duration of the trip. On exiting in Chicago, she'd locked eyes with him, and with a quiet nod, he released her from a sensual captivity, one where she relished the bonds a little too much.

Not enjoying that conclusion, Jordan caught the familiar eye of the bartender.

"Hi, it's Elle, isn't it? I'm Jordan."

Elle picked up a damp towel and wiped the bar. "So it's not enough that you feed them pizza, go to all the matches, and travel with them on chartered planes, you want to drink with them, too?"

Jordan laughed. "Yeah, my life does tend to revolve around these people a little too much, but it's all for a story. When did you start working here?"

"Yesterday. I'm trying to get enough cash together to move out of Hunt's. I mean, he's not shoving me out or anything, in case you're thinking there's some story there."

Jordan hid a smile at Elle's guard dog loyalty. "Didn't think there was. He said you two were good friends."

"Yeah, he's the kind of guy who's always stepped up. But he has a hard time letting people see that." She leaned in. "Whatever you write better make that clear. He's one of the good ones even if he is beating down on whoever deserves it in the hockey match."

"Game."

"Whatever. What are you drinking?"

"IPA times two, please."

Elle squinted over Jordan's shoulder. "Well, here come the freakin' All Stars."

Jordan looked behind her to see the crew walking in, led by Theo. Jorgensen, Burnett, Petrov were in tow, but no sign of Levi, which was good because she wasn't sure she'd be able to remain neutral in his presence.

She turned back to find two bottles of Sam Adams IPA and Elle sizing her up. "On me. Don't be a bitch, 'kay?"

"Okey dokey. Thanks." Note to self: do not piss off the woman in combat boots.

Kinsey elbowed her. "I'm disappointed there's no Levi, but why didn't you tell me that Theo Kershaw is so gorg— oh, God, here he comes!"

Theo swaggered over. "Howdy, Hockey Grrl, you here to watch us score off the ice?"

"Oh, I'd *love* to see that, Superglutes! Please show me how it's done."

"Superglutes?" Elle yelled. "That's your nickname?"

"No, it's—"

But Elle was too busy laughing her head off to hear Theo's denials.

"Thanks, Cooke," he muttered out of the side of his mouth.

Jordan grinned. "You're not digging it? I heard you were having trouble getting pants past your manly thighs and gluteus maximus."

"Hell. No." Elle stood on something behind the bar that gave her a foot in height as she leaned over to ogle Theo. "Your ass is too big to handle?"

"The struggle is real." Theo gave a booty shake. "And every part of my anatomy is too big for you to handle, cupcake."

"Cupcake? That's the best you got?" Elle turned to Jordan. "You have *got* to put that in your article." She dragged a palm across an imaginary billboard. "'Hockey player's ass too big to fail. Subtitle: Thinks cupcake is an insult.'"

Another customer snagged her attention and she went off, shaking her head and chuckling.

"Didn't mean it as an insult, *Sergeant* Cupcake," Theo muttered, then louder, "And I was here first to order, you know!" Sighing, he took a seat beside Jordan. "So, traitor, how's your day been?"

She couldn't help her laugh. Theo was such a hoot and not even the ruptured aneurysm that put his career on hold for almost two years was enough to change his fun personality. He reminded her of Josh.

"Sorry about that. Honestly. By the way, this is my friend, Kinsey."

Theo shook Kinsey's hand. Jordan had never seen her so shockingly starry-eyed. With a zillion hot brothers-in-law, the woman should have been immune, but Theo's glimmer blinded even the most jaded.

"Hi! Big fan!" Kinsey gushed just as her phone rang, the screen lighting up with an image of her handsome firefighter husband.

"That's right, friend," Jordan said. "Don't forget the old ball and chain, the father of your children. How old are they now?"

"Oh, shush." Answering the call from Luke, she turned away from Jordan and Theo. "Babe, remember when we were talking about celebrity hall pass choices? I may need to mix things up a little ..."

Theo nudged Jordan and jerked a chin at Elle. "When did Sergeant Snippy start working here?"

"Never mind that. So, you and I haven't talked much."

"For the profile on Army Dude?"

"Correction. He was a Green Beret, the most kick ass military force on the planet."

"More than the SEALs? I thought those guys were the bomb."

Jordan shook her head. "The Green Berets go through the most physically grueling training program ever created, plus they have to be able to speak another language, scuba dive, jump out of planes, and know how to deal with the locals in hostile climates. It just so happens that this one on the Rebels can do all that *and* play hockey."

Theo rolled his eyes. "So he's a superhero. Why the hell do you want to talk to me?"

"Just curious about how he's fitting in. That kind of thing."

"Well, he's already beating my ass at video games after only his second try. First shooter ones because, military, natch." His gaze strayed past her shoulder to where Elle was busy chatting with a customer. "Quality selection of cheese in his fridge. Poker face to beat the band. Above average tipper. So-so cook but I guess he's keeping the good stuff for the homeless volunteer stint."

Jordan's ears perked up past her hairline. "The homeless what now?"

"He makes breakfasts once a week at a shelter in the city. He's trying to keep it on the down low so it's not over-whelmed with women looking to impress him or draw the wrong kind of attention to the cause ..." He trailed off, his attention refocusing on Jordan. "Shit, I wasn't supposed to tell you that. He let it slip one night because he had to get up early. You need to keep it to yourself."

She plated up her sweetest smile. "Me? I wouldn't tell a soul. Where did you say this shelter was again?"

"I didn't and I need to get this round in, so kindly leave me alone."

LEVI REPLACED the empty coffee urn with a fresh-brewed one and tidied up the sugar packets while he was at it. He liked this time, that early morning hum of quiet before the guests came in hungry. With his mind so full of everything these days—the games, the profile, but most of all, Jordan—this was the one place he didn't have to feel so on.

Since returning from New York four days ago, he hadn't heard from her or even spotted her around Rebels HQ. He was trying to give her space so she wouldn't feel hounded, when really not seeing or tasting her made him tenser than his bomb disposal days.

"Think those sugar packets are arranged just fine, Levi."

He blinked at his big paws mauling the condiments and turned to Lucy. "Sorry, mind elsewhere." The room was starting to fill up and he watched the entrance for Joe.

Reading his thoughts, Lucy said, "They take off sometimes, worried they're getting too comfortable or are being watched. He'll probably be back in a while."

"Would you text me if he shows? If I'm in town, I'd like to come and talk to him, give him some assurance."

"In town? Off on a secret mission, are you?"

"Something like that."

Lucy narrowed her eyes. "Sure, I'll let you know. But be careful about getting too close. Making promises you can't keep. I know your heart's in the right place—"

"Front and back of the hand right there."

She grinned. "Just some advice, that's all. Now, let's get serving."

Levi kept his eye on the door during breakfast. He'd even made his *huevos rancheros*, an invitation to the universe to cut him a break and deliver Joe from the streets. As the line was wrapping up, he saw someone he recognized, just not the person he'd hoped.

Jordan.

She wore yoga leggings—those ones that should be illegal—along with Chucks, a hoodie, and a baseball cap pulled down low, as if it were an effective disguise. But he'd know that rumpus of fire-hot hair anywhere.

"Back in a sec," he said to Lucy, sprinting out from behind the counter and barreling down on Jordan.

"Levi!"

He grasped her arm and steered her back the way she'd come. "What are you doing here?"

"I should really be asking you the same question. I can't believe you didn't share this."

"*This* doesn't go in the profile, Jordan. *This* is private."

She stared at him. "One, nothing is private. Two, you are actually doing a good thing here so why wouldn't you want to share that? Your connection to this charitable organization, if known, would probably increase donations tenfold. In fact, keeping it to yourself is pretty selfish."

"They're not wanting for donations."

Her face brightened with the thrill of discovery. "So as well as donating your time, you also cut them a check. That's wonderful."

"Yeah, wonderful," he said sarcastically.

"Levi, everything okay?" Lucy appeared at his side, looking like she wanted to protect him, which, coming from the one hundred pound woman, was hilarious.

Jordan pushed him aside and held out her hand. "Hi, I'm Jordan. I'm a ... friend of Levi's." The pause was unmissable.

"Here to volunteer?" Lucy asked, ignoring Jordan's hand. "We don't hold much truck with observers."

"Sure I am," Jordan said with a sunshine smile that ripped his heart to pieces. "Lead the way."

JORDAN WASN'T QUITE sure what she'd landed herself in, but elbow-deep in sudsy hot water wasn't what she'd expected when she popped into the Uptown Mission this morning looking for Levi. Not that she doubted he was volunteering, but she needed to see it with her own eyes like a good little reporter. Her story putting himself out there instead of writing a check like every other pro athlete?

Human. Interest. Gold.

The fierce woman acting as Levi's bodyguard despite being half his size had shoved her in the back and put her on dish duty. It still gave her the perfect view of the man himself working the distribution line.

And she meant working it. For every one of the Mission's patrons, he had a few words of encouragement and a couple of strips of bacon, a killer combo that should probably go into some life coaching manual.

"You really a friend of Levi's?"

Levi's guardian angel-slash-bodyguard had materialized and was now pulling plates from the industrial size dishwasher, which Jordan hadn't noticed before. Why the hell was she washing these dishes by hand?

I see what you did there, Mission Lady.

"I heard you guys needed all hands on deck," Jordan replied, all smiles.

"He didn't look too pleased to see you."

"Does he ever look pleased to see anyone?"

The woman's mouth quirked in understanding. "Poor

guy's looking for a quiet life. Thinks he's flying under the radar. Our guests don't watch a lot of TV."

"Perfect cover for Levi, then. So you know who he is?"

She folded her arms. "My brother is an Army reservist and a huge Rebels fan. Levi Hunt is all he talked about when he was acquired. But when the man himself showed up here just over a month ago, he didn't lead with his—"

"Big stick?"

She laughed. "Right! Figured he had his reasons for laying low."

And here Jordan was blowing it. "I'm a reporter doing a profile on him, following him around, embedded with the team. I got a tip he was here and thought it would be good for my story, but now ..."

"You're wondering if it's worth it."

"He's rather closed off." Except in bed. Between the sheets, he was more expressive. More open. Was that the only place she could get to the core of Levi Hunt?

"Maybe figure out what he cares about."

She thought it was hockey, and while she knew he loved it, it wasn't producing the result she wanted. "Why is he volunteering here?"

"People have all sorts of reasons."

Ain't that the truth. "Okay if I take these out and help out there?" Jordan nodded at the stack of plates waiting to be returned to the front.

"Sure. And I'm Lucy."

"Nice to meet you, Lucy. Thanks for letting me stick around." Jordan headed out and stowed the plates at the end of the counter.

Levi was smiling at one of the patrons while he piled his plate high with scrambled eggs and bacon.

"Need any help?"

Levi peered down at her, all traces of cheer evaporating. "Thought you were on dish duty."

"I was so good I already got a promotion."

"All right, then, super sleuth. How'd you find out I was here?"

She smiled. "Can't reveal my sources."

"Kershaw?"

Which led to a call to Tommy, Levi's agent, who was more forthcoming, given that he didn't understand Levi's motivation to keep it under wraps. *I already told him that shit is perfect publicity, Jordan!* She made a lips-zipped motion across her mouth.

He shook his head but his eyes lingered on her mouth. And lingered. And *that*, friends, was exactly why she'd been avoiding him for the last few days.

"You're killing me, Cooke."

"I don't mean to! I even wore my least sexy outfit so there'd be no risk of temptation."

"That's your least sexy outfit? Leggings that make your ass look like a dream?"

She preened a touch, might even have cocked her hip for maximum ass displaying effect. "It's just an ass. Nothing to see here."

"I've missed you in my bed," he murmured, all gravelly and sexy.

Oh, baby. "Well, technically it was the Hilton's bed." When he just kept up the Levi-intensity, she added guiltily, "And we—we can't."

"'Cause it was a mistake?"

"No, never that. It just wouldn't look good if someone found out." She bit down on her lip, not liking the conclusion but resigned to living with it.

He swore and moved along the line to help someone.

Coming to her senses, she looked up to find a bearded man with fierce blue eyes staring at her intently.

"Hey, there. Would you like some eggs?"

He smiled, then offered a quick nod.

"Joe, good to see you, man," Levi said, back in her space. "Getting worried about you."

"I was down in the Bahamas for a while. Just got off the jet."

Levi laughed, which made Jordan turn her head in surprise. Seeming to realize his mistake, he frowned at her. "Not a word."

"Wouldn't dream of it." She turned back to the man, who was still waiting on his eggs. "Hi, I'm Jordan." Should she be telling her name to the strange homeless man? She wasn't sure of the etiquette here, but Levi seemed to like him. He seemed to like Lucy, too.

Huh, Levi liking people. What was that about?

Gently, he nudged her aside and built a mountain of food on the plate. "Here you go. We can chat later if you like."

The man merely nodded, took his plate, and went on his way.

"One of your favorites?"

"Just one of the guests." Levi was still standing close, his exposed forearm touching hers. Thick as her calf, it had the perfect proportion of dark, springy hair. Thank God she'd pulled up her sleeve so she didn't miss any of the electricity.

It was the little things.

"You seemed friendly."

"Merely giving him the respect he deserves. He's a vet."

She side-eyed him, wanting to see in profile that serious, intent look on his face, the one he got when he was focused on a problem or a play or ... her. She'd missed it and even though he no longer would give it to her, *for her*, she'd enjoy it vicariously.

He caught her looking at him. There was no softening, which is what she'd wanted at one time, a hint that he was human. She was starting to understand that this was Levi's default expression. Intense, driven, on fire, and possibly more expressive of his humanity than a smile or laugh.

"You really care about these people, don't you?"

"There's no story here, Jordan. Just doing a good deed, like plenty of others."

There was something else. Something that held the key to Levi Hunt, and she was determined to oil the rusted-over lock.

"HI THERE!" Jordan plunked down opposite Joe, the homeless guy—though here they called them guests—who Levi had seemed to connect with earlier.

He looked over his shoulder dramatically, then back to her. "Hi yourself."

"How's it going today?"

"Better now that I've had breakfast."

"Oh, I brought over a donut." She pushed the napkin-wrapped pastry forward. "Figured no breakfast can finish right without a little sweet."

"That's a good rule." He took the package and placed it in his pocket. "You friends with Levi?"

Good, he brought it up so she didn't have to make the awkward segue. "I know him." Close up, she could see that he was younger than she'd assumed. More like mid-twenties.

"So, I saw you guys talking earlier. Seems like you're someone he pays attention to around here."

"Wouldn't say that. He's a worrier, is all."

"He got reason to be?"

He sniffed and sipped his coffee. "Gettin' colder, so he probably wants to make sure I've got my ducks lined up. He knows what—"

"Hey, you guys plotting something?"

Jordan looked up into Levi's blue eyes, now flashing like a fire engine siren in warning. "Just how to snag more donuts without Warden Lucy watching."

Joe chuckled. Levi did not.

"Could I have a word?" Levi squeezed her shoulder, giving her no option but to obey. He steered her over to the coffee section. "Whatcha doin'?"

"Just chatting."

"Jordan ..."

"Don't be so suspicious, Levi. I'm here to help and maybe see what makes you tick."

"Told you before. I'm an open book."

She snorted. "Are you kidding? The only time you were open is when you—" She stopped right there, thankyou-verymuch.

"When I what?" His eyes lit up in recognition, a smirk teasing his lips. "You think that's the way into my brain? You think having me explode inside your body will get me to be more responsive to your probing questions? I can guarantee that the path to my mind is not through my dick."

"Oh, I dunno, you were fairly chatty in the post-coital phase."

"Is that going in the profile?"

She shook her head, marveling at his ability to be sweet

and flirty while uttering such dirty, delicious words. "Trying to keep it separate. Professional."

"It's hard, though, right?" He stepped closer, bringing with him a sexy menace she hadn't realized was missing from her life. "Tell me this is as hard for you as it is for me."

She peered up at him, taking in his rough-hewn jaw, his sharp cheekbones, his blaze-intense eyes, so blue, so hurting with lust. Desire licked through her, not the sweet tingle of wouldn't-it-be-nice, but the savage burn of need.

Nodding, she surrendered to the moment and let herself bask in the consensus between them. It felt good to agree on something even if no joy could come of it.

"You've been thinking about it? About that night?"

"Of course. Believe me, I don't have much of a sex life. When I get some half-decent action, it keeps me going for weeks. Months." She put her hand over her mouth. "Look, that's not to say I've been thinking about you *specifically*—"

"No?" He stepped in further, imposing but not scaring. Her heart jumped all the same. "You think about mouths and fingers and touching and tasting, but there's no face or voice? I'm not even the one delivering the goods?" He looked incredulous as well he should.

"Just thinking about the act itself," she said, deflecting. "Not the actor."

Somewhere between his pointed offense and her sloppy defense, his mask slipped. He'd thought of something—damn, he was always thinking of something—but hell if he'd share it with her.

"What, Levi?" She placed a hand on his arm and he pulled away.

"Think it's time you headed out. You've had your fun. Show's over."

Show's over? "Are you seriously evicting me from the homeless shelter?"

"I'm saying it's time you were on your way and I'd appreciate it if you kept what you've seen here to yourself. This isn't going in that damn article. Just stick to fucking hockey."

What had happened here? One minute they'd been luxuriating in the lovely sensation of mutual, frustrating-as-all-get-out lust, the next he was steering her out the door. Literally.

Strong, formerly orgasm-producing fingers curled around her arm and *march, march, march.*

"Levi, what's going on?"

He'd already turned away.

16

LEVI SLID the puck to Petrov on his left and skated too far ahead to get the pass-back. Because it was that kind of day.

"Open your freakin' eyes, Hunt," Coach yelled. "That's the third pass you've missed."

"You okay, New Guy?" Vadim skated close enough so the query was unheard by the rest of the team.

"Just not firing on all cylinders, Cap. Sorry, I'll get there."

The big Russian patted him on the back. "I know. But maybe get there soon before Coach has a heart attack."

Focus, man. He needed to excise from his brain everything not related to hockey which was a big ask when all he wanted to do was think about Jordan.

Levi was under no illusions about what she wanted. He was the itch she needed to scratch, the story she needed to tame. Whether she knew it or not, she'd poked him with that comment, the one where she wasn't fantasizing about him, only about sex in general. As if it didn't matter who was delivering her orgasms.

It made him think that maybe, just maybe, she had

someone else in mind when they'd slept together and whenever she thought of it since.

Maybe she was thinking of Josh.

They'd talked so little about Cookie since reconnecting, a deliberate tactic on Levi's part. He didn't want to suffer through the obvious comparisons. He didn't want her thinking of her husband while she was with Levi. And he certainly didn't want to think too hard about having the hots —and maybe more—for his friend's widow.

He'd been doing a pretty good job of staying in denial so far. The truth was he wanted more from Jordan. Getting a taste should have satisfied him—it was way more than he deserved—but no. She was the thirst he couldn't quench.

For the next hour, he put his head down, his stick to the ice, and he bashed every puck like it was a demon he could destroy.

You're not worthy of this shot in the pros. Whack.

Jordan is only interested in you for the story. Thump.

It should have been you on that mission. Bash.

Amazing what a little self-loathing can do for your game. By the end of morning skate, he was back in Coach's good graces and wasn't getting weird looks from the rest of the team—at least no weirder than usual.

They were playing Nashville at home tonight, so he headed back to his place for a nap. Opening his front door, he found Elle on her laptop with the screen facing him. She snapped it closed, but ... was that a grid of shirtless guys?

"Need some alone time?"

Her mouth gaped. "What? No! Of course not!" She shot a guilty glance at her laptop. "What the hell are you doing here in the middle of the day? Thought you had practice."

"I'm here in the place *where I live*, for a bite to eat and a nap. Wasn't expecting a porn party in my living room. Just don't make a mess, okay?"

"Hunt, I am not looking at porn! Not that there's anything wrong with that but if I was I'd have the decency to do it in private."

Struck by another option, he folded his arms. "Was that a dating site?"

"It was nothing." She stood and headed toward the kitchen. "Want a sandwich? I went grocery shopping this morning."

"Sure. Let me know what I owe you." He followed her in. "Did you get that Gouda that Kershaw likes?"

"Yeah, yeah. That guy's eating you out of house and home, you know."

"He's just a kid. I think he misses his grandma." Levi leaned against the kitchen island, watching Elle take out the sandwich ingredients.

"You were always a soft touch, Hunt." She grinned to let him in on the joke. *Chez Hunt, home for Waifs and Strays.*

"So, I need advice. A woman's opinion."

Pulling her T-shirt neckline out, she checked inside. "Still a card-carrying female. Shoot."

"I was kind of a jerk. To Jordan."

"About the profile?"

"That, and well, I might have a thing for her."

He had to give it to her. She didn't look smug or immediately utter I-told-you-so, though she'd be within her rights to.

"Jerk to the girl you have a crush on. Sounds on brand."

He deserved that. "We got together in New York."

"And the problem is?"

He walked to the fridge and grabbed a bottle of water. "It was a one-time deal. It's tricky for her, ethics-wise. Can't be seen with the subject of a story." Also, she'd set aside her career aspirations for the love of her life seven years ago. No way would she let a man derail her again, and understandably so. A niggling voice acknowledged it was more than that, but he'd keep it simple for today's lesson. "I threw a mini-tantrum about it. Didn't explain it to her so well." Or at all.

She bent her head in sympathy. "You can see her side, right? Screwing around with her story might make her look bad. But hey, screwing around in secret is also kind of hot or so I hear. Maybe it's not a complete disaster?"

Maybe. But even if he could convince Jordan to take another spin on the Levi love-coaster while keeping it on the down low, could he trust his heart not to get the upper hand over his dick?

Heart vs. Dick. A cage match for the ages.

"I need to fix things."

"What a very male thing to say." Elle slathered Hellman's on the whole wheat bread like she was celebrating the end of a mayo drought, then dropped in a few spinach leaves to make it healthy. "I assume you're underplaying this and that you were a monster to Jordan, so first you should apologize for being a total and utter dick. Then you need to figure out your hard limit. Should you be shutting these little tête-à-têtes down because it sucks to be around this woman who doesn't want you the same way? Are you going to take your butt-hurt feelings out on her because she's established the boundaries and you don't like them? Or are you going to be a fucking grown-up and own your shit?"

"Wow, so glad we chatted."

She smiled. "See, that wasn't hard! Now, work the knife, Hunt. That cheese isn't going to slice itself."

THREE HOURS LATER, Jordan still wanted to throw something. Anything.

She paced her apartment, realizing that she should have just gone into the Chicago SportsNet offices, but needing familiar surroundings to center herself after what had happened this morning.

What *had* happened?

She replayed the conversation with Levi. Something about not thinking of him, thinking of sex but not with him, thinking of anyone as a stand-in. Was the man that humor-deficient that he couldn't see right through her ridiculous charade?

I'm fluent in body language, Jordan.

Apparently not, Sergeant.

Of course she'd done nothing *but* think of him since New York. Every waking second was spent with Levi Hunt's built-to-please-her body pleasing her in her fantasy. The vibrator wasn't holding up its end of the bargain either—she needed a real, live man.

She needed Levi.

It couldn't happen, so she'd brushed her desires aside. Did he not see the difference? Weren't men supposed to be easy to figure out? Why did this one insist on breaking her lady brain?

She had just set the coffee pot to do its thing when a knock on her door pulled her out of her thought ditch. Pulse quickening, she groaned at the sight on her threshold.

"Sorry, we're all stocked up on dickheads, thanks."

Levi's stupid, hockey-playing foot stopped her door from slamming in his stupid, hockey-playing face.

"I'm busy, Levi. And how the hell did you get into my building?" Or even know where she lived?

"Someone didn't shut the door behind them. Major security hazard."

"Well, yeah, there's an asshole on my doorstep."

A-plus level glowering ensued. "Jordan, I'm sorry. I was a jerk."

She folded her arms. Not good enough.

"A big ... dumb ..." He squinted, feeling her out. "Piece-of-shit ..."

"Getting warmer."

"Should-fuck-off-and-die jerk?"

"Ding ding ding, we have a winner! Is this the part where I try to figure out who hurt you? I use my woman's intuition to get to the heart of your man problem, whatever the hell it is, because your ego must be stroked and feelings validated now that you vomited your so-so apology out?"

He did that hot, broody thing with his mouth and muttered, "I don't need to talk about my stuff."

"So, you just want to mic-drop your lame-ass sorry, add nothing to the conversation, and expect me to be okay with it?"

"Getting mixed signals here."

She sighed, knowing he was right—about this *one* thing. The man was damned if he shared, damned if he didn't. Talking it out, however, was more her style.

"Tell me what made you go cold like that."

He blew out a breath. "I wasn't a fan of how we left things in New York, and I let that get under my skin. I know this is what you need, this separation. I get that. You're not obliged to give me the time of fucking day, never mind be still using me to ..."

"Get myself off?"

His nostrils flared and his jaw tightened. "You don't have to think of me when you ... do whatever. If you just want to use the what of it and not think about the who of it, that's fine. I'm not here to tell you how to fantasize. I know you want to draw a line under it, but hell, Jordan, not sure I can be as professional as you. 'Cause when I think about that night, I've got a host of very specific memories to keep my right hand busy."

Her breath hitched. *Tell me. Tell me everything.*

Encouraged by her silent plea, he went on. "You've got this freckle high on your inner thigh, this sweet little beauty that tasted so good. Your skin's the softest I've ever touched, but especially that gorgeous ass of yours. It was like touching an overripe peach. And the memory of being wrapped in you—your pussy hugging my cock, your body consuming mine—has kept me up, twisting and turning in the bed that never knew it needed you to feel right. That sigh you made when I licked you through—Jordan, I don't think any sound could top it. Not the slide of a skate, not the blare of the goal buzzer, not the cheer of the crowd. It's the sound I want to hear all night, every night."

Okay. That was probably the hottest thing she'd ever heard.

Something struck her strange. "Aren't you left-handed?"

"Only on the ice. One of my early coaches recommended switching, kind of like the Rafa Nadal effect."

And now all she could think of was his right hand doing things. To himself. To her. And then his left hand joining in because *skills.* Maybe hunky Spanish tennis player Rafa Nadal might be involved because dammit she deserved it ...

"Sounds like I was right. You are quite chatty when it comes to sex."

His mouth twitched. "When it comes to sex with *you*. There's a difference."

She was beginning to see there was, just as she was beginning to see that this was a problem. Something about their charged conversations tapped into hidden recesses of their brains where they started to reveal things they hadn't told other people. This was wonderful when you were a reporter looking for the inside track but not so great when you were a woman looking to guard her heart.

"I'm sorry for wanting another taste," he said. "I'm not really built for casual." He shook his head, like that was the hardest thing in the world for him to admit.

Levi opening his heart opened something inside of her.

"Anyway, I got you a little something." He gestured to a shopping bag at his feet, which she'd not noticed before. "Dante said you like macarons. There's a Vietnamese bakery on Broadway that does great ones."

He turned to leave which prompted her panicked chirp. "Levi. I—I lied."

He whipped around. "About what?"

This story. How I feel. Everything.

"I *have* been thinking of you."

He shook his head. "You do not need to massage my ego here. It's okay for you to have put what happened behind you. I'm a big boy and am perfectly capable of working through my stuff by myself."

"No."

His brows slammed together. "No?"

She stepped toward him, each step feeling like a mile. "Work through it ... with me."

"Jordan, I get that you're about the nicest and most cheerful fucking person in the world but that's no reason to think you owe me a—"

"Hot, slow fuck."

His hand went to her jaw, clamped tight and pulled her in toward his mouth. But no kiss. "Woman, you are killing me."

"Let's die together."

She anchored her hands to his hips and on tip-toes met the mouth that didn't seem to be kissing her fast enough, slow enough, just enough. His groan vibrated through her body, setting off sparks and little fires that would turn into full-scale conflagrations any moment. Their tongues tangled while their mouths slanted first one way, then another, looking to explore and find the perfect mating.

"I'm not fantasizing about anyone else when I'm with you," she said when he let her up for air. "And when I'm not with you, you're the face I see when I touch myself."

"Tell me you want this."

"I want this. I want you, Levi."

He closed his eyes briefly, then opened them to reveal midnight dark depths. "One hot, slow fuck coming up."

Oh God … well, that is what she'd said! And Levi, she was finding, was quite a literal person. He recalled everything, dismissed nothing, considered all the things she'd said and figured out a way to use it against her. The man was relentless.

He turned her toward the hallway wall, pushing her flush while grinding against her ass. The white-hot heat of him branded her.

"You feel so good," she whispered. "So, so good."

He rolled her pants down to her thighs, baring her ass. Falling to his knees, he yanked the pants down to her ankles, and she obliged by stepping out of them.

They were still in the hallway outside her apartment. "Levi, maybe we should—"

He slipped a finger between her legs and dragged it through her soft, wet, sensitive flesh. *Yeah, maybe we should.* With a gentle tug, he placed her foot on his shoulder, which gave him all the access he needed. "Hold on, baby."

Surely, he wasn't going to ... "Levi, what—oh, God!"

His mouth connected with her pussy, his tongue spearing, licking, owning, earning a climb-on-the-coaster, drop-off-the-cliff orgasm that made every extremity ignite with pleasure.

Then he pulled her to the floor and started all over again.

17

JORDAN COULDN'T BELIEVE that she'd had two top-of-the-line orgasms in the middle of the afternoon. Hockey players get things done!

Realizing that (more) sex in her building's corridor might be considered a tad too extra for her neighbors, they had finally retreated to her sofa for a post-coital canoodle and macaron feast. Well, Levi limited himself to one bite because the zero-body fat physique didn't happen by itself. She'd dragged her clothes back on; he wore jeans and nothing else. Neither of them had spoken much in the last fifteen minutes.

"How'd you find out where I live?"

"Dante told me after he mentioned you're a fiend for these macaron things." His breath ruffled the hair at her temple. "Sorry about before. I know you're in a tough position with your job and I was kind of cranky about being left on the wrong side of that equation."

She circled his nipple with her finger and traced over his tattoo. "There is that. But I'm more concerned with the idea you'd assume I'm thinking about someone else while I was indulging in a little me time."

"Okay. You specifically said that."

"Hello! Deflecting over here. I didn't want to give you a big head or make myself vulnerable. Did you really think I ..." She paused, awareness creeping up on her. "Is this about Josh?"

His brow crimped. "He is what connects us. Whenever you run into me, that has to be foremost in your mind. We know each other because of him."

"Before. That's how we were connected before. Don't you think enough things bind us together now to not have Josh be the current glue? Our jobs. Where we live. Pizza."

"Pizza?"

"I have delivered pizza to you with mine own pizza-providing hands. That has to count for something."

"The foundation of every relationship." His voice sounded rusty. "You want more of this?"

This. As appropriate a label as any. "A woman has needs. Only no one can know."

"Just the standard terms and conditions—use, abuse, don't text me in the morning?"

"Is it such a terrible offer?"

He stared at her, as if willing her to fall for him when she was already halfway there. Finally, he dropped a soft kiss between her eyebrows. "Love that little divot."

And it seemed that was all he had to say on the subject of their new no-strings agreement.

She snuggled into him, preferring to get the topic off them and back onto him anyway. "Care to tell me why you don't want anyone to know about your volunteer stint?"

"I just prefer to keep that under the radar. Less complicated."

From the man who became more complex with each encounter. "It's time you started giving me some good stuff. This pillow talk has to eventually graduate into beefy gossip." She winced at how that sounded, like she was using him for what he could do for her career.

Before she could rephrase, he murmured, "One question."

She could get her phone to record but she didn't want to break the connection. "Why did you go into the army? You had this shot at a life most people would dream of, this talent you could use to become adored and wealthy. Most people wouldn't think twice about that."

He paused so long that for a moment she thought he hadn't heard her. Finally he exhaled a deep breath.

"When I got to college and saw how athletes were treated, I couldn't believe how lucky I was. I could do anything I wanted, have any woman I wanted, could get by on C's in classes as long as I produced on the ice. And I knew it was only going to intensify in the pros. More adulation, more money. I saw first-hand how that affected people. The players, the coaches, the fans, the groupies. I wasn't ready to change who I was. I wasn't even sure I knew *who* I was yet. My upbringing had been fairly unorthodox."

"In what way?"

"My dad drank hard, played hard, fought hard. He wasn't around much, so I learned to stand on my own two skates from a fairly young age. Because it didn't seem like a regular way to grow up, I wasn't sure I was ... complete?" He shook his head, searching for the right way to frame it, perhaps. "Wasn't sure I deserved to be successful."

Impostor syndrome again, which astonished her coming from a man with such amazing gifts. "Even with all that talent?"

"I loved hockey. Loved working with a team. Loved people telling me I was amazing, and then I realized that maybe I could get to love it a little too much. One day, I was no one. The next, a hockey superstar. It could skew my life a particular way, mold me into the wrong person. Twenty-year-olds are still kids, really."

Sheer wonder caught in her throat. "But the fact you even thought about those things means you were mature enough not to let your mind be swayed. Yet you still gave it all up to enlist?" She drew back to look at him. "You're unbelievable."

"Because I didn't want to get rich quick and become an asshole?"

"According to you, you've always been one. Sounds like money and fame wouldn't have changed a damn thing!"

He squeezed her tight and added a butt pinch for good measure. "That mouth of yours."

"Just repeating what someone told me. This guy said you were an asshole through and through and I'm inclined to believe him. Very reliable source."

His laugh, such a rare sound, sent her heart into a funny flip.

"You think I'm a reliable source now?"

"I think that when you open your mouth I can usually trust most of what comes out of it." She applied a light kiss to that trustworthy mouth, letting him know she was teasing.

"Look, I don't regret my time in the service. It made me a man. It shaped me in ways I wouldn't have learned on the ice. I had a great team, met some amazing people. In fact, if I hadn't done that, I wouldn't have met Cookie. Or you."

It always came back to Josh, their link.

"We might have met—me as a reporter, you as a player —under these or different circumstances."

"Maybe." He sounded doubtful. Clearly it still bothered him that he was lusting after his best friend's widow.

She'd made peace with it a long time ago because such was life: a never-ending series of bargains with your hormones, heart, and conscience.

JORDAN HAD to give it to the Rebels organization: they knew how to rock it when it came to executive suite washrooms. Aveda soap and lotions, one-use hand towels, quality mints! Not bad, not bad at all.

Levi's revelations about his upbringing had thrown her and had her rethinking the thrust, so to speak, of the profile. Living his life according to a certain code was no different than possessing values that guide you, like religion or recycling. Growing up as he did, no one would have questioned him taking the easy(-er) route of fame and glory instead of service and mortar attacks.

Yet, Levi thought he would have been twisted the wrong way if he turned pro at such a young age. The bright lights and unlimited offers to polish his stick would have set him on the wrong path.

Every conversation revealed another version she could profile, each more fascinating than the last. Yet it'd result in another draft she'd have to trash because God forbid anyone see the great guy underneath.

In the stall, she adjusted her skirt just as her phone buzzed. She slipped it out of her Kate Spade (*so pretty!*) and her heart jumped in recognition: Levi.

Bad news, Ms. Sunshine.

Oh, no! She waited for him to fill her in on the gossip ahead of tonight's home game against New York, her pulse rate climbing with every second passed. Was he injured? Scratched?

Dot dot dot. Nothing. Then more dots, and ... Still nothing. She was going to kill him.

What?!!!

Finally, he responded: *Just heard they've run out of mini-macarons. They can't keep up with the press box demand. Customer of one.*

She giggled. *Skirt's getting too tight, anyway.*

IDK. That ass feels perfect in my hands. I'll bring over a box for you later.

Her heart squeezed. She was going to journalism hell, but at least she'd be well-fed and fucked.

Don't you have a warm-up to get to?

On my way.

She sent a couple of hockey stick emojis, thought about adding hearts, and opted for flames instead. Just about to slide her phone back into her purse, she stilled at the sound of voices in the restroom.

"You mean you're lining up a three-way trade? Does Dante know?"

Trade talk? Stealthily, Jordan stepped back and God forgive her, lifted her Keds-shod foot quietly to the toilet seat. Then the other. Because that voice belonged to Isobel Chase—Olympic medalist, hockey phenom, middle sister, and co-owner of the Rebels.

"He knows it's an option," the other voice said. *Harper fucking Chase.* "He fell in love with a player, Iz—a player on the team he manages. He can't seriously think that if an opportunity came up for me to trade Cade for someone more effective that we wouldn't take it."

"But that means you'll lose Dante! He's not going to stick around if Cade's in LA or New York."

Were they seriously talking about trading Cade Burnett, Dante Moretti's partner?

"You don't think I've thought about that?" Harper said impatiently.

"Would you get rid of Vadim as quick?"

When Harper didn't answer fast enough, Isobel was all over it. "Oh my God, you would! Your own brother-in-law. You know I'd go with him."

"Of course you would. Look, these guys are family, but they're also very valuable assets."

"That you're happy to move around the chess board."

"Because it's my job, but let's be realistic: Vadim's knee isn't going to last more than a year or two. I know he loves hockey, but dammit, he's rich enough to retire and start seeding you."

"Eww! Seeding me? That's gross! And I'm happy being the favorite aunt, thanks. But I see your point about his knee. The rehab's getting longer every time."

"It is. And as much as I love him, as much as I love them all, we're running a business here. I have to start thinking of the next generation. Who's going to lead."

"Still think Hunt's your man?"

Harper hummed. "I do. His stats have improved in the last few games. A goal, three assists, killing it in all his face-offs, and he just seems happier out there, don't you think?"

"You're not wrong."

"But I need to see him taking a firmer hand with the younger players. I'd hoped his military background would bring the leadership skills we're lacking."

They were grooming Levi to be captain? He had defi-nitely come on by leaps and bounds. With each shift, he was a half-second quicker, all sleek muscle and taut sinew as he glided around the rink. Realizing that she had her phone in her hand, Jordan pressed the record button while maintaining the perfect hunker-squat above the toilet seat.

No one in journalism school had told her she'd need this kind of flexibility.

"Someone has to make the tough decisions," Harper was saying. "That first year out with you, me, and Violet was lightning in a bottle. We need to recreate that magic and it might take a mix up of these proportions to make it happen."

There was a pause before Isobel spoke again. "You okay? You seem on edge."

"No more than usual before a game."

"I know what's going on here," Isobel said. "You saw Stroger out there and it's thrown you. You think you have to be the hard ass business woman who'd sell her own grandmother to prove you won't wither in the face of that dickwad?"

Stroger? Jordan racked her brain, assembling the pertinent facts. He had a brief run with the Rebels about ten years back. Then there was that throw down between Billy and Harper's now husband, Remy DuPre, a few years ago during Remy's first season with the Rebels. Stroger got his nose broken and Remy got a two-game suspension. Add to that Harper's OTT reaction at the sight of that dick pic on Jordan's phone ...

More evidence that Harper and Billy had been in a relationship once?

"I heard he's engaged or close to it," Harper said. "I saw her out there heading into the visitors' box. I just ..." She broke off.

"What?" Isobel's voice was soft, concerned. "Hope she's okay?"

Harper sighed. "I know it only happened once and maybe he never hit another woman after me but I sometimes wonder if we should have done more than threaten his career."

Jordan tensed. No, surely not.

Isobel was still talking. "You're not responsible for Billy Stroger's behavior or for any of the women he saw after you."

"But I don't know what he's done or who he's hurt. If I'd come clean, even after Remy pounded on him, then I'd know I did the right thing."

"What's the right thing? You did what was right for you at the time. Dad didn't even defend you, just traded that piece of shit out. Remy and Bren took care of it, and Stroger knows you're not alone. You have people who will stand up for you. You have people who care, Harper. But be prepared to enter a world of fucking hurt if you trade Cade Burnett because I'll cut you if you do."

"I'll think about it."

Laughing as one, they left the restroom and Jordan reeling with all this new information. As if the trade rumor and Levi on tap for the captaincy wasn't enough, that Stroger bombshell had rocked her. Her heart ached for Harper and the trauma she'd endured at the hands of that asshole. To look at the powerful CEO, no one would have ever guessed that she was a survivor of domestic abuse. But then everyone had secrets.

How had the Rebels managed to keep this one? And how could Jordan thread this into her smash-the-NHL-patriarchy story without betraying Harper's trust?

18
———

LEVI STACKED the plates on the crockery shelving unit and wiped his brow. He smiled at Lucy. "A lot of happy campers out there."

"I'll say. Thanksgiving is always a tough day, so anything we can do to make that easier." She pushed a plate of pumpkin pie toward him. "This is pretty good."

It should be. Levi had done a pie run around every grocery store on the North side after the donation the Mission had expected fell through. Those pies were gathered with grit and love.

He took a bite, figuring one morsel was enough. Another pie sat in his fridge at home awaiting Jordan's return. She was flying home from DC tomorrow and he missed her like fucking crazy.

"Where you headed this evening?" Lucy asked, mischief in her eyes.

"I have offers."

"Plural? Nice!"

"Quiet, you." Elle had headed to Florida to visit her family. Most of the team were off home, and anyone

Chicago-based was at a big party at Chase Manor. He'd received an invite but was weighing his options.

"Got a big game this weekend, Mr. Hockey?"

He blew out a breath, not completely surprised that his cover was blown since Jordan had shown up a couple of weeks ago. "How long have you known?"

"Long enough. Don't worry, I haven't spilled the beans about our celebrity short cook."

He gave a grateful smile. "Just prefer to keep it private. I've been getting a lot of attention lately and too much information gives people another way to label you. Neither do I want this to come off as performative."

Lucy nodded in understanding. "Better to keep the worlds separate?"

"Yeah. This is personal for me, and I'm already too exposed in my day-to-day." Lately, his nights, too, which required him to endure Jordan's probing. The price of keeping her close and in his bed.

"I'm not going to blab."

"Thanks, boss. Now, I expect your family's waiting," he said. "You should get out of here."

"Plenty of turkey at mine if you're at a loose end."

"I'll be okay." Levi had somewhere to be.

THE TENTS HAD BEEN MOVED to the west side of the Wilson Avenue viaduct after the city said they wanted to build bike paths. Flaunting his nice SUV was probably not the best way to make friends, so Levi parked a couple of blocks away on Broadway and walked down. The wind sliced through his jacket, an icy stab he felt in his marrow, and guilt gnawed at him that this was the first time he'd come down here. In truth, he'd been avoiding it. Worried that it would spark memories he'd prefer stayed buried.

He pulled his baseball cap down when he passed by the first tent. Most of them were zipped up, but a small gathering up ahead gave him hope that he'd find the man he was looking for: Joe.

He hadn't stopped into the Mission for dinner. Hadn't been there in a couple of weeks according to Lucy, and that had Levi worried. After kicking an empty water bottle to announce his presence, Levi strode with purpose toward the group. No need for anyone to feel ambushed. A couple of people turned, one of them Joe.

But Levi's gaze slid right by him to the woman standing beside him, her fiery red curls tumbling from her baseball cap. A Rebels one, which added insult to injury.

Irritation dueled with protectiveness in his chest. "What the hell are you doing here? I thought you were in DC."

"Levi!" Jordan grinned at him. "Happy Thanksgiving!"

"Hey, Levi," Joe said. A scrappy piebald Jack Russell terrier on a leash jumped up on Levi's legs.

"Hey, Joe. Hey, fella." He caught Joe's eye. "You own this little guy?"

"He owns me." He pulled on the leash. "Cookie, don't be gettin' Levi's jeans muddy."

Levi shot a look at Jordan, just in time to catch the shock on her face. *Cookie.* What were the odds?

"That's okay." Levi hunkered down to rub behind his ears, which right now was about the only thing stopping him from going ballistic on Jordan. He flicked a glance up to find her watching him, her shock dissipated, now assessing his reaction. "So, Joe, haven't seen you over at the Mission for a while. Getting kind of worried."

"Yeah, Cookie wasn't feeling so good. There's a place on

the southside that looks after the homeless guys' pets so I headed over that way for a few days."

"You can keep the pets there overnight?"

"Yep." Joe covered his mouth, the sound of a wicked cough breaking up his speech. "A vet over there gives them shots. Got him some pills and now he's right as rain."

The people who had been standing with Jordan and Joe moved off.

Levi pulled himself upright. "Explain."

"You talking to me?" Jordan fanned a hand over her collarbone.

"You said you were in DC with your family."

"I was. But I thought I'd head back early and come down to see Joe."

Did she have no idea how dangerous it was down here? If anything had happened to her ... One fire at a time. He'd deal with her later. "Joe, it's going to be below freezing tonight. I can drop you off at the Mission."

"No can do. They won't take Cookie."

Pieces slotted into place. "That's why you won't stay there?"

Joe looked incredulous. "And leave Cookie on the streets? No way, man."

"Most of the shelters won't take animals," Jordan cut in. "Liability reasons. Other guests being allergic. Health and safety. The ones that do fill up fast."

Levi had only one choice here. "You can stay with me."

Joe stared at him, as did Jordan. Levi didn't blame them.

Joe shook his head like this was the worst idea and started coughing again. "That's cool of you to offer, man, but no."

"I can't have you on the streets, Joe. Not in these temps and with that cough. At least ..." Shit, what was the answer here? People got sick on the streets. People fucking died on them, a harsh reality Levi was all too aware of. His dad's pneumonia had started with a cough like that.

Finally, he looked at Jordan, because as loath as he was to admit it, she seemed to have a better handle on the situation.

She searched his expression, wrinkled her brow, then turned to Joe and grasped his hand. "How about you stay at the Mission tonight and Levi looks after Cookie? I know you don't want to take a handout, but what about your buddy here? This way, you're both out of harm's way while we work on a more permanent solution."

No way would Joe go for that. The whole point was that he didn't want to be separated from his best friend.

"Okay," Joe said because he was as ornery as fuck.

Ten minutes later, Levi had dropped Joe off at the shelter where he was soon sitting down to a hot turkey meal. Levi had also asked if they could get his cough checked out at the 24-hour clinic a couple of blocks away, and luckily they had a volunteer on hand for that.

With fury still blazing though his veins, he hopped into the driver seat of his SUV where he'd left Jordan with Cookie, who incidentally stunk to high heaven. Jordan had taken an Uber down to the viaduct and was car-free. So, another reason to be mad at her.

"You and I need to talk."

"Sure, can you drop me at home while you ream me out?"

"What the hell were you thinking, Jordan? Tent City at night?"

"It was perfectly safe." She rubbed behind the dog's ears. The stinky beast loved it. "This little guy had my back."

Perfectly safe. So blasé about it, too. "And what were you doing there? Pumping Joe for information about me?"

"Oh, don't be such a drama queen. I visited the shelter on a morning you weren't there and found out where he was living. I just wanted a little background information to see if it was worth following up on for the profile."

"I told you that's off limits. How about you stay inside the lines?"

"I missed you," she said, not looking at him, her attention still on the dog.

Oh, Christ. Just three little words, and he was putty. "Don't try to get on my good side."

"Well, if that won't work, how about pie?" Cookie yelped. "Really good pie." Another yelp.

She made it sound like something else, something illicit and sexy and gooey. And Lord help him, he wanted in—her pie, her body, her life.

But he had responsibilities and he was still mad at her. "I have to take this guy home and give him a bath."

"Got any dog food?"

"Not on me, no."

She smiled and he was lost. "My place is closer and my neighbor has a dog so we can borrow some food. And eat some pie."

Cookie barked at the third mention of pie. This dog was onto something.

"Fine. A bath and P-I-E. That's it."

~

JORDAN HAD JUMPED out of her Frye boots at the sight of Levi striding purposefully down the street under the viaduct, looking like he was on a mission. She had to admit feeling a little unnerved down there—sure Joe and his puppy were fine but it was still sixty-five shades of sketchy in that area. Seeing Levi had made her heart skitter with joy and her skin prickle with relief.

For the self-proclaimed "most boring guy in hockey" he sure excited the hell out of her.

However, right now, he was making her wet—from the dog bath, guttersnipes! Cookie was unimpressed with the rules of the house. He had already escaped the bath twice.

"Dog, you will not get pie or any food until you stop being so damn stinky." Levi lifted Cookie into the bath for the third time and set him down. "Got any soap?"

"Bath gel?" Jordan grabbed the bottle from the caddy and dribbled some over Cookie's fur.

Levi got busy scrubbing, his big hands gently yet firmly mapping the pup's little body. Cookie's eyes started to glaze over—Jordan knew that look—and he relaxed as any creature would do when under the care and ministrations of one Levi Hunt.

"Aw, he likes that. Good puppy."

"He definitely smells better."

"Sure does." Jordan stroked his head. "His name, though."

"I know," Levi said. "Kind of looks like him, too. All excited and happy to get attention."

Never a truer word. Josh always had a bounce to him, so animated and friendly.

Levi slid a glance at her. "How was your half-holiday? Parents good? Still setting you up with hotshot lawyers?"

"It was fine. Mom's gone quiet about my dating which generally means she's planning something." All through lunch, Levi had been uppermost on Jordan's mind along with a heavy dose of guilt that she was sleeping with him and hadn't invited him to DC when she knew he'd be alone for the holiday. But that would have put what was happening firmly in dangerous meet-the-family territory.

They'd met him at two of the most important events of her life: the wedding that began one stage of her life and the funeral that ended it. He'd made an impression, that was for sure. Would they think it off she was "with" Josh's friend? She suspected her dad would like him if given the chance because Levi was such a straight shooter.

Slow your roll, Jo-Jo. She refocused on the task at hand. "Did you have a dog when you were younger?"

"Yeah, but I couldn't keep him."

"Oh, how come?"

"We moved around a lot and it was tough to bring him with us."

So far, she'd heard about Levi's upbringing in patches. Unorthodox, he'd called it. There was the mom who jumped ship, the boxer father who died of pneumonia, the childhood he'd grown out of too quickly. He found hockey and it saved him, as sports saves a lot of kids.

There was something almost scripted about it. Not that she doubted it, but Levi had a way of doling out information stingily, all the better to keep those walls in place.

"We'll need an old towel," he said. "Something you don't care about."

"I'll have you know I care about *all* my towels." She grabbed a fluffy bath towel hanging on the rail. "This little guy could do with some luxury."

She put it down on the mat while Levi maneuvered Cookie out of the bath and onto the floor, then scrubbed him dry.

"Look at him! This face is getting pie tonight." Cookie yelped in joy.

Levi frowned, and wouldn't you know it Jordan loved that, too? "I know we promised P-I-E but it's probably not good for him."

"I'll check with my neighbor. See if he has a couple of tins of the gourmet crap to spare."

Two minutes later, Jordan was back with something meaty and fancy for Cookie, gifted by Seth, her next-door neighbor and owner of an Irish setter as big as this building. Seth had said "no sugar, you monster!" and gave her a bag of doggie treats, which Jordan would call pie from this moment forward.

She grabbed a bowl and no sooner had it hit the floor of her kitchen than Cookie was in nose-deep, chowing down. She turned to find a shirtless Levi leaning against the counter, wiping himself dry, so casually delicious.

"So, why do you think Joe wouldn't take you up on your offer to stay at your place?" She couldn't believe Levi had done that, but then he continually surprised her.

"Because he's proud and accepting that kind of help is a bridge too far."

"Even though he'd be safer with you than at a shelter?"

"He's got his coping mechanisms. I'm not going to mess with that. I'll bring Cookie back to him tomorrow, though he might not even recognize him he's so clean."

"You care about him. About Joe."

Levi shrugged one broad shoulder. "He's a vet, had a rough time of it. I've been there."

"As a vet?"

"That and ... you've never gone hungry, have you?"

"Are you calling me fat?"

He smiled. "I'm saying that you grew up in an upper-middle-class family where there was never any question about where your next meal was coming from. The fridge was full, the hearth was warm, the sheets were clean."

Jesus, Jordan, those are some reporter instincts you've got. "Are you saying you've experienced some of what the homeless have experienced?"

His eyes met hers, deep, blue, troubled. He didn't want to share, but part of him—she could tell—needed to put it out there.

She maintained eye contact, letting him know that she might be tasked with unmasking his deepest secrets but this one was safe with her.

He gusted out a breath. "My dad wasn't the most stable guy. Mom had already left, done with his drinking. Done with ... life, I suppose. And my father was making a living, if you could call it that, getting his head pounded in illegal boxing matches. He earned some extra cash mopping the gym and I'd help him out after school. But it was never enough. Wasn't long before we were out of a place to live but Dad would sneak us into the gym at night and I slept in the locker room for a few months."

"Oh, Levi, that's awful."

"Yeah, not great, but good practice for sleeping anywhere once I deployed. These beds in civilization?"

"For wimps, right?"

"Totally." He kept his gaze trained on Cookie. "Sometimes Dad couldn't get me into the gym and we'd find somewhere—an alley, bank lobby if we could sneak in late. Easier to do that back then. And when he got sick, it started like what I heard from Joe tonight. The cough of a three-pack-a-day seal, only my dad didn't get help. He was a proud guy. That sound? It's the sound of failure, of despair. The sound of death."

Her heart melted. "That's why you help at the shelter.

You don't want anyone to ever suffer like that." The way his dad had. The way fifteen-year-old Levi had.

"We live in this world where one person is paid millions because he does one thing well, yet we can't feed kids or look after our vets or put roofs over everyone's heads. People will pay two hundred bucks to watch a hockey game, will read about the diet of a guy who bashes a puck around for a few minutes a night, but they're fine with their fellow citizens dropping dead around them. Priorities are so fucked up."

He was talking about *his* talent, *his* priorities.

"You can't save everyone, Levi. You've been blessed with a skill that people are willing to pay for, and you have the ability to pay it forward. Yeah, it's messed up, but at least you're using it to honor your father and help others."

He blew out an annoyed breath. "Yeah, maybe. And I'd rather do it without a whole lot of attention. Which means a nosy, smart-ass reporter I know should not be trying to turn this into feel-good, human interest shit and relating it back to my hardscrabble upbringing. Don't need to share that, okay? And I especially don't need to use a guy who's down on his luck as a way to make *me* look like a hero. I'm not. I'm fucking blessed."

She threw her hands in the air. Just when she thought she had a vein she could mine, he detonated the TNT at the cave's entrance. "You're officially the worst story subject ever."

That earned her a smile. "I *did* tell you."

"You told me you were dull and uninteresting, but nothing could be further from the truth." Moving in, she curled a finger in the belt loop of his jeans and rubbed his chest. So many people these days wanted play at virtue-signaling, to brag about their good deeds, yet here was a man who walked the talk and zipped his lips. "I think you really are a superhero disguised as a mild-mannered hockey player."

He grunted. She smiled. They kissed.

Oh, how they kissed. Slow, deep, filled with an earnest longing.

"Did you mean it?" he murmured. "About missing me? Or was that just to get me to stop yelling at you?"

She rubbed her finger and thumb together. "A little bit of deflecting, but I meant it. I came back early, hoping to see you. Hoping to ..." She trailed a hand down his unyielding chest, tangled a finger in the goodie trail, and stopped at the waistband of his jeans.

"Get a little pie?"

She chuckled. God, he could be so adorable sometimes. All that gruff, I-ain't-no-hero swagger muffled a softy at his core, one who was knocking at the door to the heart she'd walled up all those years ago.

19

Levi awoke with a start.

The TV was on, and he was fairly certain he'd not left it that way. Something warm and soft was snuggled into his side, and while he wished it was Jordan, he knew better. Cookie. Joe had been diagnosed with bronchitis and was told he needed to stay in a warming center during the cold snap. The center didn't allow pets, so Levi was on the hook for the dog's care.

He turned his head. Theo was sprawled on the other end of Levi's leather sofa, a sandwich in his left hand, the remote in his right. Another orphan that Levi had taken under his wing, it seemed.

"Trying to nap," Levi muttered.

"Imagine I'm not here, dude. Just grabbing lunch and catching up on my stories."

Levi rubbed the sleep from his eyes. He'd been up since five to work out at the rink and was only now getting some Zs before tonight's home game against Detroit. "What stories?"

"*Days of Our Lives.*"

Levi took another look. Dr. Marlena Evans was floating about in a white suit with Tony. Or maybe it was Andre, who was Tony's cousin, but for some reason looked exactly like him. Stefano's doing, of course. Levi and his unit used to watch this show back on the base at Campbell.

"Why is Hope speaking with a terrible British accent?"

"She's channeling Princess Gina. Marlena's about to cross to the other side after getting poisoned by penicillin and Tony's trying to convince her to go back. Don't go into the light kind of thing. He's showing her bits of her past to remind her that life's worth living."

"Love the flashback episodes."

Theo grinned. "Me, too! They showed Marlena's devil possession a couple of minutes ago."

"You should have woken me."

"Didn't know you were a *Days* fan! Oh, man, I hope they flash back to the Cruise of Deception." Theo munched on his sandwich, which looked a lot like Levi's bread and Levi's turkey and Levi's cheese, and they watched while Marlena weighed the pros and cons of leaving purgatory, which looked like a doctor's office waiting room. When the show went to commercial, Theo took a break from chewing to ask, "Where's your roommate?"

"Working."

"You ever figure out what happened to her?"

"What makes you think something happened to her?"

Theo shrugged. "She seems guarded, like she's hiding something."

Levi's thoughts exactly. Those were unexpected observation skills from Theo, but the glow of mutual consensus was ruined with his next query.

"She have a boyfriend?"

"Not that I know of. And she's not looking for one, either."

Munch, munch. "Did she say that?"

"I said that."

"Who's your buddy?"

Levi stroked the dog's warm body. "This is Cookie. Looking after him for a friend."

Theo stopped mid-chew. "Cookie? Like Ms. Cooke?"

"Merely a coincidence." Levi wasn't superstitious. He didn't see faces in toast or signs in clouds. But meeting a dog named Cookie had thrown him.

"And how *is* Hockey Grrl?"

Levi's nerves pinged. "Theo, any chance you could eat more and talk less?"

"I didn't talk this much before my aneurysm ruptured."

The verbal diarrhea was a medical problem? "Your brain blew up and it made you chattier?"

"It made me ... think more. I've got a lot of stuff going on in my head and talking helps me puzzle it out. Like coming up with your nickname."

Levi's heart squeezed and a curious sensation warmed his chest. Maybe he should cut the kid some slack. "What happened to Kraken?"

"Not feeling it. How about Duke?"

"John Wayne, Green Berets movie?"

Theo pointed a finger. "Exactly!"

That made Levi think of Jordan. *As if you're not always thinking of her.* She'd made that joke about his tattoo before he stripped during their first time together in New York. He'd wanted to ease her into it, let her know that he was honoring his service, his unit, and Josh with that ink. Holding her tight while she fought through that moment had felt like his reason for existing.

He was in so much fucking trouble.

"Not sure I want to be associated with Wayne. Guy was a dick."

Theo nodded, and for once remained quiet. *Days of Our Lives* returned, and they watched it in companionable silence.

Mission Make a Rebel

Levi Hunt is a man of many parts: NCAA All-Star, former Green Beret, and now the latest centerman for a team that's looked directionless for the last couple of years.

{insert some stats about the Rebels' early games here}

What does a man like Hunt bring to the team? He's known hardship, both personal and professional. Living on the streets with his dad as a kid except for when they were lucky enough to sneak into the gym where his father worked, and the death of that same man from pneumonia have forged Levi into a man who takes nothing for granted. He's here to earn his place. He doesn't want anything handed to him.

That work ethic, so refreshing in this age of entitlement, makes Levi stand out in a sea of spotlight-hogging, butt-grabbing pro-athletes. Levi Hunt works hard and still finds time to volunteer at Uptown Mission where he's a regular on the breakfast crew and wows with a much-lauded recipe for huevos rancheros.

He's the hero the Rebels have been waiting for.

Jordan reread the sixteenth draft on her screen and let out a long sigh. How could she talk about Levi without revealing all this fantastic character-building fodder? She wanted to think his stint in Special Forces, his improvements on the ice, and his aura of solid, masculine good guy was enough to fuel the story. But the devil of an excellent story was in the details, and these juicy ones he wouldn't let her use would make all the difference. Stubborn man!

Her buzzer sounded and she closed the laptop. Maybe after tonight, she'd have a better idea of how to reframe the profile. Jumping up, she pressed the intercom talk button.

"It's Harper."

"Come on up!" Jordan threw a quick glance over her shoulder at her apartment, not that she could do anything to make it more presentable now. It still looked like she'd moved in last week instead of a couple of months ago.

She opened the door to find Violet Vasquez, youngest daughter of Clifford Chase and the silent partner in the Rebels ownership, raising her hand to knock. "Hey, there! I'm Violet, the one who doesn't give a shit about hockey but is here for the wine." She cocked her dark head, streaked with pink. "There is wine, right? That wasn't just a typical Harper bait and switch?"

"Oh, there's wine. Vats of wine."

"You've got class tomorrow, Vi." At six feet tall, Isobel Chase towered over all of them. "And don't you have to do some practice teaching with a bunch of kidlets?"

"Believe me, better when I'm hungover." She winked at Jordan. "I'm in an early education graduate program at Loyola. Don't fret. Your future spawn is safe with me."

Harper brought up the rear. "Sorry we're late. My little ones needed baths and usually I miss it with the games and all, so I couldn't resist. Oh, cute place!"

"Thanks, I'm still figuring out its personality before I try to impose mine on it."

Violet frowned, bringing her brows together. "That fire-place says do-me-lumberjack but the kitchen island is giving off Barefoot Contessa."

"Barefoot Lumberjack. I'll get right on it."

Isobel laughed. "So how does this podcast thing work?"

"Well, audio set up is in the office back there and I have mics for you all. We can have a drink and chat first out here and then get started in ten—sound good?"

A couple of minutes later, they were all seated around Jordan's coffee table, extra-large wine pours in tow. Harper had also brought cupcakes from Sweet Mandy B's.

"I'd rather not talk about hockey so we can keep the good stuff for the podcast, so ... been to any good restaurants lately?"

Violet scoffed. "Let's talk about boys. Harper says you and Hunt have history."

Jordan glared at Harper, only to get a small, oh-so-innocent smile in return. "He was a friend of my husband."

"Right." Violet looked like she was expecting more.

"Vi, leave her be," Isobel said. "Sorry, she has no filter."

Harper cleared her throat. "So how are the interviews going?"

"He's started to open up a bit. How he found hockey. Why he headed into the army." And so much more that she couldn't reveal because she'd started to care. "I mean, it's a slog but—"

"Someone's gotta do it, right?" Isobel grinned. "He is pretty hot. Got that grouchy, needs-a-hug thing going on. Total GILF."

"GILF?"

"Grump I'd like to—well, you know," Violet said. "Though maybe we should pronounce it 'jilf.' Like a gif versus jif situation."

"He's started playing better," Harper said with a disapproving glance at her sisters. "Thank God."

Violet snorted. "I should hope so given the early morning sexfests he's depriving me of."

"What's that?" Jordan asked.

"He's practicing with Bren and Remy a couple of times a week at the ass crack of dawn. I tell you, I thought Bren's retirement would mean more orgasms but no. Between school, my wicked stepkids, and that broody Scot unable to pull himself away from the ice, the old hoo-hah is getting lonely."

Early morning practices with a couple of Rebels legends? Jordan would have to work that in, and because Levi hadn't told her himself, she might be able to get away with it. She picked up her phone and mimicked pressing a button. "So, say that again. Slowly."

Forty-five minutes later, the recording was completed. Jordan had *almost* extracted some hints about upcoming trades from Harper but the woman was too good at keeping her cards close. While Violet was in the restroom (*we're BFFs now, Jordan, so I'll be checking the medicine cabinet for secrets!*) and Isobel took a call from her husband, Vadim, Harper helped Jordan bring the glasses into the kitchen.

"So, I wanted to run something by you," Jordan said to Harper. With the wine and convivial conversation, this might be her best shot at getting Harper to let her guard down. "I've been doing a little research about women in the male pro-sports space and I was hoping to interview you on the record about it. Different from the podcast. This would be less about the team and more ... hard-hitting."

"Well, it's no secret that I've been treated differently as a franchise CEO because I'm a woman. But I'm in a position of power, so my voice might not be what you're looking for."

Jordan chose her next words carefully. "But you weren't always in that position. Back when your dad was alive, you weren't quite so influential. I'm guessing you probably had your own run-ins with asshole players."

Harper turned on the faucet and rinsed out her wine glass. "Oh, plenty of those. For every gentleman like Remy, there are three brutes without manners waiting in the wings."

"Like Billy Stroger?"

The color draining from her face indicated that Harper was affected by the mention of his name, and Jordan felt a twinge of guilt. "Sure. He was on the Rebels several years back. Traded out after eighteen months, I think."

"A source tells me there was more to his departure. He hurt you, and not just emotionally."

What Harper lacked in height, she made up for in the ability to add inches with a spine-straightening move. "What do you think you know, Jordan?"

Jordan had the goods on tape but the manner of retrieval wasn't exactly above board. She needed something on the record. "There was the headline-grabbing fight between him and Remy during that first season you were in charge. A three-game suspension for Remy that was reduced to two when Stroger admitted to provoking him, which was odd given Billy's reputation for never backing down. Rumor has it that it was over you, and not just because Remy was jealous."

Harper was still rinsing her glass, now the cleanest thing in Jordan's apartment. "Just a little muscle-flexing between boys. It's in the past."

Jordan stepped forward. "I know this is difficult for you, but if Stroger is dangerous, then maybe people need to know that."

"What makes you think he's dangerous?" Harper's tone was sharp. "Has he done something recently?"

"Just cyber harassment as far as I know. But do you honestly think Stroger stopped the physical stuff with you?"

Harper's eyes widened in shock and Jordan's gut churned at her own dirty tactic. *You're going to hell.*

"What are we talking about?" Violet appeared at the door, dividing a look between Jordan and Harper.

"Jordan's trying to make a name for herself in the big leagues," Harper said icily, her composure returned. "I suggest you stick to the story you were assigned."

"Just make your rookie look good and the Rebels with it?" Oh, Jordan understood now. Harper had seen the sparks flying between Levi and Jordan in the locker room after that first game and thought she'd found the perfect person for a feel-good profile. The newbie beat reporter, desperate for her first big story, would never say a bad word about a guy she was attracted to.

Harper knew exactly what she was doing.

Anger flared. It seemed everyone was determined to tell Jordan how to do her damn job. "What happened to reporting the bad actors to management, Harper? Isn't that what you said when you saw that dick pic on my phone?"

The second the words left her mouth, she realized her mistake. Harper might have been receptive if Jordan had framed it as a mentee looking for help from the big-shot CEO. Backing this woman against the wall was only going to piss her off.

"If a player is harassing you," Harper said slowly, "then you should report that instead of using it as leverage to find a juicier story. I don't have anything to say to the press about past players."

She walked to the door where she was bookended by her taller sisters. Not unsubtly, both of them moved in to protect the queen.

"Thanks for including us in the podcast," Harper said,

her tone friendly once more. "It was fun. I can't wait to see what you write about Levi."

And that, ladies and gentleman, was that.

JORDAN SHOULDERED her way through the DC press box door ten minutes before the puck drop for the Rebels away game against the Congressmen.

"Evening, boys, would anyone care for a classic Chicago treat?"

DC locals wouldn't recognize the familiar-to-any-Chicagoan red, blue, and yellow design, so she opened the box to let the sticky-sweet scent of Ann Sather's cinnamon rolls mix with the scotch fumes and musty aroma of dudes watching hockey. It had been a struggle to keep Theo's fingers out of them on the plane ride in, but she'd managed. Just.

"Help yourselves!"

Not even the supposedly arthritic knees of Mark Carriger, the *Washington Post*'s hockey reporter could stop his jump into action. Formerly of the *Trib* in Chicago, he knew the score. "Cooke, I think I love you. But I *know* I'll love you if you tell me you have extra icing."

She removed a bag from her purse. "Is Wayne Gretzky the best to ever play the game?"

"We're not doing that again. You know it's Bobby Orr." Mark took a knife and sliced off a corner to the giant cinnamon roll, slathered it with icing, and placed it on a paper plate. "Why so generous? You get your copy in on Hunt?"

"Not yet, but it's shaping up nicely." She grabbed a soda, took a seat, and set up her laptop.

Reporters trickled in, stopping by to pay homage to the cinnamon rolls before settling down for the game.

"Hunt's on the first line again," someone commented. "He looked good at that last game."

She hummed noncommittally. Lately, he looked good at every game, which made her think of other places he looked good. Her bed, her shower, on the kitchen table—ahem. *Let's keep the mind clean while we work.*

During the first intermission, the box emptied out while the old guys with enlarged prostates did what old guys with enlarged prostates needed to do. One of the more pleasant aspects of being a woman in a man's world were the shorter lines for the women's restrooms during breaks—though she usually kept her ear to the tile, listening in on the WAGs as they gossiped about their men. Always be eavesdropping.

On arriving back in the press box, she found the seat beside hers occupied, and she instantly recognized the back of Coby Dawson's head.

He smiled up at her. "Jordan, how goes it?"

"Hey, Dawson. Three times in six weeks. If I didn't know better I'd say you were following me around, looking for a story."

"Don't worry, I have plenty of stories. Sorry, I needed access to the juice. I'm only at 15%." He gestured to her laptop which had been nudged a few inches aside so he could plug his own Macbook into their shared outlet. "Speaking of stories, here's one for you. Little birdie told me about an upcoming move."

Her heart sank. Were Harper and Dante considering trading Levi out? Or maybe this was about Cade Burnett?

"Is my story already in danger of becoming a different story?"

He cocked his head. "Hunt? Nah, or not as far as I know.

But before I give you the details, I wanted to run something by you. Heard you're working on something bigger than Mr. GI in skates."

The back of her neck tingled. "You've got a whole flock of birdies chirping in your ear."

His smirk was half-charm, half-smarm. "One of the girls at ESPN HQ said you've been getting chatty with all the lady reporters. Information-gathering chatty."

"We women do like to talk." Offering up that rusty stereotype grated but was necessary to throw him off the scent. "We especially like to talk about co-workers and bosses and who did what. Just girly gossip."

"Not a story about the trials and tribulations of your tribe? We've all seen how the female reporters get dumped on. You might have something there."

"You mean bite the hand that feeds me?" The words mixed with bile in her throat. She couldn't even get the great and powerful Harper Chase to see the bigger picture. "I'd like to keep my job, thanks."

"Maybe I could help you out. Give it the coverage it deserves. I do have a bigger platform."

Coby Dawson offering to use his national platform to call out his fellow male reporters, the athletes he covered, and the front office staff who kept him juiced with information? She thought not. More likely he was thinking up a way to throw shade so her story on Levi landed with minimal impact.

Curious, she played along. "Let's say that hypothetically I was working on a story like that. Why would you even want to touch it?"

"These toxic environments make it hard for everyone to do their jobs, Jordan."

She could feel her eyes grow large. "Wow, Dawson, you sound almost like an ally."

"Is it so shocking? I've got sisters, female friends, co-workers. You think I like seeing how they're treated? No woman should have to put up with half the shit I see some of these guys pull."

These guys were obviously anyone but Dawson. Admittedly, she'd never witnessed anything disqualifying other than those sly texts congratulating her when she got the Hunt profile. Perhaps she'd misinterpreted them, looking for micro-aggressions that didn't exist. Not every man in the business was the enemy. Neither had she heard a word against Coby during her multiple interviews. Either he was Teflon or a good man to have on her side.

Needing a moment to digest that, she changed the subject. "So what's this scoop you're dangling?"

He worked a beat for effect. "It's unconfirmed but word has it that Gunnar Bond is back in play."

"Where?"

"Chicago."

Jordan let out a low whistle. This was huge. Gunnar Bond had been the top goal scorer for two seasons running three years ago when he played for the LA Quake. A family tragedy—the loss of his wife and four-year old twins in a car accident which he survived—had destroyed him. He'd left the NHL, dropped off the grid, and as far as she knew hadn't spoken a word to anyone in hockey since.

"Where'd you hear this?" And why was he telling her?

His crinkly eyes said he wouldn't dream of revealing his source. "As you know, the Quake let him go after a year. Only so much grief a franchise will tolerate. But the Rebels seem to be making a business out of picking up orphans and has-beens."

"They're all for giving people a second chance. Redemption is their cornerstone." She should put that somewhere in the article. Is that what Levi was looking for? For his dad? For Josh?

"Maybe now that you have an in with Harper you could pump her for information?"

"Maybe." She refocused on the rink, where the second period had begun. Levi had just won a face-off and was zipping down the center, waiting for Callaghan to pass it back.

Here it comes ... and nothing.

She side-eyed Dawson. "Looked like you're just as tight with the Rebels management. Why not go to Harper yourself?"

"Favor is so fleeting in this biz."

True, but it still didn't explain why he was dropping this juicy AF goss on her here and now. Unless ...

"Did Bond and Hunt graduate in the same class at Dartmouth?" she asked, testing her theory.

"Yes, they did." He grinned at her.

"Sheesh, Dawson, if you want me to ask him, just say so."

He laughed and she joined in, enjoying the camaraderie of holding a secret and gossiping with a big shot. This was the level she wanted to attain.

"Bond's not been heard from for over a year," Coby continued. "Someone said he's living in a shack in the woods of New Hampshire. Real mountain man stuff. I figured your boy Hunt might have some insider knowledge."

"Which I extract and pass on to you?"

He shrugged. "What you do with it is up to you. We could help each other out. Either way, I'm serious about giving your story—whatever that story might be—a signal boost."

"Why?"

"Because the world's changing. Sports are changing. The demographics of sports are changing. Close to 40% of our viewership on SportsFocus are women, with millennials leading the charge. Only a fool refuses to acknowledge numbers like that. I'm not planning to go down with the dinosaurs you see here." He waved a hand around the press box, just as Ernie Cross, who was seventy if he was a day, hacked up a juicy gob of phlegm. She didn't want to know what he did with it but the man used cloth handkerchiefs. Enough said.

Dawson was still talking. "We're always looking for new on-air talent at SportsFocus, Jordan. I've listened to your podcast, read your columns. You have a great voice and good instincts. I think our viewers would really respond to you."

An on-camera gig at ESPN? That was unexpected. Her heart boomed, swelling with excitement at the thought of working for the premier sports broadcaster in the country.

The freakin' dream.

Despite the compelling conversation with Dawson, she couldn't take her eyes off the Rebels' new center. Couldn't stop admiring all that strength and grace and power. And then five seconds later, she couldn't unsee that hit.

DC's Dimitri Sokov had smashed into Levi, a hit so hard that the Rebels center dropped like a sack of icing-drenched cinnamon rolls.

"Whoa! Down goes your man." Coby chuckled malevolently beside her.

Her man. She covered her mouth, barely muffling her shocked gasp. Oh, God, was he unconscious?

"You okay, Jordan?"

She blinked at Coby, who was looking at her curiously. And why not? She was peering down at him because, not only had she gasped, she'd jumped to her feet the moment Levi sustained that vicious check. *Excellent undercover props, Cooke.*

When she returned her focus to the ice, Levi was upright, skating around like nothing had happened.

"That looked rough," she said with a nervous chuckle while she retook her seat. "Don't know how they do it."

"I'd swear you've never watched a hockey game before." Dawson shook his head in pity at poor, fragile Jordan.

More like her poor, fragile heart.

20

JORDAN POPPED four slices of bread into the toaster and depressed the button. Should she go with lightly-done or medium?

"What do you think, Cookie? Light or medium on the toast?"

The puppy gave a yelp, which he always did whenever she said his name. Or pie. Or anything, really. Levi had brought him over last night, not wanting to leave him alone at his place while Elle was working. Poor Joe was still under the weather.

"Medium? Gotcha."

She stirred the eggs, thinking about Levi. About where this was going. About the mess she'd gotten herself into because this was quite a mess. Last night, when Levi was checked hard—which was basically fifty percent of his job —she'd almost given herself away to Coby Dawson, of all people. *So long, objectivity.*

A movement behind her made her turn, while the gorgeous, shirtless man made every part of her hum. *Hello, hot stuff!*

"Hungry?"

He answered with a ravenous, all-consuming kiss that turned her knees to jelly. Fortunately, he was holding her upright, hands on butt, just how she liked them.

"Starving." Burying his lips in the crook her neck, he inhaled her skin, laying butterfly kisses where she was so sensitive. "Those eggs look done."

She spun back, noting the eggs were browning around the edges, and quickly flipped off the heat. The toast popped. "Coffee?"

"I can get it. I think." He squinted at her Keurig, on the same counter as the box of mini-macarons he'd picked up for her yesterday. So sweet. (Both the treats and the man.)

A minute later, he'd worked it out and they were seated at the kitchen island, tucking in. Cookie sat at Levi's feet, waiting for scraps because the man completely spoiled him. Such picture-perfect domesticity. She hadn't indulged in this since ... she was married.

It felt good. Intimate. A little bit terrifying.

"I assumed you'd be heading into practice early this morning."

"Morning skate's not until ten."

"I was talking about the extra practices with DuPre and St. James."

He paused, delivered that trademark Wild West squint, then went back to chewing. Once he'd swallowed, he sipped his coffee. "Where'd you hear that?"

"A little, pink-streaked bird told me. Her bed is cold but the gossip is hot."

"They're just getting some exercise the same time as me."

Oh, to be a fly on the wall. "Learning anything while you

all skate around the rink avoiding each other? Those guys are legends after all."

"Just French curses and how to play dirty. St. James has a bag of tricks for how to start a fight while coming off smelling like roses." He leaned back, that Green Berets tattoo emblazoned across his chest announcing loudly his hero status. "What other things have you heard?"

She slathered Nutella on her toast and took a bite. "Gunnar Bond. Rumor has it the Rebels have him in their sights."

He held her gaze unerringly. "Good player."

"And in your class at Dartmouth. You two still friendly?"

"Not especially. What happened to him was awful." He shook his head. "I hope he makes it back. And no, I haven't heard from him or any rumors about where he's headed."

"Useless."

"Baby, I told you I'm not the guy you want for heartfelt secrets and insider gossip."

"Oh, I dunno. You've come up with some good stuff."

He reached out and took her hand. "C'mere."

She went to him, sat on those thick-as-ancient-oaks thighs, and enjoyed being held while she munched on her toast.

His hand grazed the back of her thigh in erotic, sensuous strokes. "You almost done with this profile?"

"Close," she said around her chewing. "You can read it before I turn it in if you like."

"Is that typical?"

"No, but then you're not typical."

"And once it's done, then what?"

Did he mean them or her next story? She couldn't say for sure what exactly was happening, but seeing Levi checked hard last night had unlocked something soft and fragile inside her. With Josh, she'd existed in a constant state of anxiety about his safety, and while an ice rink was nowhere as dangerous as the Middle East, the possibility Levi could be badly injured was exceptionally revealing. Acknowledging this made her feel exposed in a way she hadn't felt for years.

Eager to move on, she centered the conversation on a topic she could better grasp. "I've been doing some research on the place of female reporters and professionals in sports. Harassment, come-ons, that kind of thing."

His hand stopped. "You said something about that before. What kind of harassment are we talking about?"

"The usual."

"Enlighten me."

Best to keep the specifics to herself. "Guys sliding into my DMs."

"Players?"

"Some. Mostly trolls and fanboys."

"Close your DMs."

Easy for him to say. "You wouldn't tell that to a male reporter."

"I would if he was being harassed. You don't need to keep your DMs open."

"And what about email or comments on my column or podcast posts? Do I get someone to read it for me, like the equivalent of a medieval royal taster? I have open lines of communication so I can work with players, agents, managers, and coaches to get the information I need to do my job. Shutting down the platforms on which jerks can insult me is not the answer."

"You sure about that? How about some names, Jordan?"

She stood—or tried to. He kept her steady in his lap, his palm flush against her hip.

"I shouldn't have said anything to you. I knew you'd just see one angle."

"The angle where you're getting harassed. Yep, that's what I see and I'm suggesting a solution."

"And I'd rather come up with a different solution. Education. Awareness." When his expression remained immobile, she tried another tack. "Coby Dawson said he'd give me a spot on SportsFocus so I can shine a light on the problem."

"Dawson? *That* guy wants to help you?" His tone basically accused Coby of wanting to help in ways that would likely only help Coby—or Coby's penis.

So she'd also been incredulous, but she didn't have to take it from Levi. "Not every guy is trying to get in my pants."

"They are, Jordan. Every single one of them."

Some women might take that as a compliment, but Levi hadn't intended it as one. It reduced her to a set of genitals and men to rutting beasts.

"This could be huge for me. Coby said there might be a chance of interviewing for a national correspondent spot at ESPN. It's like the Holy Grail for sports reporters."

"And in the meantime, you do what? Flirt with guys in your DMs to get your story?"

She pushed back against his chest and stood, putting necessary distance between them before she cold-cocked him. And she could do it, too, given that the press box dessert table was helping her bulk up.

Cookie looked up, sensing the tension in their previously happy little trio.

"You're very close to sounding like I'm asking for it, Levi."

Exasperation pleated his brow. "That's not what I mean. I

don't like seeing you in positions where you have to play along with some leering joker in a locker room or some shithead sending you 'hey, baby' messages on Twitter. Or worse, because I know you're sugarcoating it. I just don't want to see you hurt. You can protect yourself, Jordan, and still do your job."

"Why is that the message here? Why do I need to modify my behavior and not the guys who do this?"

His sigh was long-suffering. "Because that's the way of the world."

That wasn't the world she wanted to live in. Shunting the responsibility to *not* be harassed off to women should not be the answer. How about education, awareness, responsibility? How about making our next generation of boys understand respect?

She was in a unique position here: inhabiting both the story and the person who could report on it. This was her lived experience, and to have a man tell her the equivalent of "don't get drunk or wear a short skirt" to ensure safety on the job, made her eyeballs burn with the heat of a thousand suns.

"That might be the way of *your* world, Levi, but it's not mine. Did you treat Elle differently on the base because she was a woman?"

"I looked out for her because the reality is that there aren't enough of the good guys to achieve critical mass. Yet. And until there are, a woman in all walks of life, but especially male-dominated ones like the military and pro-sports, needs to take extra precautions."

"Can't change the world, so change myself?"

"If need be."

Oh, for fuck's sake. "Well, this woman has changed something—her mind about continuing this conversation.

I'm hitting the shower. And I really don't need to see your knuckle-dragging ass when I come out."

THE NEXT MORNING, Levi plunked down on a bench in the locker room and unlaced his skates while breathing his way back to normal.

Remy peeled off his jersey. "What's up, Hunt? Too much for you?"

Bren took a seat. "He got you good on that last run, DuPre. A little credit, now."

Levi smiled, grateful that Bren had his back. The early morning workouts had been a three-time a week occurrence for over six weeks, and it was paying dividends during the games with a 15-11 record on the season. He wondered if the guys really did stop by the rink this often or if they were just worried about their wives' investment.

"He's gettin' a little trickier with those dekes for sure," Remy said. "Almost like he's paying attention to what us giants of the game have been sayin'."

"You don't have to do this," Levi said.

"What?" Bren asked. "Whip you into shape, soldier?"

"It's getting cold out there. Can't believe you'd rather be here than in a warm bed with your women." Hell, if he had a choice, he'd be snuggled up with Jordan, even though she wasn't talking to him right now because of his "knuckle-dragging ass" as she politely termed it.

"Nah, this is good for us." Bren rubbed his beard. "Keeps me fit for my hot trophy wife. You got a woman keeping your bed warm, Hunt?"

Not one he could talk about. "Nope."

Bren slid a glance at Remy, who smirked back.

"What's that for?"

Remy shrugged. "*De rien.*"

"Didn't look like nothing."

"Just thinking that pretty reporter seems to be your speed. Kershaw said—"

"Kershaw is a gossiping old woman and he'd better keep his mouth shut about Jordan."

Bren and Remy stared at him, then each other before bursting out laughing. Wonderful.

"Look, we understand wanting to protect your woman, especially when it looks like lines are being crossed." Remy crossed his arms. "I went through that with Harper."

"That's not it. Or not the only thing."

He figured these guys knew all about taboo workplace relationships, but that wasn't the only issue here. Originally, he'd worried that Jordan's natural cheer would (a) piss him off and (b) piss her off when he didn't respond, but once he'd accepted his fate, he'd leaned into it. He looked forward to seeing her smile, talking hockey with her, touching her with abandon, even though he could only do it in private.

"I like Jordan. Shit, I really like her, but that's not what she's doing with me. Aside from the fact it wouldn't look good for her to be with the subject of a story, she's pretty focused on her career."

Bren frowned. "So?"

"So, getting close to me is more of a career move. It's a reflection of our proximity. I don't doubt she's attracted to me but it's not more than sex."

"For you?"

"For her." As for him? His heart pounded, just talking about it.

Remy rubbed his chin. "You sure about that? Maybe you're reading it wrong."

Usually, Levi didn't give a flying fuck about changing anyone else's mind but explaining it would be a good way to pound it into his own thick skull. It was bad enough he was doing this to Josh, the fact that nothing could come of it made his sin even more egregious.

"Jordan and I have history. She was married to a close friend of mine who died."

"Saw that somewhere," Bren said. "A guy in your unit."

"Yeah, Josh. And this guy was the best. Shirt off your back, funny as shit, biggest heart of anyone you'd meet, and perfect for Jordan. She has a type. Guys who can make her laugh, who can match her bubbly personality. That's not me. So when I say that Jordan is using me, it's not a criticism."

This breakdown of his doomed relationship with Jordan rendered the guys silent for a spell.

"You know, opposites attract," Bren finally said. "Violet and me are living proof. You won't find two personalities more different."

"Except for Harper and me." Remy grabbed a towel. "I'm pretty laid back and well, Harper, she's not."

Bren snorted. "Testify."

"Your point?"

"This idea that Jordan needs a guy who's a clone of her husband doesn't really wash," Remy said. "People fit together for lots of different reasons, and sometimes the yang and the yin is the thing."

No. He had nothing to offer Jordan but the comfort of his body and a few sound bites to give her career a boost. He might want more, but that was never going to be in the cards.

"I'm not her favorite person right now, anyway."

Bren chuckled. "There's a very slim window for when

any man is a favorite of his woman's. Wouldn't worry about it."

But he did, especially as it was something into which he could legitimately pour his frustration. "Part of it is her job. She's good at it, really good. But it puts her in positions where guys get to be assholes, and she's too nice or too concerned with losing an opportunity that she plays along. I hate that. I just want to protect her and I want her to take precautions, like not letting fuckers DM her with proposals and more in the name of a story. She thinks that's me policing her behavior instead of theirs."

Remy frowned. "Look, there will be times where you stepping in to help or even offer your help is the last thing she wants. What she really needs is for you to listen to her."

Bren nodded. "Been there. You can still be pissed, but she's looking for something more evolved."

"More evolved?" Levi could be evolved. He could be so fucking evolved those Twitter assholes wouldn't see him coming.

"We get it," Remy said. "My wife runs a pro-hockey franchise and gets dragged by *couyons* on a daily basis. I can't jump in and answer every comment on a newspaper article. I can't burn down the Internet though that would probably do the world a favor. But if I see she's being hurt and I have it in my power there and then to do something about that, I will."

"You have," Bren interjected.

Levi shot a hard look at Remy. "You've taken some shit-head to task for talking smack about Harper?"

"More than talking. A few years back, during a game, I cleaned the clock of a guy who hurt her in a way no man should hurt a woman."

Levi knew the game and hit instantly. It had always struck him as hinky at the time. "Stroger."

Remy gave a short nod. "He hurt Harper. I hurt him. It was pretty simple math."

"If you have names, we can deal with that," Bren said. "If it's fanboy trolls, let it be. Keep your fire for problems you can solve and never forget that your woman is likely stronger than you think."

21

Levi knocked on the door to Lucy's office at the Mission. "Could I have a word?"

"Hey, it's the middle of the afternoon. What are you doing here?" Her bright smile dimmed when she saw his companion. "Really?"

He looked down at Cookie, whose tail was wagging and tongue was lolling.

"Don't worry, buddy. The mean lady won't hurt you." He stepped inside. "I wanted to talk about making this place pet-friendly for the guests."

"Of course you do." She gestured to him to take a seat. "I'm guessing this is Cookie."

"Hear that, Cookie? Your rep precedes you."

Cookie gave a friendly yelp, as he always did when anyone paid him the slightest morsel of attention.

"I heard you dropped Joe off Thanksgiving night and took care of Cookie for a few days while Joe was under the weather," Lucy said, her gaze sussing out the puppy for trouble. "I appreciate that, but we can't afford the liability insurance to have pets on the premises. They might bite other pets or guests, they usually need shots, and they make a godawful mess."

Guessing there'd be pushback, he'd come armed with a plan. "What if I could raise some funds? I've been doing some research with a charity called Pets for the Homeless. They offer veterinary clinics for the animals, give them check-ups, and they can also send crates to keep the animals and guests safe. We'd need funds for a pet liaison, someone who could manage the program and—"

"Clean up the dog shit?" She sent a glare Cookie's way.

He smiled at her, tongue out, a complete doggie-doofus. How could someone not love that face?

"Because, Levi, honey, that's what I'm seeing here. Mountains and mountains of dog shit."

He grinned at her plain speaking. "I hear you. We'd figure out a way to keep it environmentally safe that will not require you to personally shovel shit."

She still looked skeptical. Levi knew that breaking the homeless cycle depended on people moving into shelters where they could access other services, but someone like Joe wouldn't leave his best friend behind.

"Let me work on it, Luce. I might be able to get sponsorship from the team."

She sighed, recognizing that he had the bit between his teeth and this would end when he ended it. "My door's always open to meaningful solutions. Not so much for visits from dogs, though, even if they are cute. And thanks for the good coffee, by the way." She held up her cup. He'd talked the local Starbucks into donating to the shelter any coffee beans they didn't deem worthy.

"Gotta keep you juiced, Luce."

"Just what I need, better caffeine delivery methods. Now don't you have rehearsal or whatever it's called to get to?"

"You're not a hockey fan, are you?" He figured not, but maybe it was an incorrect assumption.

"Me? God, no. But my brother is."

"Game on Friday, if he's interested. Text me his name and I can leave tickets at will-call."

She smiled, smug as a bug.

"What?"

"Worlds colliding, Levi. Proud of you."

"Oh, shut up."

On his way to his car, a text from Jordan made his phone buzz and his heart leap. He hadn't spoken to her since yesterday. Correction: he'd tried, but she'd gone dark until now.

Figured you should get to see this before I turn it in, with a link to a Word doc.

He opened up a preview of the profile. *Uh oh.* Given the fight they just had, dread shivered through him at how this was going to turn out.

Levi Hunt: A Man on a Mission

That was the title? Army, mission—not terribly original but he guessed that wasn't important. He'd read her game reports. She had a good eye, a nice turn of phrase, and a knack for homing in on an angle that someone might not have noticed, but a long-form piece required a defter touch. For a moment, he worried he might not like her writing. But even if he didn't, it wouldn't change his like for her.

> *Clifford Chase once famously said "hockey's not for —" (Insert a word not suitable for primetime here). And it seems we've come to the point in player recruitment where regular*

old athletes are no longer good enough. No.
The NHL is now in the business of drafting
superheroes.

Okay, that was a cute start.

Levi Hunt would laugh if someone called him
that to his face. Or not laugh, exactly. He'd
stare at you hard, knowing his ability to wait
you out would force you to backtrack and
make you unsure of what you'd previously
been so certain of. But make no mistake, the
man is a bona fide hero.
Rather than go pro, Hunt gave up his spot in the
NHL draft and enlisted in the army. Rather
than sign a lucrative contract, he became a
grunt on a grunt's pay. Rather than skate
onto a rink to the soundtrack of sliced-and-
diced rock classics and rowdy cheers, he chose
to place himself in harm's way. That rink
would have been a lot safer.
I know this intimately.
You see, Levi Hunt is not a stranger to me. He
served with my husband, Sergeant Engineer
Josh Cooke in the Special Forces, also known
as the Green Berets. I didn't know him well
back then. I still don't know him, but I think I
understand him better. Levi's not in this for
the money or the glory or the adulation. He's
here to serve. It's what he does. Serve his
country, serve up goals. Be useful.
The Green Berets' motto is Sine Pari—Without
Equal. But they also have another one: "De

Oppresso Liber," Latin for "To Free the Oppressed." They are considered the first line of defense in any conflict, and while Levi Hunt is not a D-man, he certainly doesn't shy away from conflict on the ice. Green Berets are also known as "warrior-diplomats." They enter a region and act as bodyguards, take out targets, build houses, befriend children. They are nimble, adaptable, jacks-of-all-trades. Their presence is felt, but rarely acknowledged.

Levi brings these skills to the ice. He's everywhere at once, making trouble, fixing mistakes, protecting his teammates, being as solid as they come.

He's also kind of a dick.

Levi burst out laughing. "Jordan, baby, you did not just call me a dick in your article."

Maybe she didn't hate him after all. Which was good because he was head over skates for her.

JORDAN HAD EXPECTED that her weeks embedded with a pro-hockey franchise would have a lot of downtime, likely filled with poker, foosball, and listening to Theo Kershaw bemoaning his clothing struggles. Not expected? That she would become familiar enough with the storylines of the team's favorite soap opera to be able to hold up her end of the conversation.

In the player lounge at the Rebels practice facility, the big screen TV was tuned to *Days of Our Lives*.

"I don't understand how the former serial killer is finding true love," Erik said morosely. By all accounts, the Rebels' goalie had the worst luck with women, surprising given his Swedish good looks and big bank balance. Seeing a fictional murderer getting some was obviously an affront.

"He's been rehabilitated with drugs that ensure he won't kill again," Cade said. "Now he deserves to be happy."

"But what about the people he killed?" Jordan asked, questioning, not for the first time, the soap's believability. "And their families? He's running around scot-free, falling in love with hottie motorcycle chicks with no recognizable source of income, and no one's saying, that's the Necktie Killer!"

"Her mother is," Erik insisted. "Hope hates Ben. You know she's going to frame him for whoever's murdered next."

"Everyone, even the Necktie Killer, deserves a second chance. A little empathy, Jordan." Theo shook his head, disapproving of her unwillingness to get with the program.

"Besides, Will was one of his victims," Ford commented, "and he came back from the dead and forgave him."

"True," a deep, familiar voice observed. "No harm, no foul. Except to the other victims who *didn't* come back from the dead using Dr. Rolf's wake-up juice."

Jordan turned to Levi, remembered that she was still mad at him, and turned back. Unfortunately her booming heart was thrilled to see the jerkface.

Speaking of thrilled ... Cookie jumped up in her lap and the rest of the team went wild for their four-legged visitor, which only excited the dog more.

"Hey, puppy!"

"Who's this little guy?"

"We need a mascot! Hey, let's call him Rebel!"

"He's already got a name. Cookie, meet the team. Team, meet Cookie." Levi placed a big box on the table behind them. "Kershaw, got a little something for you."

Theo's face lit up. "You did?"

"I heard it's your birthday tomorrow—"

"Only because he won't stop gabbin' about it," Cade interjected.

"And because we'll be traveling, I figured we should celebrate today." Levi lifted the lid on the box to reveal a cake shaped like ... a giant peach? "Happy birthday, Superglutes."

Jordan got it now. Not a peach, but—

"An ass cake! You got me an ass cake for my birthday?" Theo sounded both horrified and ecstatic.

"I figured you deserved it for having the most powerful ass in the NHL."

That cracked the team up, and Theo blushed to the tips of his ears. "Thanks, Hunt," he said, sounding shyer than Jordan had ever heard him.

Within seconds, someone had produced a candle and the lounge was filled with the off-tune warbling of eight guys singing "Happy Birthday."

A lump the size of a puck had somehow lodged in Jordan's throat. How would she ever finish this damn article when the man kept presenting a hundred different versions of himself?

Jordan felt a shoulder nudge.

"Could I have a word?" Levi's gaze bore into her, and then he turned and walked to the other end of the lounge, giving her no choice but to follow.

Oh, another face to the marvelous Mr. Hunt. What a penis!

He kept going down the corridor with the massage and rehab rooms. Inside one with an examination table, he gestured to the seat in the corner, waiting for her to take it before he sat himself.

"That was nice of you. The cake for Theo."

"He's a good kid. Annoying as hell, but a good kid all the same." Inhaling deep, he took her hands in his. "I'm sorry."

"For?"

"Being a jerk who implied that *you* need to change instead of the whole damn world of sexist morons out there."

She pressed her lips against a smile, not wanting to make it too easy for him.

"Go on."

"I just want you to be safe, Jordan. I read some of the stuff people say on your columns and I hate it."

Now might not be the best time to mention that Chicago SportsNet moderated those and that they were often much worse pre-approval. Every ugly, misogynistic insult you could think of found its way into those threads.

"Even if I was a man, I'd have people disagreeing with me. That's the Internet in a nutshell."

"What about the emails and the DMs? You want to share those with me?"

"They'd just make you angry. Most of them are from anonymous egg accounts set up to troll. I report them, they get closed down, another one pops up like a game of whack-an-asshole." She rolled her eyes like it was all a joke to minimize and keep him sane. To be a woman online was to be at constant risk of harassment. Fact.

"What about dick pics? Kershaw said he saw something on your phone, unless that was something else."

"Pretty much every woman gets those, and when you're in the public eye, it's worse. But I can handle it. They're kind of sad, really." She'd blocked Stroger after what she overheard in the Rebels' executive box washroom. So far, there'd been no fallout.

"Are you saying you wouldn't be receptive to a photo of me in all my naked glory?"

"Well ..." She giggled, and he smiled, and it felt like she'd dodged a bullet.

"Read that draft you sent me. Made me laugh."

"And I missed this blessed event?" She grinned. "It's not done. I'm not sure how to end it."

"I liked that you called me out for being a dick. I like that you don't let me get away with anything."

She stroked a thumb along his cheekbone, then over his lips. "I've only been calling you out since Day One. God, you were so grumpy when I met you and your crew in that bar, and I just loved poking the bear, trying to provoke a reaction. But you refused to relent. Gave me nothing. But since then, I've seen a different side to you. A softer side." Not to mention that part of him so ready to lose control, to get down and dirty. Every night with him peeled back more layers and revealed this man she was starting to care for deeply.

"No soft sides. I've got a rep to maintain."

She smiled, seeing right past his gruff exterior. "Sure, keep it up but I know who you are, Hunt. The stalwart friend. The attentive listener. The player who buys ass cakes for his teammate. The man with a big heart who doesn't want anyone to know about it. And here's me, with a platform where I can tell the world what a good guy you are and you won't let me!"

He pulled her from the chair into his lap and brushed his lips across hers. "Just because you can doesn't mean you should. I'm trusting you on this, Jordan. You're skilled enough to write around the edges."

"So, I just keep this secret? Be the one person who knows about your soft, gooey center?"

"Why not? No one else needs access to what's in here." He placed her hand over his heart, guiding her fingertips to absorb the thrum of power within. "Only you, Jordan."

Only you.

She was beginning to think that the warm glow created by this private knowledge was brighter than the need to sprinkle her story with the journalistic gold dust he gave her every day. So, basically a death sentence to her ability to finish this assignment with any semblance of objectivity.

And while his heart beat strongly beneath her touch, her own was a mushy mess when it came to Levi Hunt.

22

"JORDAN! GET IN HERE!"

Jordan knocked over her coffee cup, cursed loudly, and tried to mop it up. She rarely came into the Chicago Sports-sNet offices, preferring to work from home, which was fine with Mac as long as she turned in her assignments on time. Today, she'd stopped in to chat with Rebecca Voigt, the other female reporter at the network, only to find she'd left early to pick her sick kid up from daycare.

"I haven't got all day. Now!"

Muttering, she headed into Mac's office.

"Shut the door."

She did as she was told and took a seat even though he hadn't asked. This was how one of the reporters out in the pen would behave: assume the male privilege of seat-taking without invitation.

"This Hunt story..."

"Yeah?"

"It's good. Nice phrasing, sharp insight. Your game reports and columns have been on the nose as well."

"But?" Because she heard it loud and clear.

"I expected more ... dirt. This is on the wrong side of respectful. Too much hero worship."

She squirmed, because that was her take on it, too. "He's a private guy. This was like pulling teeth."

"What about the other story?"

"What other story?"

He raised a caterpillar-like eyebrow, or she assumed he did. It actually didn't budge a millimeter. "I heard you're working on something else. Maybe a players-behaving-badly angle?"

How would he know that? Maybe Dawson had reached out or one of her sources had tattled.

"I've got a few irons in the fire." Likely he thought it was something about one of the players screwing around or conduct unbecoming. Would he be as receptive to a story where female reporters were the victims?

Not victims. She hated that word, so laden with misery. Given how Mac had framed the terms of her employment on Day One, she didn't think he'd be interested in this angle anyway. She'd come out of it as a bad sport, branded a troublemaker.

And likely without a job.

If only she could convince Harper to go on the record about Stroger. Mac would be all over that.

"For now, I'm focusing on trying to get the inside scoop on the next big trade into the Rebels. Rumors abound."

Grunting his semi-approval, Mac held out a marked-up paper copy of her article. "Take another stab at this. See if you can add a bit more shading."

"Will do."

She left the office, her mind a whirligig. She had plenty of anecdotal evidence about female reporters getting shafted (professionally) or offers to be shafted (sexually), but throwing up a blog post on CSN or a podcast on Hockey Grrl might not get the exposure a story like this deserved. She needed advice—and she knew just who to call.

JORDAN WAVED her coffee cup at Kinsey as she entered the Starbucks to let her know she was covered. Once Kinsey had her caramel macchiato in hand, she kissed Jordan hello, and took a seat at the window.

"Hey, it feels like ages since we last talked! How goes it in the world of big-time sports reporting?"

"It goes. I've got a few things in the hopper—dick stuff, trade rumors, dick stuff."

Kinsey shook her head. "Still with the pecker pics? I'm telling you: name and shame."

"And get my social media accounts closed down?"

"Put it out there with a blur filter but name those asses and cocks now!" A few people sent disapproving glares her way, but Kinsey ignored them. "Unless you think it's not that serious?"

"Right now, I have bigger dicks to fry. I need your wise counsel, friend."

"Okay, unload, shoot, ejaculate. I'm listening."

Jordan grinned. "So I've probably got enough data points on the reporter harassment story to do something with it. I could post an online article or a podcast but Coby Dawson offered me an interview spot on SportsFocus. Kind of like a *Sixty Minutes*-type deal. More publicity. A bigger platform."

Kinsey nodded. "Sounds good. What's the problem?"

"I can't help thinking it's a trap. Something's in it for Dawson. He says he's an ally but it feels off."

"Maybe you should go with your gut."

"Maybe." She mulled it over for a moment. "Levi was suspicious, too, but that was probably typical male cynicism."

Kinsey's internal antennae must have gone *zing* because she sat up straighter. "You've run this by Levi?"

"Yeah, and he thinks Dawson has an agenda. An in-my-pants agenda."

Kinsey cocked her head and stared.

Busted.

"Okay, we've done the deed! And before you tell me that I'm now incapable of being unbiased about my story subject, I'll have you know that ... you'd be absolutely right." She mentally curled up, bracing for Kinsey's response.

"Not gonna judge, babe."

No worries, because judgment protocol was already activated in Jordan's muddled mind. "I have great stuff on Levi to make his profile so much more. Upbringing hardship. Current good deeds. Ass cakes! But he doesn't want me to talk about anything other than hockey. And my editor wants dirt."

"Ass cakes?"

"He bought a birthday cake for Theo shaped like an ass. It was actually really sweet."

"Theo's ass or the cake?" Kinsey sipped her coffee. "Okay, don't answer that. Sounds like you can't be unbiased. The heart has no objectivity. I've been there."

She passed over the *heart* comment. "Really?"

"Yeah, it's how I met Luke. He'd gotten into a brawl at his bar involving the Chicago Police Department and CFD, and I was brought in to make his firehouse all shiny again."

"With a firefighters and kittens calendar?" Jordan remembered it well. The entire country swooned for a week.

"One of my finest days on the job. And in the meantime, I got involved with him and his family to the point where I had to take sides, and I took theirs. His. And lost my job in the process."

Jordan hadn't known any of this. "Weren't you working for the mayor of Chicago at the time? You mean he fired you?"

She rolled her eyes. "And now that same ex-mayor is my brother-in-law and one of my closest friends. Never a dull moment with the Dempseys."

"So, it was worth it?"

"Oh, yeah. But at the time, making that choice was tough. My career was—is—really important, and having to subsume my ambition in deference to a man I was falling in love with was so hard. I'd already moved cross country for my previous fiancé, who promptly dumped me. And now here I was faced with an impossible choice: love or duty."

"I'm not in love with Levi." It was a reflex, more a thing you say rather than mean. She couldn't deny that she liked him. A lot. But love? No.

"Maybe not yet, but I can tell there's something there. Something that's holding you back from delivering the killer blow. If it was just sex—how is the sex by the way?"

"Adequate."

Kinsey smiled slyly. "If it was just *adequate* sex, you wouldn't be letting him dictate the story. You'd be writing it your way."

The truth was an ice-cold latte in the face. Shocking and eye-opening, but probably delicious when you licked your lips. Jordan couldn't mine the story's nuggets because she had deep feelings for Levi.

She'd not dated seriously since Josh died. Losing him had hurt so much and laying her grief to rest had been almost as difficult. Turning over and offering her underbelly with a new romance was pretty low on her list of priorities. Just have fun was the name of the game, even if 'fun' wasn't exactly in Levi's vocabulary.

Yet, she loved spending time with him and challenging him to crack, when really she was the one softening. She was the one unfurling under his warm attention.

"I don't want to hurt him." With the story, or in any other way.

Her friend squeezed her hand. "I know. And you don't want to get hurt, either. But let's face it: you haven't responded to any of my efforts to set you up on a date. Or, your mother's. Sure, you're busy and you're focused on your career, but maybe it's because your heart is otherwise engaged?"

"No. Just my hormones," she said stubbornly.

Kinsey scrutinized her closely, but didn't push, thank God. And if she had ... Jordan was unsure her rickety defenses would have held.

23

Tonight on @HockeyGrrl: the man, the legend,
@TheTheoKershaw tells all. #ChicagoRebels #Superglutes

"THEO, WELCOME TO HOCKEY GRRL."

"It's great to be here, Jordan." He fluttered those pretty eyelashes over even prettier green-gold eyes. "At last. I've been trying to get a spot on your pod-thingy for months now, but it seems you'd rather interview everyone else but me."

"Maybe because everyone else is the warm-up act and you're the headliner?"

Theo flashed a toothy grin. "Nice pick-up."

She patted his hand. "Theo, we're seven weeks into the season. How would you assess the Rebels' play so far?"

"A big improvement over the first few weeks. Man, we stunk like Jorgenson's jock strap there for a while. But we always knew it was going to be tough to find our rhythm after DuPre and St. James retired. Feels like we're getting into a groove now."

"I imagine it's been tough for you to get into a groove

yourself. Eighteen months off to recover from your setback—"

"Brain explosion, Jordan. Let's use the scientific term."

"How are you feeling these days?"

"Pretty good. Kind of expectant, though."

"How so?"

His brow wrinkled. "Like I'm waiting for something to happen. Maybe it's with the team or the season or—hell, I don't know. I've been having this weird dream where I'm outside a closed door. I'm searching for the key but my pockets are empty. I try the door knob but it won't turn." He set his jaw earnestly. "What do you think it means?"

Jordan had to cover her mouth to stop from laughing.

Theo gestured "what?" with his hands. He truly had no idea he was podcast gold.

"I don't know much about dream theory, Theo, but it sounds like you have some ideas yourself."

He sighed. "Expectant's the only word I can think of. Something's around the corner—"

"Or behind the door?"

"Right. Maybe it's the Stanley Fucking Cup." He slapped a palm over his mouth. "Shit, sorry. Agh, I'm really sorry!"

"That's okay," she said around her laugh. "We're not monitored by the FCC and I have a warning about salty language at the beginning of every episode. Now I hear you have strong opinions about suit pants and NHL player physiques. Tell me more."

Seventy-eight minutes later, the recording was in the can.

"Hey, that was fun," Theo said, stretching his arms above his head to reveal very nice abs. She loved her job. "We could make a whole series out of my dreams. I've started writing them down."

"Maybe. Good stuff tonight, Theo. Really."

She grabbed his empty beer bottle and headed to the kitchen, throwing out over her shoulder, "You want another one?" *Please say no because Levi is waiting for me to text him when you leave.*

"Probably should head." Dragging a finger along the mantle above her fireplace, he looked at the photos of friends, family, and her wedding day lining the shelf.

She leaned against the entrance to the kitchen, sensing he had something on his mind. "Everything okay?"

"Yeah. So what gives with you and Hunt?"

Her head jerked, her heart with it. "Excuse me?"

"Excuse you? Come on, Hockey Grrl, you know what I'm talking about."

"Really, I don't." She hated denying Levi in this way, but it was necessary for her professional reputation. "We're just working together for the profile. It would be unethical for anything to happen between us."

"Why?"

"Because he's the subject of a story. Because I'm trying to present an objective piece. Because anything more is not a good look."

"Yet, he can't take his eyes off you. Gets moody—or moodier—when you're mentioned. And I see how you sneak those glances at each other on the plane. Is it because of your husband? Is that why you won't jump?"

"Theo! How is that"—she waved a hand ineffectually —"relevant? I just got through saying that I can't be in a relationship with the subject of a story I'm covering."

He nodded slowly, like he was trying to appease the crazy woman in the room. Picking up the photo of her wedding day, he studied it for a few seconds.

"What was your husband like?"

"Josh? He was funny, sweet, a real joker."

"He and Hunt were close?"

"They were, but they're so different from each other. Josh was chatty, easygoing, always up for a laugh. With Levi ..." She considered how to phrase it. "With Levi, every word is precious, every smile earned a prize. He's funnier than I expected, dry and sharply observant. And so stubborn. I want to strangle him sometimes he's so damn stubborn. He gets this look on his face when he's going to tell me something good. Like he has this secret and I need to guess it. And that's usually when I want to kill him the most. Either that or ..." She caught herself, unsure what was coming next but knowing it would reveal too much.

Knowing she already had.

Theo put the photo frame back and for once in his gabby-as-all-get-out life, didn't speak.

Shitshitshit.

This was an absolute disaster. Surging forward, she grabbed the lapels of Theo's leather jacket. "You didn't hear that."

"Think I did." His grin was DEFCON Obnoxious. "I think Hockey Grrl is in love with the NHL's oldest rookie."

Holy Gretzy, she was! For all her denials to Kinsey and her heart, she could no longer keep it buried. "You can't tell him. Please don't breathe a word, Theo. If this got out, my career would be toast. No one would take me seriously in this business."

"Why the hell would I tell him? I'm not going to steal your thunder." He patted her fists, currently crumpling the baby-soft leather of his jacket. "But anything could happen, Jordan. Run over by a bus. Salmonella poisoning. Brain explosion." He pointed at his head and unfurled his fingers. "Maybe go for it because life's too short."

It couldn't be that simple. Nothing ever was.

Especially not with something so complicated as falling in love with your dead husband's best friend who happened to be the subject of a career-defining story you were trying to cover objectively and failing at dismally.

Theo merely smiled, for once not overdoing it. She'd almost rather he teased her to death. He chucked her chin, like she was a kid and he was the wise old gramps who had all the answers. "I'd best be off now. My work here is done."

"And what about you, Theo? Are you going for it now that you have a second chance?"

One hand on the doorknob, he grinned like he was a man with a plan. "I'm not missing a thing."

Levi jumped because someone had thumped the driver side window of his car.

Outside, Kershaw was laughing his head off, so Levi jerked opened the car door, not caring that it slammed right into the defenseman's body.

"Hey, watch the nads!"

"Maybe don't frighten the bejesus out of me." Levi climbed out. "What's up?"

"Jordan's free," Theo said with a knowing grin.

The mere mention of her name sent Levi glancing up to her apartment. He should have parked around the corner and waited for the text, but this neighborhood blew chunks when it came to parking spots and he took the first free space he saw.

"You're smiling like a crazy person, Kershaw. It worries me."

"Have to say I'm enjoying this dance between you two

lovebirds. I just got through trying to get her to fess up. Then what do I find but you waiting here like a lovesick teenager ready to climb the balcony. New nickname, effective immediately. Romeo!"

He knows nothing. "You were talking about me with Jordan?"

"Don't worry, she stuck with name, rank, and serial number." He waved at the car. "Looks like your Special Forces skills are rusty. You suck at the covert ops thing."

"I was just coming over to do more interview stuff." *Extra weak sauce on that shit burger, Hunt.*

"Sure you were. Enjoy your chat." He turned to go then spun back, hands in pockets. "Is Elle at home?"

"Think she's working tonight. Why?"

"Just thought I'd check in on her."

Levi didn't care that he might sound ten grades above hypocritical here. "That's a hard no. You will keep your roving eyes, hands, and dick to yourself, Superglutes. You're the last thing she needs."

"Sure, Dad."

Levi took a step forward. "I'm serious. She's like a sister to me, so you know what that means."

Theo didn't back down. "I know what it means if this was high school."

"Imagine we're still in high school." He didn't feel bad saying it. Elle was family and he sure as hell had known her longer than Kershaw. She'd probably kick this dude's my-pants-don't-fit ass if he made a move, but you never knew when the right combination of factors would point someone down the wrong path. Usually involving tequila.

He watched Theo head down the street, whistling like an asshole. Levi hadn't been lying about the interview—there was some of that to give their meet-ups the gloss of respectability, but it wasn't long before all respectability flew out the window and they were clawing at each other with so much thirst.

He wanted her a little too much.

His phone buzzed with a text he didn't need to see. *Coast is clear.*

But was it? He couldn't claim her properly, shout from the rooftops that she belonged to him. Even when the story was done and the conflict she claimed to care for so much had passed, he doubted he'd get a look in.

It was with this mood that he walked into her apartment. She must have sensed it immediately because her expression turned concerned.

"You okay? Saw you ran into Theo on the street."

"Yeah, he knows about us. Or thinks he does." He stomped into the kitchen and helped himself to a beer. Knocked half of it back while she watched.

"I'm sure he's just guessing, and even if he knows anything, he'll be discreet."

"Kershaw? Discreet?" He shook his head, pissed they were even having this conversation because ultimately he didn't want discretion.

He wanted her and he didn't want to hide it.

"Listen, I need to make sure my audio files are good. Give me a couple of minutes?"

He nodded, not trusting himself to speak.

The few times he'd been here over the last couple of weeks, their time had been frenzied, get-to-the-good-stuff, and he was usually out the door quicker than Petrov's slap shot. Now, he spent a moment getting a feel for Jordan's space, still filled with unpacked boxes. One foot into her new life, one foot in the old.

A quick circuit took him past the mantle, lined with

photos. Her parents and brothers, who he remembered from the wedding and the funeral. A cute photo of her on her graduation, her smile big and infectious, her red hair uncontainable by her cap.

He took a seat on the sofa and placed his beer bottle on a coaster. A photo frame sat face up on the coffee table: Cookie and Jordan on their wedding day.

The silver gilt frame singed when he picked it up, so he put it down immediately. A flash recce told him there was a spot missing on the mantle, which meant that she'd brought it over to the sofa to look at it.

Fuck, what was he doing here again?

She walked out of her office and he knew why: because he'd loved her from the first moment he heard her laugh in that bar and he was biding this time on the off chance she might eventually feel the same.

This shouldn't have been news to his dumb brain. He thought of himself as fairly self-aware so the sight of her now with her fire-red waves and blue-on-blue eyes should not have taken his breath away. Neither should the memory of his friend's wedding day be the catalyst to that heart-destroying realization.

She sat on the sofa and curled her legs up underneath her body. "Tell me why you're in such a bad mood. Don't say Theo pissed you off."

"Wouldn't be hard."

"He was hilarious on the podcast. Every word out of his mouth was gold."

She chuckled to herself, and while he knew his mood was not down to Theo, there was a yearning inside him that was starting to ache unpleasantly. It seemed his heart was beating out his dick in the cage match.

"Remember that day?" She nodded at the photo on the coffee table. "Josh was so nervous."

"You weren't?"

She shook her head. "Not at all. I was so ready to begin the next stage of my life, so excited to be with this one person who got me."

Josh had been as jumpy as a puppet, constantly asking Levi if he was doing the right thing given that he was rarely stateside. Torn between telling his friend he needed to lock this woman down because he was the luckiest sonofabitch alive and a heartsick desire to not bear witness to what would happen next, Levi had asked him the only question that mattered.

Can you imagine a life without her?

Josh—funny, gregarious, loyal Josh—had smiled, a calm infusing him, and that was all she wrote. And when Jordan walked into the army chapel on the base, Josh had muttered "holy shit" loud enough for the entire congregation to hear, which made Jordan laugh all the way down the aisle.

The couple that laughs together …

This was all wrong. "I need to go."

She frowned, producing that little dent between her eyebrows that he wanted to kiss. "What did I say? Was it talking about Josh?"

"No. In fact, you don't talk about him at all. I don't want you to have to tread on eggshells around me."

"Five years is a long time. I'll never forget him but he's not always on my mind." She narrowed her gaze. "When you spend time with me, is it a constant reminder of Josh?"

That was the problem. He rarely thought of him anymore because Jordan was *all* he could think about. She pushed out everything else.

"If being with me just brings up bad memories or guilt,"

she said, "then we should talk about that." Always with the talking. "Do you feel like you're betraying him?"

He couldn't answer that directly, the truth of it too jagged, so he came at it from another angle. "He was my partner. You know how the Special Forces teams are built, with redundancies." The twelve-man detachment consisted of pairs who could each perform the same job. Both Josh and he were engineer sergeants, logistics, demolitions, and sabotage experts.

"You were trained for the same thing," Jordan said. "Doubled each other's skillset, so the team could be split up for missions, if necessary."

"Right. Which means it could just as easily have been me in his place, on the mission that got him killed. Instead, I'm here." He let that hang, the implication crystal. He was Josh's replacement, in the man's life and bed.

Worlds crashed and planets burned while she considered him. He tried to gauge her mood. Guilt. Censure. Hurt.

When she spoke, he heard the note of accusation, just not about the crime he'd expected. "That's not the first time you've said that. Implied that Josh's life was larger or worthier, and no one would mourn you if you were gone. Do you really believe you didn't deserve to come back, Levi? That you don't deserve good things? Because you do. So much."

Sure, life throws curve balls, people end up in places miles from where they started, and you need to work with the gifts you're given. Accept them with some semblance of grace. That didn't mean you had the right to wring every ounce of joy from it.

"I wish ..." The words refused to come.

"What, Levi?" So gentle, so understanding.

"I wish I could have done something different that day

and I don't even know what. Just some other decision that would have resulted in a better outcome. I wish I hadn't envied him so much. That easy laugh, that untroubled air. But the worst of it is that if he was here, I wouldn't be. Not that I'd be gone or dead, but I wouldn't be with you. Like this. Mostly I wish I was a better person, who doesn't rejoice at the opportunity to be with his best friend's girl when his best friend can't be."

Her eyes filled with liquid pain. "Oh, Levi."

Comforting her was his overwhelming instinct, but it would also be a sneaky way to make himself feel better. He didn't deserve that.

"I should go."

"Levi, don't."

"Don't what?"

"Leave."

Oh, he heard too much in that plea, and though the core of him knew she just meant now, tonight, this painful moment, a small, usually inaccessible part of him wished it meant never.

"Jord—"

She kissed him, cutting off her name, all rational thought, and any hope he had of surviving her. He pulled her over his lap, so she straddled him, and gripped the hem of her T-shirt. Up, up, and away over the back of the sofa. He wanted to take his time, enjoy the sweet taste of her skin, how she melted under his tongue, but she had other ideas.

Grinding into his erection, she moved her mouth to his jaw, his earlobe, his neck and sucked on the pulse beating here. It drove him wild.

A plump of her breast popped it out of the cup, so he took the gift on offer and sipped on one rosy nipple.

"Levi," she moaned, and the way she said it cracked

something inside him. Life and love poured out, flooding his veins with hope. He was here. He had survived.

And she was his prize.

No contract, no goal, no cup could compete.

There was an excellent chance they were going to dry hump each other to completion. Nakedness was the next objective, and he achieved it for them both in record time. No question of heading to the bedroom. They had all they needed right here.

Each other.

Once he'd secured the condom, she eased onto him while he thrust up, their desire meeting in the middle. A slow, languid fuck. But this was more. Looking into her lust-stoked eyes, he tried to hold on to this moment. Imprint his love on her because there was no question he adored her.

He pressed a hand between their bodies, seeking her clit, needing to see her go over. This is what he could give her. Those smoky blues ignited just as her pussy clenched hard and fluttered on her moan.

Her mouth sought his, a kiss deep and true. Still, she moved up and down, up and down, bringing him closer, binding him to her. Words had no place here. Nothing he could say would ever top what his body communicated. His physical prowess was the only foundation he could rely on.

That's where he was these days. Sure in the Berets, surer on the ice, but a mess of indecision around her. Yet he knew that this was what he was built for.

She was what he was built for.

With her wrapped around his body, he let himself believe he deserved her, here, now, and forever. He let himself believe.

24

Tune in to @SportsFocus in prime time for @BigDogDawson's interview with @HockeyGrrl. We'll be talking women in the media, the bad boys of hockey, and the dirt on the @ChiRebels' Levi Hunt!

JORDAN WISHED to hell and back she hadn't worn this suit. The skirt was too tight. (*Press box mini-macarons, why can't I quit you?*) The fabric was supposed to wick but not today, apparently. Sweat poured off her, rivulets of stink flowing toward Fear River.

She took off the jacket ... and immediately put it back on. Those pit stains were not how she wanted to make her national TV debut.

Her phone rang and she answered because talking to someone, anyone, was better than confronting her underarm situation. In ten minutes, Coby Dawson would interview her live on SportsFocus.

"Baby, how's it going?"

Oh, God, that voice. "I'm a mess, Levi. A sweaty, shaking,

tongue-tied mess." She continued to babble. "I'm too hot but I can't take off my jacket because it's bad."

He chuckled.

"Not funny. I stink, both literally and figuratively!"

"No, you don't. Well I can't say for sure on the literal. But for the figurative, I know for a fact that you are amazing. You have something important to say and you have a big forum in which to say it. I'm so proud of you."

Hearing him say that didn't exactly calm her down but it helped. He always did. The man had become her rock.

Two days had passed since he'd confessed to his guilt over Josh and they'd not had a chance to truly debrief. She could have shared the depth of her feelings for him then, but it seemed too convenient, a way to make him feel better in that moment instead of a true acknowledgment of her love.

And yes, she was in love.

She didn't want to be, not because Levi wasn't wonderful. He was. But this profile demanded a more critical eye and not the love/lust-goggles she was wearing at the moment. Her fledgling career would die in a fireball of you-did-*what*-with-your-subject if she came clean now. Any heartfelt confessions would have to wait until she and her career were on firmer ground.

This was also one of the reasons why she'd agreed to come on SportsFocus, despite her gut warning her against it: if she could score a win with a more newsworthy story, then people might not question the fluff factor of her too-friendly profile on one Levi Hunt.

She blew out a breath, feeling clear-eyed and focused for the first time in months. "Thank you for talking me down, Levi. For being here for me."

"Don't forget the orgasms."

She giggled. "And for the orgasms."

"Jordan, two minutes," an assistant called out. She'd already forgotten her name which demonstrated how truly nervous she was. She never forgot people's names!

Thinking about normal stuff might help her jitters.

"You feel good about tonight's game?" The Rebels were playing in Boston, a mere two hours away from where she was taping the interview for SportsFocus. Levi should be getting ready for the warm-up instead of talking to her.

"Yeah, but Petrov's knee is acting up. He's on IR."

"Oh no! Who's got the captain's patch? You?"

"Not a chance. Burnett. He totally deserves it."

"Right, that's good." She'd never revealed that she'd overheard Harper discussing Levi as captain material. He was under enough pressure. "It'll be you one day."

"I expect so."

This was different—Levi sounded more confident in his ability to tread that path.

The assistant called out, "Jordan, we need you!"

"I've got to go," she whispered. "Wish me luck."

"You don't need it. I'll be watching you after the game and imagining you naked."

She giggled. "That's supposed to be my coping strategy. Bye, Levi."

"Bye, Ms. Sunshine."

COBY HAD his thoughtful face on. "Tell us more about what you and your colleagues—our colleagues—have experienced."

Our colleagues. Nice.

The studio was pumping out furnace-levels of heat and

Jordan suspected her face looked like a shiny balloon in a red wig. But Coby had put her at ease, so other than her sweat glands working overtime, she felt good about the interview so far.

"Female sports reporters across the board are feeling the pinch, Coby—and often that's literally from some handsy player, coach, or agent. I'm not saying that every man in professional sports is guilty but it's enough of a problem that women in these careers are reconsidering their tracks, ambitions, and futures."

"We've heard stories about pro-athletes behaving badly," Coby said. "The NFL has a domestic violence problem. The MLB and NBA aren't immune, either. We don't hear as much about it in hockey, maybe because the guys are able to work off their energy more effectively on the ice." He tilted his head, watching for her reaction to that cockamamie theory.

"Talk to the women reporting on the NHL, AHL, and even NCAA. Hockey is just as problematic."

"You've experienced it?"

"I have. Sleazy comments. Inappropriate invitations. Information requests that invariably demand something in return."

Coby looked puzzled. "But this is a quid pro quo business. Every relationship where information has value will expect that."

"Where the currency for that information is sex? Why is that acceptable? There's an abiding attitude of boys will be boys, mostly because the stakeholders are by and large in possession of a penis." She winced. "Sorry, can I say penis?"

"Say it all you want, Jordan."

So she'd walked into that one. Remembering the conversation they'd had in the DC press box and the argument he'd made to entice her onto his show, she switched to a language all businesses could understand: money.

"The leagues need to start realizing that the demographics are changing. Women often control household budgets, and they decide where discretionary income should be spent, whether that's after-school sports clubs for their kids, tickets to the pro games, or pricey merch. Female viewership is increasing and parents won't stand for letting their daughters participate in a sport that doesn't step up and show respect."

"But it's not just a woman problem, is it, Jordan?"

She exhaled, relieved he'd taken the baton and run with it. "No, Coby, it's a human problem. We need to be setting examples for our children that guys shouldn't get a pass on obnoxious behavior because they have skills with a hockey stick or a pigskin or a bat. And it applies across the board—on the field and in the front office."

"Speaking of diverse front offices, maybe the Rebels can set the example for other teams." He followed that with another understanding head-tilt. "You've been working closely with the Rebels this season. Are things different over there?"

"It might be the influence of all the estrogen at the top, but this team seems to have it right when it comes to gender dynamics. I haven't witnessed any examples of toxic masculinity. The guys were nothing but respectful to me at all times."

"So they had no idea you were spying on them, investigating this story on players-behaving-badly while ostensibly working up a profile on Levi Hunt?"

Ping. Her threat alarm sounded, not at full-scale but enough to put her on defense. "They knew I was a reporter. It was hardly an undercover gig."

"Sure, but shooting the breeze to get a feel for the team dynamic as color for your piece on Hunt is a bit different than having a female reporter note everything out of the players' mouths to check against an anti-feminist bingo card. Or some people could see it like that."

Some people? "Like I said, the Rebels approved my being embedded with the team. Nothing was off the table. Harper Chase was very clear about that."

"Well, they probably have little to fear in terms of toxic masculinity. Some people might say it's because there isn't any masculinity over there at all."

Jordan pulled up short. Again, there was the mention of *some people*, this time tied to a snide comment about masculinity. "I don't follow."

"The team is run by women who seem to have all the players under their heels." He laughed. Jordan didn't. "It's certainly introduced an unusual culture and might make fans question the team's killer instinct."

Was this a Devil's Advocate strategy with him deliberately taking the counterpoint so her argument stood stronger? If so, she wished he'd run it by her first.

"If you're implying only men can have killer instincts, you must have been under a rock four seasons ago when the Rebels won the Cup the first year the Chase sisters were in charge. They also have Dante Moretti as their GM, a former defenseman with a great record before he turned to management."

"Easily attributable to a fluke. The stars aligned for one good year. Now they've lost two of their prime players who are staying home to play house husbands instead of out on the ice where they're needed."

"Coby, with all due respect, you sound like an idiot."

He laughed again, holding his hands up in that age-old

gesture of *Whoa, calm down, hysterical female*! But there was something else, a deadening of his eyes. He didn't like being called out on his own show. Good old Coby was not such a friend to the ladies after all.

It was at this point she realized that she'd brought a knife to a gunfight.

"Fair enough." Coby gave that sly smile that told her she'd better don her catcher's mitt because here come the fastballs. "Harper and company have certainly done wonders for the Rebels, which is amazing considering what happened to her."

"What happened to her ...?" Jordan prompted when Coby left it hanging.

"It's a true testament to her strength or maybe the Chase genes that she was able to rise above being assaulted by a player before she inherited the team. Anyone would understand if she wasn't able to assume that mantle."

Jordan's blood turned to ice in her veins. "I'm afraid you have me at a disadvantage, Coby."

"Oh, really?" Coby looked down at a piece of paper, consulting notes she suspected he knew by heart. "My source tells me that Harper Chase, current CEO of the Chicago Rebels, was assaulted by a Rebels player several years ago. And that the organization hushed it up by trading him out. Essentially made him someone else's problem. Not exactly the pro-women, call-out-bad-behavior stance you're painting for the team."

She swallowed. Hard. She had no idea where he was getting his information and given that she had nothing on the record from Harper, she was not about to confirm or deny.

"You'll have to take that up with the Rebels front office.

As I said, I've witnessed nothing but professionalism in my dealings with them."

He nodded. "Right, professionalism. Let's talk about your profile of Levi Hunt, the latest addition to the Rebels. How's that going?"

Feeling whiplashed, she was glad to step out of her defending-female-run-teams role, if only for a moment while she caught her breath. "Good. It's been fascinating to travel with the team and witness the onboarding, so to speak, of a new and exciting talent in the league."

"Hunt's hard to read, would you say?"

"At first. But getting to know him and the rest of the crew over the last few weeks has been really rewarding."

"But you had a leg up there, Jordan. He was a friend of your husband's."

She narrowed slitty eyes of death at Coby, making it clear she didn't enjoy this line of inquiry. "I knew him briefly from before."

"And that helped you get this plum assignment."

"Helped *when* I got this plum assignment, Coby. That connection meant the Rebels management were more open to having a reporter embed with the team. Levi would be more likely to trust someone he knew, who understood where he was coming from and the sacrifice that he and his unit had made."

Coby reached his hand over to cover hers. "We're grateful for your husband's service."

You. Fucker. She pulled her hand away, knowing it came off as childish but not caring. "Thank you."

Anxious to get back on track after that ambush, she tried to line up her ducks. The guy had basically said she got the assignment because of her connection to Levi—which was true.

But.

This business was as much about who you knew and who you could trust. Levi trusted her and she'd worked that to her benefit. Even he knew that. What she didn't enjoy was the underlying, insidious accusation.

You beat a male reporter to this story by flashing the woman card.

You beat me.

Coby wasn't done. "What would he think of you and Hunt?"

"Me and—"

"Your husband was a close friend of Levi's. Do you think you have his blessing?"

Her heart pounded, and those rivers of sweat overflowed their banks. Surely, the man wasn't going there.

She chose to interpret it another way. "I think Josh would be happy that I'm following my dream to report on a sport I love."

"Oh, I've no doubt. Especially since you've come a long way in such a short time."

She balled her fist, then, worried about how it would look on camera, she put it in her lap. Nails dugs deep into her palms, sharp enough to break skin. "I've worked hard, as have a lot of female reporters." *Yet we're still getting dissed by pricks like you.*

"Sure. Still. As a newbie on the pro-league scene, there's bound to be a lot of jealousy and questions wondering how you gained such quick acceptance and the trust of a notoriously guarded player. But it was probably easier to gain that trust since you and he have a special relationship."

Time to shut this offensive play down. "So you've said. In fact, you've said or insinuated several times that my meteoric rise is suspicious and that there has to be a reason why

I've been blessed with this assignment. Maybe you should be clearer about what you're accusing me of."

Coby's expression said that crazy Jordan must be completely misunderstanding him.

Bring out the oil for the gaslights, buddy.

"Not accusing you of anything, Jordan. I think it's great that you've found happiness again, though I'm guessing there might be some infraction of an unspoken code here. Perhaps it doesn't bother Hunt and you've every right to seek solace where you can. *I* don't have a problem with it, but given some of concerns you brought to light here today about female reporters being expected to provide favors for information, some people might say a relationship with a player you're covering for a story weakens your argument."

Not me, though, his expression said. *I'm on your side and the side of women everywhere.*

Shock throttled the words in her throat.

Dawson filled the silence. "With a man as private as Hunt, he's not going to reveal his troubled history to just anyone. The tough upbringing that included homelessness, losing his father to pneumonia while they were both living on the streets, and then the death of a fellow soldier, your husband, who was also a good friend."

Her mind whirred, fumbling for the correct response here. As far as she knew, Levi's history was not common knowledge. His friendship with Josh was known but everything else? This was Levi's very private life that Dawson was splashing around on live TV.

"I'm not here to talk about Levi's past or my relationship with him. I'm not sure where you're getting your information—"

"From you, Jordan." He held up the paper in his hand. "This is all background research *you've* done on Levi Hunt."

No no no ... "I—I didn't tell you that."

"So, it's not true, then? How Levi's mom left him when he was a kid, his dad drank his way out of a roof over their head, they sometimes stayed the night at a gym where Hunt Sr. worked. It's all in your notes, Jordan." He consulted those damn papers on his desk.

Were those her notes? But, how?

"Now he's paying it forward by volunteering at a Chicago homeless shelter. Of course, you wouldn't know any of this if you weren't so close to Levi, so kudos there. It's just ..." He grimaced, like this was *so* awkward to bring up. "It looks like you're getting that scoop any way you can."

Fury fueled her response at last. "You pri—"

"Hold that thought, Jordan. Let's take a break and delve deeper when we come back."

Later Jordan would learn that her lunge for Coby Dawson was *not* caught live on camera. Damn seven second delay.

She tightened her grip on his tie, choking it good, hoping that, by the time the commercial break was over, she'd manage to extinguish all life from his smug, entitled, assholic face.

He sputtered. "Hey!"

Someone restrained her, forcing her to release the turd. "Who the fuck do you think you are, Dawson? Are you really so pissed that I got this story that you'll do anything to take me down?"

"Come on, honey. We all know how you got this story. Maybe you and Hunt recently reconnected. Maybe you've been banging him since your husband bought the farm. I don't know and I don't care. But don't tell me that you got it from *working hard*"—he added air quotes—"and following the story where it leads. You opened your legs and the words started flowing."

She suspected her gaping mouth made her look oxygen-deprived. What a vile, disgusting excuse for a human being. *Should have trusted your instincts.*

"I didn't tell you anything about Levi. Where did you get that information?" It was far too specific to have come from anyone but her.

"A reporter can't reveal his sources, Jordan. Even if it's another reporter." He winked and she threw up a little in her mouth.

Then it hit her. The DC game. She'd stepped out of the press box, and when she returned, her laptop was a few inches out of place while Coby "accessed" the outlet. Accessed her files, more like.

He must have seen those early, aborted drafts and read her take on the Harper/Stroger situation. She'd made notes of her recording, noodling about a strategy to bring the Rebels CEO into her confidence.

Then the icing on this shit cake: Coby Asshat Dawson had capitalized on the opportunity by dropping a juicy nugget of gossip about the acquisition of Gunnar Bond and flattering Jordan with an invitation to go national with the story of her heart. To maybe even get an on-camera gig at ESP-fucking-N. And she'd fallen for it like a dog in heat.

She was the reason Coby knew about Stroger assaulting Harper.

She was the reason he had the inside track on Levi's deepest, most painful secrets.

She was the reason she'd be remembered as the reporter who tanked her career on live TV.

"Everyone can see what you did here, Dawson. You flashed your tiny dick because your ego got hurt."

His smile was oily. "When we come back, Jordan, we'll be running a story we did earlier on LeBron. I'd ask you to stay but I'd rather we didn't get into a mud-slinging match that detracts from the important issues that you've raised today. Thanks for doing your part."

He gestured over her shoulder to a pair of beefy security guys, on hand to escort her off the set.

Perfect.

25

Go @BigDogDawson! My man rips @HockeyGrrl a new one and
shows why girls should stick to tennis and soccer.
#TheMenAreTalking

ONE GOAL and two assists in a 5-2 win against Boston was undoubtedly the highlight of Levi's so-far brief professional career in the NHL. Afterward, in the visitors' locker room, he sat on the bench, breathing slowly and letting his body absorb the changes. He felt hopeful, like he finally knew where he belonged.

It might have something to do with his practices with DuPre and St. James. It might be the fact Coach had given him multiple shifts, and he'd honored that choice with his play. It might even be his progress with the pet program at the homeless shelter—Harper was considering making a donation on behalf of the team.

But deep down, he knew why hope was truly springing and his heart was brimming over.

This rookie was in love.

Hearing Jordan tell him that he was as deserving as

anyone of good things had unraveled something, like a thread on a sweater. She hadn't recoiled when he expressed his envy of Josh's life, just understood that this ugliness was part and parcel of who he was. He'd always glossed over his shame at where he came from, assumed his God-given talent on the ice was accidental, taken for granted that a woman like Jordan could never accept him as worthy of love. Worthy of her.

As soon as that damn profile was done, Levi would be telling Jordan Cooke exactly what he thought of her. Until then, he'd love her on the down low, like he'd been doing for years. He could be patient a little longer.

First they had some locker-room press stuff to get through. He'd become better at this, which he credited to his regular grilling by his favorite lady of the press. He couldn't wait to see how her interview went because damn, she deserved it after all her hard work.

The guy from the *Boston Trib* spoke first. "Care to comment on reports of your rumored relationship with sports reporter, Jordan Cooke, who was married to one of your unit mates in the Navy SEALs?"

Wait, what? He opened his mouth to respond only to hear, "It was the Green Berets," in the dark voice of Dante Moretti. "Levi won't be taking questions tonight."

Scenting blood in the water, the rest of them descended.

"How has your stint of homelessness as a kid shaped you, Levi?"

"Would Sergeant Engineer Cooke have given his blessing to you and Jordan?"

"Is it true that's how she got her job at Chicago SportsNet? Her connection to you?"

He turned at that last one, ready to answer in a way that would satisfy his gut, only to be led away by Dante.

"Come on, Hunt. Time to head to the airport."

"What the hell was that about? How did they know about ...?" Any of it?

Dante remained stone-faced. "I'll tell you on the bus."

Ten minutes later, Levi had watched Jordan's Sports-Focus interview on Dante's phone and was trying to make sense of it. He peered up at their GM, the only other person on the bus. Apparently his teammates had stayed behind to draw the fire that should have been coming his way.

"What a prick."

"Dawson? Oh, yeah, the guy's a *gabbagul*." Dante took back his phone. "I assume you gave her all that information?"

Levi's pulse boomed, scrabbling to defend his woman. "The background stuff on me, yes. But she promised not to use any of it. She swore she'd only stick to hockey."

"And you believed her?"

Of course he did. They were operating at a level of trust he'd only ever had with his team back in the Berets, but more than that. He trusted Jordan with his heart.

"Jordan wouldn't do that."

Dante looked skeptical. "I've had my fair share of dealings with the press. They're not the most ethical bunch, so assuming anything is off the record is usually a mistake. When I came out, they were vicious. And as for Cade ..." He shook his head, remembered anger setting his mouth in a grim line. "To be honest, what Dawson said about you is less of an issue than the story he has on Harper. It was before my time but the organization should have reported what happened to her and punished the player in question."

In the heat of thinking how this affected himself, he'd forgotten about Harper. That must be related to what Remy had told him—how he'd smacked down Stroger for hurting his wife.

"Remy mentioned the Harper incident to me, not in any detail. But I promise I didn't breathe a word of it to Jordan." Anger surged in his chest. What was more concerning is that he might have eventually told her. He'd felt comfortable enough with her to confide his deepest fears, his heartfelt dreams. Why not someone else's pain and heartbreak?

He wanted so badly to believe that Jordan had been ambushed. "She sounded shocked when Dawson brought it up. My stuff. Harper's."

"Maybe. But then that could be a way to keep her hands clean in all of this. She slips him the information, acts like it's being revealed without her knowledge. Next thing we see Jordan's got a job at ESPN to atone for Dawson being a jerk and ratings are through the roof."

That was a cynical take. But Dante's job was to protect the team. He was understandably upset about how the Rebels were portrayed: protecting an abuser was never a good look.

Erik poked his head above the stairwell of the bus entrance. "Can we come in? It's colder than a gorilla's nut sac out here."

"Yeah, come on," Dante said with a final nod at Levi.

Soon the bus was full and on its way to Hanscom Field, about ten miles outside of Boston, to catch the chartered flight back to Chicago. All around him, the buzz of post-win happy was keeping the team in good spirits. Levi wanted to watch the interview again, so he put in earbuds and cranked it up on his phone. Less than a minute in and before it got combative, Theo sat beside him.

"So wanna tell me what the fuck happened on Sports-Focus tonight?"

With a bud out of his right ear, Levi could hear Jordan's voice humming through the bus on some of the other players' phones.

"You need me to do a play-by-play?"

"So, is that what she's been doing all this time? Spying on us?"

The poor guy sounded so wounded. "She's a reporter, Kershaw. Her job is to prod, find a weakness, and exploit it."

That didn't come out right. He meant that was how she'd approached the embedding assignment.

"Is it true what Dawson said? About you being homeless as a kid?"

"I had a disruptive childhood. Like lots of kids." How did Coby Dawson have that information? She'd looked surprised, and if Theo would just leave him the fuck alone, he could examine her expressions and make up his mind about whether he had reason to be pissed with her.

"Yeah, I hear you." Accepting that, Theo scrubbed a hand through his hair. "She did say that we were respectful, so there's that. Maybe it's not so bad. I apologized to her that one time and she's always seemed really cool around us. Just one of the guys." After a moment he seemed to realize that this wasn't all about him. "And that stuff about Ms. Chase. You think that's true? Any idea who it was?"

"We don't know if any of it is true. Reporters make up crap all the time, Theo. Let PR handle it." He pulled out his other earbud, resigned to not getting any peace. "So, you had a good game tonight. Some great blocks in that last period."

Hoping to get his teammate's mind off the negative, Levi put his problems aside and listened while Theo launched into a debrief of the game, which lasted all the way to the airport. This late, the smaller airports were usually empty, and tonight was no different, except for the vision standing near the check-in desk.

Jordan.

She was on her phone, her expression anxious, her energy tense. All he wanted to do was hold her tight, tell her he had her back, then order the pilot to fly over Bristol so he could parachute into Dawson's back yard and take that fucker out.

Levi might be the only guy within a five-mile radius qualified to actually do that.

"Jordan." He rushed over to her, ready to take her in his arms, but she stiffened on seeing him.

Her face told him: *back off, not in front of the team.*

It's not about you, Hunt. "You okay? Did you drive here?"

"ESPN was all class. Gave me a car to take me wherever I wanted." Tears welled as she peeked around his shoulder at the team, gathered near the gate to the plane, trying not to be nosy and doing a terrible job at it. Levi wished they'd hurry up and board, so he could be alone with her.

"You got shafted, baby. Come on, we can talk on the plane. Let me take care of you."

Let me love you.

"I don't know if that's such a good idea. I came here because I wanted you to know I didn't tell him any of that stuff about your upbringing. I swear."

Relief flooded him. He'd known she never would, not even to get a shot at this interview with ESPN or the chance of a better job. Still, he had questions that needed to be answered. "But he knew about it, Jordan. How?"

She swiped at a stray tear, and his palms itched with the need to comfort her. "One night during the DC game, he was alone with my computer for a few minutes while I was in the restroom. He must have read my early drafts. My notes on Harper. I've been trying to call her but she won't pick up."

A nagging unease burned in his chest. "You had drafts of the story, ones that included all the things I didn't want mentioned, and you left them lying around?"

"They were on my computer! He stole them."

"But you shouldn't have written them down at all." Anger gripped him like a flash storm. He looked over his shoulder. The team had left the boarding area, though one of the travel assistants remained behind. "We'll be there in a couple of minutes, Amy," he called over to her, trying to use the moment of not looking at this woman he loved to calm his emotions. "Go ahead."

When he turned back to Jordan, her eyes were wild, her stance that of a cornered animal. "I wrote them down because I write everything down. It's my process—figure out what I can use, chisel away at the hunk of marble to get to the Michelangelo."

Levi hauled in a breath, running it through his mind. So she made a mistake. People made mistakes all the time.

"He saw how upset I got when you were hit hard a few games ago," Jordan said. "I think that's how he knew about you and me. Or he guessed. And he's not wrong. I slept with a player and now I have a story, just like he said. I'm a laughing stock."

His heart cracked at how she connected the dots, and his next words sounded like they came from someone else. "You're worried about looking bad?"

"Yes! You know I've always been concerned with that and how it could affect my career."

"Because I'm just a job to you."

"You—you *were*!" She censored herself, but it was too

late. She'd been about to say "are." "I care about you, too. You've got to know that, but this job is *everything* to me."

This shouldn't have been news. She was upfront about it from the beginning: why she got the job, why they couldn't be seen together, why she wasn't interested in dating. But he'd thought they were moving beyond that and that she saw him as more than a stepping stone.

"You didn't admit anything to Dawson. Just keep denying and you're fine." He hated the resignation in his tone, how the knowledge that it would come to this felt inevitable. She'd done that. Given him hope, then ripped it right from under him.

She frowned at his take on it. "The worst of it is that it drew focus from the real story. I went on SportsFocus to talk about how women should be treated equal and we shouldn't need to pay for play, where payment is in the form of our bodies."

"And here you are proving that's how a woman gets ahead. According to Dawson."

She cut him a frosty look. "That's not what I was doing. I didn't sleep with you to get a story."

"Dawson was right about why you got the job, though. Because of our connection." Levi couldn't believe he was agreeing with that jerk.

"I was honest with you about that."

She was, then she'd employed some dirty tactics to squeeze all she could from that connection when it didn't bear fruit immediately. "But when I wasn't as forthcoming as you wanted, you needled. Poked away. Kept bringing up that kiss, all to provoke a reaction. So I could think of nothing else but touching and tasting you."

"I was mad at you for being a closed-off jerk, but I didn't deliberately try to provoke you into kissing me so you'd suddenly become an open book. If that's all it takes, I'd kiss every player in the NHL! *Hey everyone, free blowjobs, I need a story.*"

He folded his arms. "If it looks like a duck—"

"How about if it looks like a dick? Don't do this, Levi."

"Do what? Call you out on your tactics? Tell me. Would you even be speaking to me if it wasn't for this assignment?"

"Probably not."

Her ready agreement surprised him. He'd expected her to be wishy-washy about it.

"But lots of people start out not liking each other," she continued. "It's the premise for every rom-com ever written. The last time we met was weird and awkward and you've always acted like you enjoy my company about as much as a bowl of dicks. Without the story, I probably wouldn't have sought you out, but the story is not the reason I slept with you, you dummy!"

"No?"

Her eyes flashed. "No! It was just the inciting event. I had sex with you because I thought you were hot and sweet, and spending more time with you—both in and out of bed— revealed a side of you I never knew existed."

"The side that could get you a scoop." The side he kept hidden along with the pain and shame.

Had he really thought he could show her all that and *not* have her use it to get ahead? Her career meant everything to her. She'd been completely honest about *that*.

"You were annoyed that I refused to give up all the good stuff, all the human interest junk. But you found a way. Certainly puts you in prime position for a job at ESPN. Not only do you have the goods on me, you also have it on Harper and the Rebels."

She threw up her hands. "Which I didn't pass on to

Dawson! Can't you see that I was screwed over as much as you here?"

Maybe, maybe not. He didn't know what to believe anymore. "I might be able to see past the betrayal of *my* secrets, Jordan. I'm just a dumb fool who fell for the wrong girl, after all. But using Harper like that to get your pound of flesh? Anything for the story, right?"

Her nostrils flared. He knew he was pushing her, but he didn't care. She would never be here if she didn't need that story, and he was a bastard for using that weakness of hers, that need to make her mark, to make his mark on her.

"Well, that didn't take long," she said.

"What didn't?"

"You reverting to your factory settings. Supreme asshole."

It shouldn't have hurt. He'd asked for it after all. But he'd spent the last couple of months upending her view of him that for it to come back around to this just proved he hadn't deserved it in the first place. One of those self-fulfilling prophecies.

"I guess Ms. Sunshine doesn't like hearing the truth. Admit it, Jordan. This—" He whipped his hand through the air between them, hard so as to stop the shake. "This would not have happened without your assignment. You needed to pry me apart to get the good stuff and you figured out a way. You knew I wanted you. That I've always wanted you."

Awareness flared in her eyes, and he realized his mistake.

I've always wanted you.

He could mean since the moment she'd walked into the Rebels locker room and they'd reconnected, but that wasn't it—and she knew it.

Even now, she was still capable of unearthing his rawest secrets.

She stepped in close, her mouth trembling so much he wanted to stop it with his thumb. Soothe and protect her from anything that would hurt her, including him.

Especially him.

"Yeah, I figured you always had a crush on me, Levi." Sarcasm dripped off words that shredded him. "I figured it wouldn't be so hard for me to turn that crush against you and get that lockbox you call a heart to open right up. A little flirting with your teammates to drive you crazy. A few prods and pokes to get you riled." She touched his chest, fanned her hand over the heart that beat for her. Broke for her. "There was never any question of me falling for you. Not really."

He couldn't help himself. Assholes be assholin'. "Why would you? You've got places to be and people to step on to get there."

That had the desired effect. Because not even Ms. Sunshine herself, a walking-talking smiley face, the woman who wore her heart on her sleeve then complained about the bloodied shirt, had armor enough for a blow like that.

She drew a shuddering breath and balled her hand, the one over his heart, into a fist. "Ah, Sergeant Engineer Hunt, you know me so well." The break in her voice sounded not unlike his heart shattering into a million fragments.

It took him a full two minutes to realize he was alone.

26

CHASE MANOR ON CHICAGO'S NORTH SHORE on a cold December morning was not where Jordan wanted to be, but alas she had an unpleasant duty to perform. The air was frigid enough to freeze her tears. Fortunately she didn't have to worry about that.

She was all cried out.

Levi had made her cry, and she'd spent half of yesterday on the phone with Kinsey—who had the patience of a saint —and the evening in the company of her good friend, Jose Cuervo. Needless to say, neither she nor her pounding head were fit for stop one of the apology tour to the burbs. She only hoped they didn't set the estate's dogs on her.

Flicking a nervous glance over her shoulder, she stepped closer to the big oak door and listened for a 'Release the hounds' order to echo through the nippy air. Thankfully, the door flew open, presenting her with a sight that should have cheered her: a shirtless Remy DuPre toting a cherub-faced toddler.

"Jordan." He frowned, then his good manners kicked in. "Come in."

"Thanks." She followed him and closed the large door behind her. "Who's this angel?"

"This anti-angel is Madeleine. We call her Maddy, eh, *petite*?" He squinted at Jordan. "You okay?"

She must look awful. "Just a bit tired."

"No, I mean after that interview. That motherfu—" He smiled at his little girl, blew out a breath, and lowered his voice. "Dawson needs to be hung, drawn, and quartered for that stunt he pulled on you."

Oh. She'd expected they'd be furious with her. Harper hadn't returned any of her messages. Only a sneaky call to Casey, Harper's PA, had revealed that the Rebels' boss was working from home today.

"Come on through to the kitchen."

In the cozy, warm kitchen with more of those French-inspired touches, Harper was busy cutting up toast for her three-year old twins, Amelie and Giselle. The Rebels CEO in a domestic setting didn't feel as off as Jordan had expected. If anything, it inspired a jolt of envy at seeing this woman who seemed to have it all worked out.

Harper raised her gaze, a humanizing smudge of Nutella on her chin. "Honey, who was—oh! Jordan."

"Hi, Harper. I'm hoping we could chat."

Remy put Maddy into a high chair. "Okay, *mes enfants terribles*, who's ready for ... waffles?"

All three kids cheered. Jordan wouldn't mind a Remy-made waffle herself.

The hot Cajun kissed his wife, wiping the Nutella at the same time with his thumb, and sucking it into his mouth. It was nothing, really, but the intimacy had Jordan averting her eyes.

"I got this, *minou*. Go make the big bucks."

Smiling, Harper grabbed a coffee mug and gestured to the pot. "Jordan?"

Happy that Harper's annoyance didn't extend to denying coffee privileges, Jordan accepted a cup with thanks. Beverages in hand, they headed to a living room/den and sat on a careworn sofa.

"What does 'minou' mean?"

Harper colored slightly. "Oh, just a Cajun term of endearment." With her usual laser-eyed focus, she studied Jordan over the rim of her cup. "Well, *that* probably didn't go the way you expected."

"Harper, I'm so sorry. I promise I did not tell Dawson a thing. He somehow read my notes—"

"So you said in your multiple voice, text, and email messages. You had these notes because you'd planned to write up a story on what happened all those years ago? And how did you even hear about it? I was too annoyed to ask about it before." Jordan's heart sank at how hurt the usually stoic woman sounded.

"I overheard you and Isobel discussing it one night in the restroom before a game. I've been collecting stories about women in the pro-sports space and what happened to you was just one more data point. I would never have revealed it without your permission. You've got to know that."

Harper held her gaze, those moss-green eyes playing lie detector. After an eternity while Jordan questioned her very reason for living, Harper said, "Unfortunately, Dawson doesn't have such scruples, and now, we're dealing with the fallout. Despite the fact it happened during my father's tenure as boss and I was young, foolish, and desperate to put it behind me, it still looks like we covered it up. We sent a bad apple away so he couldn't contaminate our barrel any longer and to hell with all the other barrels."

"People will understand you not wanting it to get out."

"Perhaps." She took a sip of her coffee, then said with feeling, "That SportsFocus interview was a complete hatchet job."

Jordan had never felt such relief. "The man was determined to get his scoop at the expense of mine."

"Any truth to the charge?"

"That I'm using my vagina to get a story? Oh, 100%!" Anger rose swiftly, though it wasn't all for Coby Dawson. She had plenty of arrows in her quiver for Levi, who had essentially jumped onto Dawson's bandwagon.

"You were ambushed so a poster boy for male privilege could make a point. Who cares if you are involved with a player? Does your ability to write a good story or game report suddenly turn to goo because you're getting some hot hockey player lovin'?"

"It's not exactly above board, Harper."

Harper's eyes almost rolled into the back of her head. "I'm living proof that it does not matter. I fell in love with a player on my team and hell, did I resist. I was so afraid I'd be judged by the all-male hockey establishment when really my happiness with Remy made me stronger. Love made me better at my job."

Agitated, Jordan stood and marched a few steps, hands on hips. "That all sounds nice, but perception is reality here. I look like a woman who can't control her hormones."

Harper gave a wry smile. "I know it's not how you wanted it to come out, but it was going to happen eventually, wasn't it?"

"I—I don't know. If Levi and I didn't have a future together, then there would've been no need to spill. We would have just chalked it up to one of those things. Hot hockey player lovin' received, story in the bag, no muss, no fuss."

"And that's what you wanted?"

Jordan shrugged helplessly. "No. I've been falling for him, but I didn't know how he felt." Until seeing how hurt he was last night.

Harper looked sympathetic, but remained silent.

"How Dawson portrayed it is exactly how your star rookie thinks it went down. That every moment we spent together was for the story."

Jordan couldn't believe that Levi would prefer to accept she'd been using him above all else. She could ignore trolls like Dawson for their snide comments about how she got stories. Fanboys calling her "whore" and worse on social media could be dispatched with a Luke Skywalker dust-off-my-shoulder GIF. But for Levi to side with the enemy and basically agree that this was her MO?

That killed her.

Harper raised her eyes to the ceiling. "Men are such dumb creatures, sometimes."

Now Jordan felt a need to defend Levi. Her brain could barely keep up. "To be fair, it started out that way ... not using, but exploiting the connection. Our dynamic. I poked him, got under his skin, hoping he'd deviate from that gruff, by-the-book, hard ass, who would never reveal a thing."

"Hmm," was all Harper said.

"You're the one who said annoying him would get him to open up, and it worked." With every kiss, with every sensual touch, she burrowed her way in, all while he was using his Special Forces skills to stealth-sneak behind *her* defenses. Fair trade? She might have thought so once, but not when her heart was shredded like mini-wheats.

"Men who are more in touch with their feelings make better players. It's been quite productive for us."

"I'm *so* glad I could help with player development, then." Jordan plunked her butt on the sofa whereupon she slumped even more gracelessly than usual.

"Levi's an insanely private guy," Harper said thoughtfully. "Right now, seeing these things he's gone to such pains to hide splashed about for entertainment is all he can think of. That you're the reason, whether it's fair or not, is particularly hurtful. I take some responsibility here. I might have misjudged how a profile like this would impact him. But ..."

"But, what?"

"He's smart enough to recognize that what happened in that interview wasn't entirely your fault. I assume there was more to your interaction than orgasm, question, orgasm?"

"Of course there was."

They'd connected on so many levels, and as wonderful as the sex was, it was a small part of it. Right now, her hurting heart brimmed over with memories. Snuggling on the sofa. Dogsitting Cookie. Laughing their heads off at Theo's absurdity. His support ahead of the SportsFocus interview.

Hell, the man went out of his way to that Vietnamese bakery to buy her mini-macarons.

Maybe that should be a black mark against him.

Something he'd said bothered her, like a nail over a raw wound. "He told me he'd always wanted me. And I think he meant from before, from when I met Josh."

Harper's lips formed an *O*. "Poor guy."

"Poor guy? He was so ..." *Cruel.* Yet she didn't believe Levi was intentionally unkind. Hurt people tended to lash out. If he'd had deeper feelings for her while she was married to his best friend, it certainly put another gloss on his self-worth issues. Was this why the so-called betrayal appeared to be magnified in his eyes?

"Listen," Harper said. "You have some things to work out with Levi, but until then, there's something else we can focus our efforts on."

Jordan tried to reel the threads of her mind back in. "There is?"

Harper had a look in her eyes that Jordan envied: the expression of a woman back in control. "I think it's time we unleashed a little hellfire of our own."

AN ICY WIND whipped though Levi as he turned the corner onto the main thoroughfare in Riverbrook. He tried the door of the Empty Net bar.

Locked.

"We're closed!" Elle's voice called out in response to his pounding on the thick oak door.

He should think so, it was 2 a.m. "Elle, open up."

Ten seconds later, she pushed the door ajar. "What the hell are you doing here?"

"Figured I'd see you home."

Frowning, she took a long look at him as he stepped inside. "I need a few minutes to clean up."

The place was dressed for the holidays, red, green, and gold decorations sprucing it up from its usual dumpster dive decor. He took a seat at the bar, furious with everything. What kind of outfit gave key privileges to a rookie bartender?

"You shouldn't be closing up this place on your own. You just started working here."

Aaaand he sounded like an idiot. Elle was trustworthy,

responsible, and could drop-kick any assailant into the middle of the next millennium.

Rather than argue with him, or more likely knowing she'd already won, she placed a beer on the bar. "You groveled your way back to Jordan yet?"

"Very funny." He took a swig of the beer.

"Is it?"

"She made her position clear. I'm the subject of a story. A means to an end. A stepping stone in her career."

Elle mimed a bored yawn.

"Found your own place yet?" he asked caustically.

"Like you could get by without me. I'm keeping you flush in blueberry pop tarts and Cheetos."

He rubbed his brow, regretting his testiness. "I'm sorry. I'm being the asshole Jordan thinks I am."

"Want to tell me how you're so sure you're just a job to her?" With an elbow on the bar, she affected perfectly the cliché of the friendly bartender, ears open for her customers' troubles.

"Because I'm not her type. Always knew that."

"Aw, Hunt, are you kidding me? This whole business has been a *Jesse's Girl* scenario?" At his blank look, she went on. "You've had a thing for your best friend's girl forever?"

"I haven't had a thing for her forever." He winced at the dark look Elle shot his way. "Okay, I've had a thing for her forever. I saw her first, but she saw Josh and that was that."

"That's kind of sad."

"It wasn't, not for them. You didn't know him, Elle. He was all teeth and dimples and such a good-hearted doofus—"

"You loved him," she whispered.

"I did."

"Why didn't you talk to her first? The minute you saw her?"

Because he'd hesitated. Too much head, not enough heart, but also ... how to explain it? "There was something so bright and good about her, not just a physical presence, but an aura about her. And I didn't want to dim that in any way."

Elle shook her head. "Hunt, what the fuck does that mean?"

"It means that a woman who burns as bright as Jordan, with that laugh and all that joy exuding from her, needed to be with someone who could reflect that back on her. Who knew what to do with it. I knew what I was—what I am— and I could never have made her happy. And the thought that I might remove even one percent of her joy didn't sit right. I didn't expect Josh to actually marry her. But he did and every time I've seen her since confirmed what I'd always known: she was never meant to be mine. So I continued my schoolboy crush by glaring at her and being an all-round dick. Standard operating procedure."

"And now?" Elle spat the words out. "Do you still think she exudes too much fucking joy—whatever that means— for you to worry that dark, damaged Levi will dim her light or whatever?"

He didn't appreciate her take on it, probably because it was a little close to the bone. "That's not what this is about. She's not in the same place as me. You saw that interview— I'm just fodder for her career."

Elle passed right over his self-pity. "Looked like she didn't expect to get her ass handed to her by that Sports-Bogus dude. Did she have an explanation for him knowing all that stuff about you?"

Levi shrugged. "She said he looked at her notes on her computer one night in the press box."

"And you don't believe her?"

"I—hell, I don't know." Doubts niggled but he slapped them away like a puck to the boards. And just like a puck, they came boomeranging back. It was much easier to succumb to the darkness and assume that Jordan couldn't possibly want Levi for himself. That her career was all that mattered.

"Don't tell me you haven't noticed all the social media hate she'd been getting?"

He'd seen it—the nasty comments on her CSN posts, the shitty responses to her tweets, all of it hateful, misogynistic, and red-misted rage-inspiring.

He growled. "I want to reach through my phone screen and break the neck of every one of those tweeting twats."

"Still think she did it for her career? No job is worth that. No woman would willingly put herself in that spotlight just to get on some asshole's payroll. Even I could see Jaw Turdson in a tie had an agenda! Instead of supporting her after that ambush on national TV, you focused on how it affected *you*. Typical man-baby."

"She's made it clear she didn't want anything real—"

Elle raised the hand of STFU. "Sounds like standard guarding-of-the-heart stuff, if you ask me."

"Didn't ask you," he said under his breath.

But a strong woman on a roll didn't care, and Elle was one of the strongest women he knew. "So you had a crappy childhood that you didn't want anyone to know about. You fell in love with a woman but were too chickenshit to go talk to her and your friend reaped the reward. We've all got baggage. But you'd rather assume that this baggage makes you unlovable or some such *male* nonsense and that

Princess Joy-in-a-Box couldn't possibly be interested in the man beneath. And you know what, why should she be? You haven't exactly given her a reason." Wiping the bar down vigorously, she muttered, "Men."

He shifted in his seat. Squirmed, more like. "You done here?" He meant Elle's shift, but he may as well be asking about the way she'd sliced and diced his balls.

"Yeah. But think about what I said. I know you hockey superstars are VIPs around here, but it's not always about you." She smiled at him, both pity and affection in her grin. "I'll get my jacket."

27

LEVI LEFT the Uptown Mission dining hall, checking his phone. Traffic back to Riverbrook should be okay at his time, given that the flow from the suburbs into Chicago was generally worse.

A familiar yelp caught his attention. Joe and Cookie were walking into the foyer.

"Hey, buddy!" Hunkering down, he hugged the pup's warm body and gave him a friendly rub. "How's your human?" He looked up to find a smiling Joe.

"We slept here last night. I'm here to see a counselor about moving into a halfway house."

Levi stood. "That's awesome. And your bronchitis?"

"Almost cured. Staying inside has helped." He shifted from one foot to the other. "They set up crates for the pets beside the beds. Cookie didn't want to go in there, but as long as he can see me, then he's all right. Lucy said you came up with that idea."

"Just a bit of research."

"More than that, I heard. They had to hire someone to watch the dogs when we're eating."

And clean up after them, too. Lucy was adamant that would be part of the bargain.

Not wholly comfortable with the implied praise, Levi changed the subject. "Tell me about this counselor."

"It's the same as the army. Someone to talk to and help you figure out what might be preventing you from succeeding. Most of our obstacles come from in here." He touched his head, then his chest. "Mine? I need to figure that out."

Don't we all. Since Elle's you're-the-asshole-here pep talk in the bar, he'd been shooting for more introspection about how he'd handled the situation with Jordan.

Why had he elected to believe the worst-case scenario?

That kind of thinking was part of his training in the Special Forces. Analyze every way a mission could fail, so you were ready when it turned FUBAR. This approach had kept him alive in the desert, and certainly stood him well when shutting down an offensive play on the ice. But glass half-empty didn't work with relationships. Assuming it was doomed before it began wouldn't win fair maiden.

"So, what are you doing tonight, Joe?"

Joe opened his mouth, closed it again. He shook his head and laughed, like it was a question he'd never given much thought to.

Serious again, he looked Levi right in the eyes. "You've been a good fellow serviceman, Levi. A good friend. I didn't adjust so well on my return and let things get away from me, but I see the light now. You don't have to keep checking up on me."

"I was going to ask if you like hockey. I have tickets to the Rebels game against St. Louis tonight."

"Really? I would, but I've got no car and there's this guy to think of." He looked down at Cookie, who was wagging his tail, friendly as ever.

"How about I take care of transport? And you can bring Cookie."

Joe squinted, clearly not buying this scenario.

"For real," Levi assured him.

Joe checked in with Cookie. "Hey, boy, want to watch hockey tonight? Don't know why they'd let a couple of jokers like us in, but Levi says it's okay."

The pup barked his approval.

Joe grinned, ear to ear. "Guess we're going to the game."

LEVI WALKED into the locker room at call time to find everyone crowded around Jorgenson.

"What's go—" The words died on his lips as he caught sight of the iPad in Erik's hands.

Jordan. That was Jordan on the screen.

For a moment he thought it was a rerun of her disastrous interview with Dawson until the camera cut to Harper Chase. "What's happening?"

"Chicago SportsNet interview," Cade said. "Your girl and Harper."

"She's not my girl."

Theo coughed significantly. "Tell it to the fucking Marines, Hunt."

"Green Berets," Levi muttered reflexively.

He recognized the backdrop—that blue sofa in Harper's office, the one where he'd opened up to Jordan for the first time the morning after he kissed her. That kiss had peeled him apart. Beginning of the end, right there.

But he'd also thought that kiss was part of some grand scheme of hers, to get him out of his comfort zone so he'd be putty in her hands. Now he was wondering if that was true, and if it was, was it so bad? If he didn't need to be kissed and caressed and hell, *loved* into a space that wasn't so secure because how else do we grow?

The interview was moseying along in the expected manner. Questions about team acquisition strategy. Who was exciting the Rebels management. Hopes and dreams of the season. And then it transitioned from Harper as an NHL boss to Harper as *the only female* NHL boss, and what that meant.

"I haven't thought too hard about what I owe to this sport as a woman in charge," Harper said. "I've been too busy worrying about what it owes me."

"In what way?" Jordan's expression was curious, a look he recognized from sessions spent spilling his guts.

"For years, I felt I'd worked my butt off to get where I was. Where I am. Sure, I had a leg up being Clifford Chase's daughter."

"Some people might say it wasn't such a huge advantage," Jordan interjected.

Harper gave a sardonic smile. "Making me share the team with two sisters I barely knew might be considered cruel and unusual. But then my father wasn't an easy man. He didn't think I was strong enough to make the team successful—and in a way, he was right. I needed Isobel and Violet because while I might own a team, it was going to take more than my name on the deed to make it work. Together we made it stronger. So, thanks, Dad, you old bastard."

She spoke that last sentence to the floor, leaving viewers in no doubt as to where she believed her father had ended up. That cracked the team up.

On the screen, Jordan laughed, too. "And what do you think you owe hockey?"

"To take it to the next level. And I don't just mean creating a Rebels dynasty, though that's one goal."

The boys in the locker room cheered.

"What then?"

"Next level in terms of who hockey embraces, who it includes, who gets to take part. I'm a woman in a predominantly male business. I have a seat at the table and I want more women to be involved in the front office, in the press box, in the coaching circle. I want to see a more diverse power structure and fan base. I have the power to make that happen, to change the rules about how this business, our sport, is conducted."

"You haven't wanted to lead before in this more meaningful way. Why is that?"

"I thought the example I was setting was enough. Women would see me, my sisters, and Dante in charge and realize that the sky's the limit. Gender, sexual identity, race —nothing can stop you. But I realized it's not enough to show, I also have to tell. My story. Our story."

Jordan nodded. "You had good reasons for resisting, Harper. There's a double standard here and the patriarchal structure of pro hockey hasn't always been kind to you."

"True. I've been pushed around, called names, disrespected. Told that being a woman disqualified me from doing what I was born to do. Neither was my father all that supportive." She paused, then set her chin. "When a Rebels player hit me several years ago, my father blamed me for being a distraction."

"Who was the player?"

"Billy Stroger, currently with the New York Spartans."

Theo stood. "What the fuck? Stroger?"

"Sit down, Kershaw," Levi grated out.

Theo glared at Levi, but did as he was told.

The interview continued. "Can you tell us what happened?"

"I was dating him, against my father's wishes, and Stroger had a temper. One time was enough. I'm ashamed to say I wouldn't even have reported it except another player walked in right after and insisted my father be told. He traded Stroger out at the first available opportunity and the incident was swept under the mats of the Rebels locker room."

Harper's eyes were shiny, and for a moment, Levi thought Jordan would pull an Oprah move and reach out to comfort her. She didn't. Just let Harper recompose before starting in on the next question.

"Did you ever feel you had a duty to warn anyone else about Stroger's temper?"

"At the time, I was only thinking about how to get out safely and how to heal. My father preferred we keep it quiet and then used it against me for years as proof I didn't have the mettle to run the team. I bought into that narrative for a while. Even imagined that it was my fault."

"Women often take that on," Jordan said.

"Yes, we do. We minimize, absorb the toxicity, blame ourselves because we smiled politely at someone in an elevator. Entered a locker room to see a guy we're dating or to get that interview. Didn't immediately block someone on Twitter."

"Ergo we *must* be willing to put up with your moods or be okay with that photo of your penis."

Harper laughed. "Splotchy, weirdly-shaped ones, too! It's ridiculous the mental gymnastics we perform so we don't have to be rude or upset the status quo."

"Gotta stay nice," Jordan said ruefully. "I know that strategy well."

"Well, we're done being nice. Where's nice ever got us?"

"Where, indeed. We're looking forward to what the not-so-nice owners of the Rebels do this season. Thanks for talking with me today, Harper."

The interview ended, but that wasn't the end of the spot. Jordan appeared again, this time alone and facing the camera directly.

"Harper Chase's experience is just one of many women in the masculine space of professional sports. If the most powerful woman in the NHL can't get respect or can't feel safe reporting an assault then what chance do the rest us have in this sport we love? The male fan base for most pro sports is largely maxed out, but the female fan base is growing and ripe for development. And it'll need help. What are the male-dominated front offices, not just in hockey, but in all the professional leagues doing to ensure women feel safe in these environments? From personal assistants to reporters to yoga instructors to coaches, every single one of these jobs can be performed, and sometimes is performed, by a woman. We're not looking to cancel all men. Instead you need to be subscribing to all women.

"You want to challenge me in the comments of an article? Sure, let's talk about whether we think Boston or Detroit can make a serious run this year. Let's discuss power plays and face-off wins at even strength. But don't tell me I don't know what I'm talking about because I'm a woman. Don't offer to give me that tip on so-and-so's injury status provided I stop by your hotel room and get on my knees. And especially don't send me pics of your junk, thinking it's the way to my heart and a good word on my podcast. It's not. I'm a macaron girl."

"You tell 'em, Jordan," Cade said.

Levi couldn't speak. He was so damn proud of her and so fucking ashamed of himself.

"We're not looking to be treated differently, guys. We can handle a flash of your butt in the locker room, though Scouts' honor we didn't go in there looking for it." She smiled, and he imagined her crossing her fingers in her lap as a joke. "We've heard every swear word there is and can use them more imaginatively than you. But if you wouldn't say it or send it to your mom or your sister, then you probably shouldn't say it or send it to one of your female colleagues. And that's what we are. Your co-workers, your fellow fans, and humans sharing the earth. See you at the next puck drop."

The screen faded into the Chicago SportsNet logo.

A good ten seconds ticked over before anyone spoke.

Theo broke the silence. "And all this time, I thought she *wanted* to check out my ass!"

"You leave her *and* us no choice," Ford said, holding his hands up and making a squeezing gesture. "Those glutes are so powerful, man."

Even with the half-jokes, it was clear that the team was uncomfortable with what they'd just heard. Somehow Harper confirming and speaking about it with such grit and bravery made it so much more real. A player—sure, an absolute asshole, but a colleague all the same—had hurt one of their own.

Erik was the first to say what was on all their minds. "When do we play the Spartans next?"

"January 30th at home," Theo said. "And Stroger better have a Beyoncé-level entourage of muscle because he's going down."

"No, he's not," Levi said. Someone needed to be the voice of reason in the absence of Petrov who was still on IR.

Nineteen sets of eyes locked on his.

"Now that it's confirmed, there might be an investigation resulting in suspensions or legal action. The boss was backed into a corner, forced to explain what happened, but she won't want anyone indulging in vigilante justice on the ice. Stroger will still get what's coming to him. We're going to play our game and win it our way."

A couple of nods, then a few more. Theo's eyes flashed, not agreeing, but he remained silent.

"Gentlemen, may I enter?" Harper's voice cut in.

The team split apart like naughty schoolboys caught looking at dirty photos. Jorgenson dropped his iPad on the bench, then decided it would be better to sit on it.

"All good, Ms. Chase," Levi said.

She walked in, somehow looking taller than the last time Levi had seen her. "Feeling good about tonight's game?" she asked.

Murmurs of agreement floated over the room.

"I just wanted to say that I appreciate every single one of you. You've all been chosen because you bring something special to this team. Something that's magnified by being here with these people, on this rink, and in this city." She looked around, her gaze touching each of them, one at a time. "Have a good game, guys."

"Nice work on that interview, ma'am," Levi said. He needed her to know that they had her back just like she had theirs.

"Thanks, Levi." She went to walk out then spun on her heels to face him again. "When you get a moment, could you stop by Coach Calhoun's office?"

"Sure."

A minute later, he was seated in the office, waiting for Coach, and wondering what was up. The door opened, and in walked Harper. He stood, and she gestured for him to sit again.

Once she'd taken a seat behind Coach's desk, she placed her hands together on the table. "Jordan and I talked. About lots of things, but mostly about you."

Not sure how much he should say or what Harper actually knew, he figured he should go with a neutral "How is she?"

"A complete pro. We've agreed she's not going to write the profile."

His head shot up. "But she already did. I read a draft of it."

"Apparently it wasn't quite what her boss at CSN wanted. Not salacious enough. Too reverential."

"The preview I saw labeled me a dick."

"And that was considered too nice." She smiled to soften it.

He sighed. "I know I screwed up, Harper. I accused her of some shitty stuff. Assumed the worst. I basically told her she'd been using me for the story and that Dawson was right." Because he didn't believe that she might have seen something more. That there *was* something more.

"I don't think Jordan has a malicious bone in her body," Harper said. "She was used by Dawson, and afterward, she could have capitalized on having the information firsthand. It would have been a good way for her deflect from what happened in the interview but she kept it under wraps."

"She's a good person. And how you handled it, back then, today—you're all class, Harper."

"Thanks. And thanks for keeping the team in check back in the locker room. They're all so young and hormone-driven, and need a lot of guidance." She smiled. "Hockey isn't just about who scores the most goals or wins the most

face-offs, though that's important. It's also about connections, on and off the ice. It's about teamwork. It's about
finding your place and knowing your worth. I think you
could do great things with the Rebels if you're willing to take
a chance on us like the one we've taken on you."

Calling him up from the AHL was a leap of faith on their
part. He knew that. He also knew he needed to take one of
his own: plunge into the ice-cold darkness and trust that
Jordan would be there to light the way with her sunny smile
and a path of glowing freckles.

"I'm ready to do this." He meant taking his rightful place
on the Rebels, but mostly he meant the hard work of
accepting the love coming his way. "I'm crazy about Jordan.
So crazy."

"Good to hear it. Men in love play better."

He shook his head, grinning like a fool. How could he fix
this yet still protect Jordan's reputation? All he wanted was a
chance to apologize. Properly.

Something sparked in his beaten-down brain. "Could
you do me a favor?"

"Anything for my favorite rookie."

28

@ChiRebels boss Harper Chase blows the lid off domestic violence in the NHL. Nice reporting from @ChiSports and @HockeyGrrl #NHLReckoning

JIM KRUGMAN APPEARED at Jordan's shoulder about two seconds after she took her seat in the Rebels press box. "Good work on that interview with Harper Chase, Cooke."

"Thanks, Jim."

Folding his arms, he peered down at her. "Coby Dawson always struck me as squirrely. No way to talk to a woman." Discomfort brushed his brow, as if he realized that singling her out as a woman was, in itself, problematic. "People have really been giving you shit, huh?"

"It's no big—" She had been about to say no big deal, but checked herself. That was bullshit. It *was* a big deal. "I'm not afraid of anyone disagreeing with my opinions or refusing to give me the information I need. But when it gets personal, I have to fight back."

Jim nodded. "You're a good reporter, Cooke. Screw 'em."

"Thanks, Jim. Appreciate it."

Both of her recent interviews, one the counterpoint to the other, had garnered a lot of interest. Subscriber numbers to her podcast were up, the name-calling on her Twitter feed was as unimaginative as ever, and Mac had called to ask about her revision to the article on Levi.

"We need to strike while the iron is hot, Cooke. While you're *hot!"*

She had yet to tell him that she was bailing on the profile. Post-LeviGate, as some wag had labeled the "scandal," the profile's objectivity was suspect. Nothing she wrote on the subject of that man would ever be taken seriously.

Which meant that she was probably out of a job. Jack Gillam had texted to tell her "good work" and to keep his seat warm. This might be her last game in the Rebels press box.

Better do the necessary while she still had a chance.

The warm-up was about to begin, so as her colleagues powered up and groused about the dressed list, she took a second to assess the pastry table, and in particular, a large tray of multi-colored macarons. A small envelope sat beside them with Jordan's name scrawled on the front in a loopy script. She ripped it open to find the following message:

Nice interview, Jordan. Enjoy the game and the perks!

- Dante

Aw! *Thanks, fellow macaron connoisseur, I will.* Not caring if anyone saw her, she picked up the tray and tipped the entire batch into her oversized Kate Spade purse.

"Wish I could pull that stunt at the shelter with the donuts, but Lucy would probably kill me."

Surprised at the sound of a voice she recognized, she pivoted. "Joe! And Cookie!"

The puppy barked at the mention of his name. Joe looked a little more groomed than usual, and was that Levi's leather jacket he was wearing?

"Did Levi get you in here?"

"Yeah, he sent a car to pick us up. A really nice car. I knew you were a reporter but I didn't realize ..." His gaze strayed to the floor-to-ceiling glass overseeing the rink, his eyes widening with wonder. "I thought he'd be meeting us here to watch the game, but a lady met us at the door and brought us straight here." He looked disappointed and that's when she realized the man had no idea that Levi was a Rebel.

This was going to be fun.

"Oh, he probably thought this would be better because of Cookie. They only let official service animals in the regular seats. Come sit over here by me." She led him to the empty seat beside her. "Just put your jacket there and then help yourself to this spread. I'll even let you have a macaron from my stash."

Once she got him settled in with food and a beer, along with a bowl of water for Cookie, she gave a visual tour, pointing out the benches, the sin bin, and the entrance for the players.

"Here they come," she said, hardly able to contain her excitement, partly because Joe was about to learn that under-the-radar Mr. Hunt was actually a hockey star, and partly because she wanted to see the man she loved despite the hurt in her heart.

The announcer called out the players' names, each more theatrically than the last until: "Leviiiiii Hunttttt!"

While Levi skated a few circles and acknowledged the crowd's roar, Jordan slid a glance to her seatmate. As she'd predicted, Joe's jaw was on the floor beside Cookie's water bowl.

"Did he say Levi Hunt?" He turned to her, eyes as big as macarons. "Jordan?"

"He did. That's why Levi can't watch the game with you." She pointed at the rink, unable to contain her grin. "He's kind of busy."

"Holy. Shit. What the hell was he doing in Special Forces?"

Being a superhero, that's what.

On her other side, Jim pointed through the window. "Looks like someone's having fun with the scoreboard."

A very cute, very familiar guest on the state-of-the-art Jumbotron over the rink was making the crowd go wild.

Was that Cookie? She looked down to verify and back up at the screen. It was!

A few seconds of video showed Cookie yelping from what looked like Levi's sofa before a red heart appeared on the screen with the text: *Ms. Sunshine, I'm an idiot. Forgive me.* Then another clip of Cookie barking his approval.

The entire crowd cheered, then the scoreboard went to its usual display of player profiles, stats, scores, and a steady stream of advertisements and birthday messages.

"Cookie, you're a star! Hey, did you see that?" Joe nudged her. "That was Cookie up there."

Jordan's heart was doing back flips. So far, the rumors of her relationship with Levi were just that: rumors. Levi had found a way to apologize without confirming them, a message for her alone. Bonus points: he'd featured Cookie, the super-pup infused with a friendly spirit, just like his namesake.

That stubborn, beautiful man might have acted like an idiot, but he was fighting for her, just like he'd climbed his way out of poverty, had honorably served his country, and in every game, battled out there on the ice.

Maybe there was hope for Mount Grump after all.

THE EMPTY NET bar was about as busy as you'd expect after a Rebels home game. Win or lose, everyone seemed to enjoy any excuse to gather and knock back a few, and even though they had the W, Levi couldn't help feeling like he was a big old L.

Jordan had been conspicuously absent from the locker room post-game. He'd asked one of the assistants to check the press box, but there was no sign of her. Looked like his message had been returned as undeliverable.

Joe had shown up, awed that Levi had managed to keep the NHL gig under his helmet. The boys already knew Cookie, so it was like a reunion with their honorary mascot. But with no Jordan, Levi's heart ached something fierce.

He'd messed up royally. He should have gone straight to the press box right after that interview with Harper aired. He needed Jordan to know that he was one hundred percent behind her, that he'd let his dumb-as-dirt brain overrule his heart.

She was right, he was wrong, and that was it.

Elle put a beer on the bar. "You guys lose?"

"This place has five TVs all set to the game. How could you have missed it?"

"I was working. You think I'm paying attention to you idiots playing with sticks and balls?"

"Maybe you should come to a game one night, Sergeant Cupcake." Theo leaned an elbow on the bar. "Nothing beats watching us playing with our sticks and balls up close and personal."

"Don't you have problems with your center of gravity, Dick-Man? Sounds like I'd just be watching you fall down on that thick ass of yours." She grinned at Levi. "On second thought, I'll come to see *that* any night of the week."

Elle flipped off Theo and headed to the other end of the bar.

Theo raised a hand. "Hey, I wanted a beer!" To Levi, he muttered, "As you can see, Hunt, your ward is safe from me because she clearly hates my guts."

Fairly pleased with that conclusion, Levi pushed his beer over. "Here you go, Kershaw. Good work tonight."

"Aw, thanks, Gigi."

"Do I even want to know?"

"Gigi, G-G, Good Guy, 'cause that's what you are. So how you doing?"

"Fine. It was a good game."

"I mean, how you *doin'*?" He touched Levi's chest. "In here."

Levi would have rolled his eyes but as strange as it seemed, Theo was the only teammate who truly understood what he was going through. Somehow, this goof had become Levi's closest confidant. "I'm trying to give Jordan some space and respect her boundaries, so no one will think she's incapable of hanging with a hockey player without—"

"Falling in love with him."

Levi spun around at the sound of Jordan's voice. She stood before him, her red hair a little wild, her eyes shining with emotion.

"Jordan." He gave her a quick nod, careful to keep his feelings contained for appearances' sake. "Can I buy you a drink?"

"Here." Theo handed over the beer that no one seemed to want to drink. "Great work on that interview with Ms. Chase today, Hockey Grr—uh, Woman. And ..." He pushed Levi aside. *What the—?* "I just wanted to apologize again for anything I might have said that in any way came off as objectifying or sexist or rude. You know I can't stop talking sometimes—well, all the time—and if I've ever made you feel uncomfortable, please know that Hunt will happily beat my ass for every transgression."

Jordan pressed her lips against a smile, and locked eyes with Levi. "Would you? Beat his ass?"

"It'd be my pleasure. However, there's a decent chance that Kershaw's glutes might be too powerful and would cause my hands serious damage. I'd risk it, though. For you."

Theo grinned. "So glad that anything I've done might have brought you two closer together. I'll just ..."

"Go," Levi said.

"Go." Theo disappeared into the crowd.

Levi moved in closer, the itch to touch her almost unbearable. He grasped the bar instead and held on for dear life.

"Good game," she said.

"Thanks." He took a step, then another. "I'd give anything to be able to touch you right now, but I know I have to keep a professional distance—"

That professional distance vanished when she kissed him, her mouth hot and sweet and yes, his end. Always, his end.

"Baby," he murmured against her lips. "Everyone can see."

"I know. Everyone *should* see."

He pulled away, though it killed him. "We need to talk."

Her eyes shone, bright and lovely and all Jordan. "Then talk."

Talk. Like that was easy. But with Jordan, it was easier, and that's all that mattered.

The bar was noisy, but no one was paying attention—or at least, he convinced himself that he was flying under the radar just like his days in the service. Just like he'd tried to since returning stateside. He could angle for a quieter spot, but life had to go on. They had to figure out how to rise above all the noise.

"You're right about me. You've always been right about me. I play this kick ass guy on TV but the real me—not even close. I didn't have the guts to make a play for you the first time I met you all those years ago. I assumed someone like you wouldn't want a guy like me. And when years later, I had a shot at this woman I've loved for fucking years, I couldn't believe it was truly happening. You couldn't possibly want me past the story, so I created a narrative that fit that. You were using me. I would never make you smile the way you need. I didn't deserve a woman like you. A bunch of lame-ass excuses to keep me from going deep into the zone and taking the shot. I screwed up, Jordan, and I'm so damn sorry."

She placed a hand on his chest. "Is that true? All this time?"

He nodded, the words to confirm his stupidity unable to form.

"You told Josh to marry me even though you felt that way about me?"

"Did he make you happy?"

Her smile, half-sad but so fucking beautiful, lit her from the inside like a love-lantern. "He did."

"And that made me happy. That's all I cared about. Back

then, I wasn't ready to be the man you need. I wasn't prepared to take a chance. To give you everything. But now —hell, it's like I have a death wish when it comes to shots with the woman of my dreams."

"But you figured it out. I can't believe you used Cookie to sneak into my heart, you bastard."

"Low blow?"

"The lowest. And I couldn't react because the entire press box would be on top of me like velociraptors."

"Just wanted to do a little something that only you and I would get."

She smiled. "A coded message."

"Yeah, but now you're here, kissing me." He kissed her because she wasn't actually kissing him in this instant, and he needed it to be true. Needed this to be his truth. "Out in the open. Ruining my plans for discretion. Why the change of heart?"

"Something Harper said about how love made her stronger. I can love you and be a good reporter at the same time. My job's important to me but so are you. So much. To hell with the haters, they're going to have the knives out anyway. I'm a woman. Multitasking is my superpower."

He closed his eyes, touched his forehead to hers. "You can love me? Did I hear that right?"

"You did. Not just that I can, but that I do. I love this strong, silent—sometimes too silent—man who's given so much of himself to everyone. Who, despite his claims to dullness, excites me like no one else. Moves me like no one else. I love his face and his smile and his big heart. I love you, Levi."

That deserved another kiss, a full, claiming one. A kiss for the ages, and this one earned sappy-happy, rom-com applause. He sneaked a look at his crew at the other end of the bar, cat-calling and hooting in a way that might have been considered disrespectful if he didn't know better. But he did.

They were a bunch of good guys, after all, not a bad bone in their bodies.

EPILOGUE

Don't miss tonight's episode when @HockeyGrrl finally gets her man!

LEVI_HUNT_PODCAST_JAN5_RAW_FILE.MP3

"HAPPY NEW YEAR, friends! Welcome to the first HockeyGrrl podcast in January. We have a treat in store for you tonight. He's a hard man to pin down, but we've managed to get Levi Hunt, rookie center for the Chicago Rebels to sit still and tell us all about his debut season so far. Levi, it's so good to have you on HockeyGrrl at last."

"Baby, it's so good to be ... on you."

"The show. It's so good to be on the show. And you can't call me baby. Okay, I can edit that out, so let's redo the intro." *Sound of a deep inhale.* "Levi, it's so good to have you on the show."

"Thanks for having me, Jordan."

"So how was your holiday break? I know you guys don't get a long one but I'm guessing you managed a few days."

"Good. Great, actually. I spent it with—wait, can I say that I spent it with you and your family in DC?"

"Well, it's not a secret that we're together. You could say you spent it relaxing and thanking your lucky stars that you came to your senses and are no longer a Grade A idiot. At least, as far as this one narrowly defined topic goes."

"Seems sort of excessive. How about ..." *Long pause.* "I spent the holiday visiting my girlfriend's family and figuring out how to impress people who don't give a flying f—fandango about hockey, mostly by cleaning up at Scrabble."

Lusty giggle. "You did! Nothing impresses my father more than a high-scoring Scrabble word."

"Quixotic. One of my favorites. Defined as absurdly chivalric, which I felt was apt."

"Alternative meaning, Levi. Prone to delusion."

Masculine growl. "Is this going in the podcast?"

"At this rate, I'll spend more time editing this one episode than recording a whole season's worth. Let's get back on track!" *Long pause.* "Before we talk about the Rebels, I know you wanted to give a shout out to the Uptown Mission and the crew there."

"Yep. It's a place that's close to my heart, offering meals, beds, and social services programs for the homeless—"

"And their pets."

"And their pets. In fact, one of my buddies down there, Joe Connor along with his sidekick Cookie, is in charge of the new Rebel Critters Program, which manages the pets at three of the shelters on the North Side. Shots, food, even matching a furry friend with a human who needs companionship. The Chicago Rebels organization has pledged $100,000 to the Mission and I'm hoping the fans will want to help as well."

"You know what it's like to go without a roof over your head."

Pause, then deep inhale. "I do. I was one of the lucky ones, though, because I had a talent that set me on another path. But homelessness is a problem that shouldn't exist and something we can solve as a community. Hey, you okay?"

"I'm fine!" *Sniff.* "Just glad people are finally seeing the amazing guy I see every day. Oh, I've made you blush."

Manly throat-clearing. "I'm not blushing."

"Yes, you are and it's so cute. So, tell us more about your season. How do you think your game has improved?"

Sexy growl. "Well, Jordan, you'll probably remember that first game where I didn't seem to know my ass from my skates. And then after, when I'm at my lowest because I think I've played like shit—can I say that?"

"You can. Because you did."

"Always busting my balls. After my debut, I just wanted to crawl in a hole. But I had to talk to the media and you know how they are."

"Scum-sucking bottom feeders?"

"Precisely. But one of them, in particular, despite her scum-sucking bottom feeder tendencies knocked me over when I saw her. She was so goddamn beautiful."

A small gasp, then a breathy: "Oh yeah?"

"Simply stunning. And smart. And skilled at poking and prodding and prying."

"She sounds like the perfect package." *Suckling sound, throaty moans.* "I can't do the rest of this interview sitting in your lap, Levi. It's not—"

"Professional? Just try it. I promise to keep my hands to myself."

"Not sure I believe that's at all possible but we'll give it the old college try. Cut here, future Jordan." *Five-second pause*. "Following your first game, you seemed to adapt quickly to your new life as a hockey pro. You definitely played better. Extra practice?"

"That. Video games with my crew. Hanging with a few Rebels legends. But mostly, opening my mind to give me a chance to be freer on the ice."

"Our listeners would love to hear more about that, the psychology of opening yourself up and how that's helped your game."

"I've lived a fairly contained life, Jordan, for both personal and professional reasons stemming from my pre-NHL career. Keeping my shit locked down was crucial for survival and self-preservation, but then I met you. Again."

Sound like a gulp? "Okaayyy. And how did that change things?"

"Talking about myself has never come easy. With that comes a level of navel-gazing that's frankly, not me. Shit, no guy wants to do that. Assuring myself that I was good enough, that I deserved this ..."

"Levi." *Thirty seconds of not-dead, very-much-alive-with-love air. Kissing sounds galore.* "You do deserve this. All of it."

"Thanks, Jordan. This is my second act. Professionally. Personally. I'm ready."

"Sounds like you are." *A sniffing sound.* "Vadim Petrov has announced that this will be his last year in the pros, which leaves the captain's patch up for grabs. Would you take it on if you were asked?"

"I'd be honored, but there are plenty of guys who would be more qualified than me. Jorgenson and Burnett have been there longer, so we'll see what the Rebels leadership has in mind when the time comes. My focus right now is on getting to the playoffs and beyond."

"And on that topic, the Rebels haven't progressed to the

post-season for a couple of years, Levi. Think you've got it in you this year?"

"I do. And if we don't make it or if our playoffs ride is cut short, I'll have something else to occupy me."

"Such as?" *Loud gasp.* "Levi! Oh my God, it's huge!"

"Please leave that on the podcast with no context whatsoever."

"Seriously, though. That diamond is gorgeous—are you —oh wow!"

"Will you marry me, Jordan? Will you make me the happiest   former-Green-Beret-now-NHL's-oldest-rookie alive?"

Longest, most-heart-stopping pause ever recorded in the history of podcasting.

"Yes."

"You're sure?"

"Oh, yes."

"Because we're not live, Jordan. It's just you, me, and that half-empty box of macarons. You can edit all this out, especially if you'd rather say no."

"Did you not hear me say yes? Twice? Sheesh, take the win, Hunt."

"Say it again."

Kissing sounds with additional engagement-quality moans. "Yes, times infinity. I love you, Levi Hunt, and I won't be editing this part out. That's a promise."

"Are you crying, Ms. Sunshine?"

"No, just some dust in my eye. I really need to run a broom over this floor."

"Pause the recording, baby. I need to do something dirty and delicious to the host and it's really not suitable for sensitive ears."

Happy giggle. Zipper scrape. Recording ends.

THANK YOU FOR READING! I hope you enjoyed Levi and Jordan in this first book in the *Rookie Rebels* series. If you did, please leave a review on your favorite book platform!

Are you new to the *Chicago Rebels* world? Three estranged sisters inherit their late father's failing hockey franchise and are forced to confront a man's world, their family's demons, and the battle-hardened ice warriors skating into their hearts. Start right now with the free prequel, *In Skates Trouble,* available on all online platforms. Then meet Harper and Remy in the first full-length Chicago Rebels novel. If enemies to lovers, strong women, and Cajun heartbreakers make you swoon, you won't want to miss *Irresistible You.*

ARE you a fan of hot and heartfelt romance featuring found families? Check out the *Hot in Chicago* series about firefighting foster siblings honoring the father who saved them while they follow in his footsteps. The Dempseys' motto: fire is stronger than blood and defend the people you love to the last ember.

FINALLY, to stay in touch and learn about new releases, sales, and giveaways, sign up for my newsletter at katemeader.com.

ABOUT THE AUTHOR

Originally from Ireland, *USA Today* bestselling author Kate Meader cut her romance reader teeth on Maeve Binchy and Jilly Cooper novels, with some Harlequins thrown in for variety. Give her tales about brooding mill owners, over-sexed equestrians, and men who can rock an apron, a fire hose, or a hockey stick, and she's there. Now based in Chicago, she writes sexy contemporary romance with alpha heroes and strong heroines who can match their men quip for quip.

www.katemeader.com

ACKNOWLEDGMENTS

Thanks to Kristi Yanta for helping me shape this book into something fabulous. I couldn't have done it without you! Thanks also to Kim Cannon for doing such a great job cleaning up all my mistakes. And to everyone who asked for more Rebels books—this one's for you.

THE CHICAGO REBELS

Three estranged sisters inherit their late father's failing hockey franchise and are forced to confront a man's world, their family's demons, and the battle-hardened ice warriors skating into their hearts.

~

Irresistible You (Chicago Rebels, #1)

Harper Chase has just become the most powerful woman in the NHL after the death of her father Clifford Chase, maverick owner of the Chicago Rebels. But the team is a hot mess—underfunded, overweight, and close to tapping out of the league. Hell-bent on turning the luckless franchise around, Harper won't let anything stand in her way. Not her gender, not her sisters, and especially not a veteran player with an attitude problem and a smoldering gaze designed to melt her ice-compacted defenses.

Veteran center Remy "Jinx" DuPre is on the downside of a career that's seen him win big sponsorships, fans' hearts, and more than a few notches on his stick. Only one goal has eluded him: the Stanley Cup. Sure, he's been labeled as the unluckiest guy in the league, but with his recent streak of good play, he knows this is his year. So why the hell is he being shunted off to a failing hockey franchise run by a ball-buster in heels? And is she seriously expecting him to lead her band of misfit losers to a coveted spot in the playoffs?

He'd have a better chance of leading Harper on a merry skate to his bed...

~

So Over You (Chicago Rebels, #2)

Isobel Chase knows hockey. She played NCAA, won Olympic silver, and made it thirty-seven minutes into the new National Women's Hockey League before an injury sidelined her dreams. Those who can't, coach, and a position as a skating consultant to her late father's hockey franchise, the Chicago Rebels, seems like a perfect fit. Until she's assigned her first job: the man who skated into her heart as a teen and relieved her of her pesky virginity. These days, left-winger Vadim Petrov is known as the Czar of Pleasure, a magnet for puck bunnies and the tabloids alike. But back then . . . let's just say his inability to sink the puck left Isobel frustratingly scoreless.

Vadim has a first name that means "ruler," and it doesn't stop at his birth certificate. He dominates on the ice, the practice rink, and in the backseat of a limo. But a knee injury has produced a bad year, and bad years in the NHL don't go unrewarded. His penance? To be traded to a troubled team where his personal coach is Isobel Chase, the woman who drove him wild years ago when they were hormonal teens. But apparently the feeling was not entirely mutual.

That Vadim might have failed to give Isobel the pleasure that was her right is intolerable, and he plans to make it up to her—one bone-melting orgasm at a time. After all, no player can perfect his game without a helluva lot of practice . . .

~

Undone by You (Chicago Rebels, #3)

Dante Moretti has just landed his dream job: GM of the Chicago Rebels. And screw the haters who think there should be an asterisk next to his name because he's the first out managing executive in pro hockey. He's earned the right to be here and nothing will topple him off that perch—especially not an incredibly inconvenient attraction to his star defenseman, Cade "Alamo" Burnett. Cade has always been careful to keep his own desires on the down low, but his hot Italian boss proves to be a temptation he can't resist. Sure, they both have so much to lose, but no one need ever know...

As Dante and Cade's taboo affair heats up off the ice and their relationship gets more and more intense, they'll have to decide: is love worth risking their careers? Or is this romance destined to be forever benched?

~

Hooked on You (Chicago Rebels, #4)

Violet Vasquez never met her biological father, so learning

he left his beloved hockey franchise—the Chicago Rebels—to her is, well, unexpected. Flat broke and close to homeless, Violet is determined to make the most of this sudden opportunity. Except dear old dad set conditions that require she takes part in actually running the team with the half-sisters she barely knows. Working with these two strangers and overseeing a band of hockey-playing lugs is not on her agenda...until she lays eyes on the Rebels captain and knows she has to have him.

Bren St. James has been labeled a lot of things: the Puck Prince, Lord of the Ice, Hell's Highlander...but it's the latest tag that's making headlines: *washed-up alcoholic has-been*. This season, getting his life back on track and winning the Cup are his only goals. With no time for relationships—except the fractured ones he needs to rebuild with his beautiful daughters—he's finding it increasingly hard to ignore sexy, all-up-in-his-beard Violet Vasquez. And when he finds himself in need of a nanny just as the playoffs are starting, he's faced with a temptation he could so easily get hooked on.

For two lost souls, there's more on the line than just making the best of a bad situation... there might also be a shot at the biggest prize of all: love.

~

ALSO BY KATE MEADER

Chicago Rebels

In Skates Trouble

Irresistible You

So Over You

Undone by You

Hooked on You

Laws of Attraction

Down with Love

Illegally Yours

Then Came You

Hot in Chicago

Rekindle the Flame

Flirting with Fire

Melting Point

Playing with Fire

Sparking the Fire

Forever in Fire

Coming in Hot

Tall, Dark, and Texan

Even the Score

Taking the Score

For updates, giveaways, and new release information, sign up for Kate's newsletter at katemeader.com.

WITHDRAWN

9 780998 517827